Strike@36

Aparna Pednekar is a Mumbai-based travel and lifestyle journalist, and has contributed to *Vogue*, *GQ*, *Travel Plus*, *Verve*, *Hindustan Times Brunch*, *Lonely Planet*, *Elle*, *OK!*, *BBC Good Food* and *Jetwings International*. She wrote a feature film script, *Dirty Little Secrets*, that was part of the NFDC Locarno Screenwriters' Lab in 2009. Later, she wrote and directed an inexplicable short film, *Fowl Men*, which was screened at a couple of festivals in Italy and Chicago. She is also an IGI-qualified gemologist and jewellery designer. *Strike@36* is her first book.

Strike@36

Aparna Pednekar

HarperCollins *Publishers* India

First published in India in 2013 by
HarperCollins *Publishers* India

Building 10, Tower A, 4th Floor, DLF Cyber City, Phase II,
Gurugram Haryana – 122002, India
www.harpercollins.co.in

ISBN: 978-93-5029-392-8

2 4 6 8 10 9 7 5 3 1

Typeset in 11/14 Joanna MT
Jojy Philip New Delhi 110 015

Printed and bound at
MicroPrints India, New Delhi

To all you contrarians

Saffron-soaked hippies
Hopeless romantics with guns in their pockets
Comedians with bleeding hearts
Cat people who love dogs
My world would be a terribly dull place without you

1

The Swinger

Shobhna

'Have you considered bisexuality?'

'Huh?'

'Sho, pass me the remote.'

'No, Rohini.'

'No to what, ma? Remote? Or are you answering my first question?'

Survey the setting. A round glass-topped table, four cane chairs and a beloved green settee. Sri Lankan shoe rack neatly stacked with newspapers and magazines. Saffron and ochre mulmul curtains. A single 60W Philips bulb bathing the room in dull orange. Four feng shui pyramids pasted on the ceiling and a vastu shastra-recommended brass turtle below. Next to the turtle, a pair of ceramic Rottweiler puppies in a china basket. Below them, my archaic twenty-one-inch-screen Sony television, two packs of Rohini's Marlboro Lights on top of it, and directly in front of it, perched on one of the cane chairs in my living room, the stunning thirty-seven-year-old mother of two – my best friend who still smokes in secret, in the comforting cocoon of her childhood friend's home.

Rohini is dressed in striped pyjamas that make her look like an item number queen who has escaped from a prison in a Chaplin movie. I'm in my trademark faded-yellow ikat kurta, the oldest item in the apartment. We've just finished nibbling on post-dinner chocolate ice-cream cones. The Sony is on heat. The mob is protesting, live, at the *Azad Maidan.* (They should really look for a new venue.) The mob is holding candles, BlackBerrys and placards.

'Quit Fucking Bombay.'

'Go back to 1920. Leave us alone, fascists.'

'Freedom. Liberty. Tequila.'

They should really get a new venue.

'What's with Veepee, da? What nonsense is this?'

Rohini was college pals with Veepee, programming director of the television channel airing the 'Quit Fucking Bombay' protest. They had stayed chummy till graduation in Bangalore, after which they parted ways mentally. Rohini made a career out of sticking needles into pained animals while Veepee struck joy into the hearts of millions of housewives who worship Indian television. Last week, when the protests started, Veepee took a leap of faith and replaced his prime-time mains of housewives-in-chiffon-saris and Naxalites-in-love soaps with lakhs of youngsters cursing the bejeezus off the city's administration. It was a risk that paid off. His revolutionary new idea of prime-time television was trending violently on all social media platforms. Veepee became the golden boy.

'Do you want to do me?' Rohini says.

Ah, but we were on the topic of my sexuality. I glare at Rohini who is ranting about Veepee's diminishing aesthetic faculties. And then, I feel smoke. The kind of smoke thrown up by machines on fantasy movie sets.

Within seconds, my living room metamorphoses into a luscious parlour, a burlesque den of sin. Red replaces green. Mulmul curtains change to scarlet velvet drapes, drowning under their own weight. Rottweiler pups transform into a Victorian couple in a position so compromising, it would shake up the been-there-seen-that beatnik. Before I can raise an alarm, Rohini slinks in, all satin gown and silver Ferragamo heels, swishing a turquoise boa. The dinner table, miraculously cleared of ice-cream droppings and Sunday newspapers, is now heaped with pink and blue rose petals. Midget men in underwear swing on fake vines across the roof. In the throes of her Lauren Hutton-meets-Silk Smitha bad girl act, Rohini plucks out a rose petal from the table garden and tickles my cheek ...

I hold Rohini's wrist at arm's length.

'We've been friends for twenty years.'

'Twenty-two.'

'We're practically best friends.'

That's a puerile concept. True, nonetheless.

A midget cupid drops down from the roof on Rohini's bare shoulder.

'I've never thought of you this way.'

The midget giggles. Little arsehole.

'I'm attracted to men, Rohini.'

Giggling Midget swings his stumpy legs down Rohini's collarbone and rests his double chin on his bow.

'But you haven't had heterosexual sex in …'

Let's not get down to counting months here.

'It happens. It starts this way, for most women. Attractive women like you, with your bee-stung lips and big curvy hips … Do you not just want to touch my …'

'I don't swing, Rohini!'

She fluffs her turquoise boa, raises an eyebrow in question. I meditate balefully on the Ferragamos. The thigh-high slit of the gown exposes Swingerella's perfectly toned legs.

'Sho?'

'No!'

'Shobhna?'

'I'm flattered but no.'

'You want to go to sleep?'

'Oh, for pity's sake, Rohini! You're a mother!'

'As are you. Big deal, lemon peel.'

The midgets disappear into the roof. Curtains and Rottweilers are restored. Burlesque set melts back to ice-cream droppings and Sunday newspapers. The mob on Veepee's channel has dispersed. It's been a long day of protests. They need their drinks, bibimbap and midnight djembe classes.

'You okay, ma?'

Rohini tries to put a comforting arm around me. I dart like a virginal pomfret across the living room via kitchen, aiming for my bedroom. Rohini gives chase through the length and breadth of my 955 square feet apartment, and finally corners me near the wash basin.

'You want to try my new face wash? Honeysuckle and apricot? From Auroville?'

Bury my head in the wash basin and turn on the tap.

Rohini continues the onslaught in the relentless spirit that characterizes married women.

'You okay, ma?'

I slink into my bedroom. The obstinate heifer follows.

'You know, sometimes I think we're not that generation.'

The bisexual generation?

'The truly post-modern, liberated generation. The hippies beat us hands down.'

Every time twenty-somethings gather en mass to behave like nincompoops, a thirty-something somewhere feels her age.

Rohini settles down on the bed, rubs delicious cream on her face and neck in uncertain triangular motions, infusing the room with the heady scent of clove.

Damn, she smells good!

'Do you want to talk?' she tries again.

'Uh-huh.'

'I think you should come visit us in Bangalore.'

'No, thanks.'

'You need a break.'

The next thing you'll suggest, Swingerella, is a threesome with the hubster.

She scratches my nose like she's checking a stray puppy for signs of viral fever.

'You don't have to be so strong all the time.'

I'm not. At all. I'm weak. Can't you see me cracking, bitch?

'You're not looking good, Sho. Look, I'm not going to impose myself ...'

Lord Ayappa, thank you!

'... but I need to know. Can you really take this, Sho?'

Take what? The lack of a sex life? Propositioning girlfriend? Shitting bullets on a fucking landmine?

'I can.'

'Goodnight, sweetie.'

Having said that, Rohini leans over and casually kisses me full on the mouth.

Fifty minutes past six on a bright September morning in an apartment in Andheri, Mumbai. I – Shobhna Ramakrishnan, thirty-five, single, quasi-delirious – sit cross-legged on my bed, while sunlight pours mercilessly through the window. The monsoon has nearly deserted us. The city has received its lowest rainfall of the season in recorded history. It's hot as hell.

Close eyes and breathe in deeply, then exhale slowly. Repeat ten times. Open eyes. Suck in belly and flap gently while breathing out in short spurts.

Pranayama exercises are highly recommended for vaata dosha (afflicted air) personalities.

Concentrate. Focus. Breathe in. Breathe out. Oxygen explodes through blood cells. Concentrate. Focus.

'*Who says I can't get stoned? Turn off the lights and the telephone,*' John Mayer announces Amma's call on my cell phone.

'How's Roja? How are you?' she demands.

'She's good. I'm fine.'

'Nee Bangalore eppo thirumbi varuve? Romba jaasti aayiduthu. That's not the sort of city you can ever be happy in.'

'Okay, Ma, naa busy. Will call later.' No inane conversations after a night of delirium. Hang up and resume vajrasana pose.

Fifteen minutes later, chai bubbles over the gas stove. Two slices of brown bread lie on a griddle on the other flame, sending the fragrance of ghee wafting to all corners of the house. A peek into the bedroom to the right of the kitchen; everything is fine. Roja – bless her little peaceful soul – is still asleep. And so is the new occupant of her room.

The previous night's episode with Rohini was entirely a figment of my imagination, which is now teetering on the edge of reason. Rohini visits often, but she didn't visit yesterday. In fact, nobody has visited over the past few months. Rohini didn't proposition me. I'm not bisexual. In fact, I'm barely sexual.

Doorbell shrieks. It is robust Punjabi woman demanding garbage and an extra something for Diwali. I hand her the garbage bin and inform her that all major festivals are two months away. When the time is upon us, extra somethings – discarded clothes, snacks and sweets – will be duly handed over. It'll be stellar if she can postpone invoking the spirit of the joy of giving until November. Punjabi woman frowns, blows her large nose and rings the neighbouring doorbell.

I smell something browning and rush into the kitchen to lather the pan-toasted bread with more ghee. Two spoons a day keeps arthritis away. A couple of months back, my inner moon let out a gentle but audible yelp in the thick of the ardhachandrasan posture during Power Yoga class. That is when Bharat, my v-shaped instructor from Rishikesh, advised me to adopt the ghee micro diet. 'You can the escape the ghee in the twenties. In the thirties, you must only adapt the ghee to keep the stretch in the oily, easy manner in the body.' To emphasize his point, he had pressed down those magnificent glutes and flapped his lithe thighs like a baby butterfly. 'I do the ghee in two cups of the hot milk in every day. I'm the forty-six.'

Thus inspired, I adopted the ghee micro diet and am already experiencing encouraging internal lubrication. On the way back to my bedroom, chai and toast in hand, I halt in front of the oval mirror. 5'9". Well-proportioned limbs. Above-average waist-to-hip ratio. Decent rack. Big black eyes with sweeping lashes. Dense eyebrows. Tight caramel skin. And a cascade of curls like someone's toppled a mound of dark chocolate shavings on the head. The woman in the mirror looks good.

I place the breakfast on the bed, open dirty blue Sony Vaio and practise butterfly wings till the machine boots up. His gluteus may be maximus, but I believe my thighs more than match up to Bharat's. True, the spine falls short of superyogic flexibility and the rapid-fire suryanamaskars lack a certain je ne sais quoi. But at thirty-five, I believe I'm a fine specimen of my generation.

The posers to coolth!

Here's the thing about celibacy. It's never easy. You're either thinking of sex or thinking of how not to think of it. You could be sitting on a time bomb, at a beloved's deathbed, or at the launch of your personal spaceship into Saturn, but sex won't quit. Even when you have the most pressing, life-altering issues at hand.

Vaio leaps directly to Facebook. A sudden ennui envelops my entire being. I reach out for the chai, cup it in both hands and look wistfully out of the window. The heat is unbearable, unexpected and unwelcome, coupled with Mumbai's de rigueur monsoon visuals of floating plastic bags and random filth.

Check two in Roja's room. All is well. It appears she is exhausted by the previous day's events and doesn't need breakfast yet. *Ting!* It's Roja's caretaker dropping in to say she'll report later in the day. But before I can shut the door on the departing lady, Luchchi sticks her head in, demanding to chat with Roja.

Green eyes, you put a spell on me!

I stay away from cats. Their self-assurance is annoying. Roja gets along with them spectacularly. I should be grateful to Luchchi. Apart from her caretaker, Luchchi is Roja's special friend. Roja is intimate only with a select tribe of severe Type A personalities. Adopted by the society watchman, Luchchi fits that mould. The dirty grey feline spends all day being chased by juvenile delinquents who screech, 'Saali kuchchi, kameeni Luchchi.' But one glower from those cold green eyes and that filthy fur standing on end, and they take a step back.

Meooowwwrrrrrrrr.

I pick up my stack of newspapers, close the door on the perennially pissed-off feline and stand in the living room that is exuding an intangible sense of impending doom.

The tabloids are full of 'Quit Fucking Bombay' protests. They're on Twitter, F-book, *New York Times*, *Aaj Ka Anand*, everywhere. There's a car rally and a bomb blast somewhere in the Middle East, and people dying in Manipur and Africa. My boss's fair, chubby face looms large on page seven, clubbed along with the nightly parade of Herve Legers, sweaty armpits, Balenciagas and male escorts in tight orange ganjis. *Damn, he was meant to be on page one!*

I reach out to dial Triple S's number, then decide against it. Bugger! The calm centre of this whole fucking maelstrom. While what I needed is tranquil, intelligent and potently persuasive force.

There is a loud noise from Roja's bedroom. The phone yelps. It's Bala, calling for the twentieth time since last night.

This might be the right time to freak out.

More noise from the bedroom. A cough. *Clang!* A bowl falling to the ground. If I'm guessing right, the plastic-covered jujubes have spilled softly.

My knees buckle.

Get here, Udayan! Now!

2

The Game Changer

Udayan

A cloud to the far end of the horizon resembles Monmoyee's left breast. I am about to drift into a deep state of arousal when two pairs of curious brown eyes attack me.

'Are you Pakistani?' It is the boy.

'No.'

'What's your name?'

'Udayan.'

They're desi kids. On the row in front of mine. The girl must be eight and the boy five. Resting their arms on the backs of their seats, they appear to have decided on most of their in-flight entertainment plan.

'I'm a Pelican,' whispers the boy, eyes wide.

'He means he's American,' the girl adds with sisterly disdain.

Then she comes striding and literally kicks the Eagles-sweatshirt-sporting, forty-plus, important-looking gentleman settled comfortably by the aisle in my row. He frowns at me like I'm personally responsible for spawning the tyke who has decided to occupy the empty seat between us and is burrowing into her DSi. Emboldened, her baby brother hops over from the seat in front and, with no more than a second's hesitation, finds a cosy spot on my lap and looks curiously at what I'm reading. The mother turns around, a petite woman in her twenties with big, apologetic eyes. 'Shaan. Sona. Come back here. Chalo. *Now!*'

I assure her all's well. Her bundles of joy aren't causing me much grief. She's relieved. The father sulks at the window seat in front.

The airhostess tells the man next to me, now fiddling with his Kindle, that he may shift to business class and informs me I can still choose to upgrade. Sona declines on my behalf and orders 'pooranpolly with cream cheese' for dinner.

The lady smiles. 'Not on the menu, sweetie. How would you like some awesome chicken tikka and biryani?'

After being told by Sona where she should stick her biryani, the airhostess turns to me.

'Is she yours?'

She isn't, but I still have to make up, so I shut the script. 'No. Do you have kids?'

'Yes, you?'

'No. I'd love to. Some day.'

The airhostess' pupils dilate. 'You'll make a great dad,' she says with a smile that loses some of its vigour as she notices the brat seated next to me placing her hand on mine territorially.

Shaan declares he wants to watch a 'Shallouk Kahn' film. I adjust his earphones and he settles down to three hours of song-and-dance on his mom's iPad. Sona lapses into an inexplicable bout of silence, which gives me enough time to do some rapid reading. Their father gets up to pee and passes us by without so much as a glance at his daughter. Ill-fitting grey corduroys, striped white tee, leather jacket, and generous paunch over his Gucci belt. He must be around thirty. He is exactly the kind of Indian man that drives robust Aussie blokes like Callum insane. I thank my stars that my rambunctious co-worker is not on this flight. Another scene is the last thing I want.

Almost eight hours ago, Callum had stared at the crowd in front of the Air India check-in counter at JFK and blurted, 'Mayte, that's the saddest thing I've evuh seen.' Testosterone levels already high thanks to a battle of words with the Sikh driver who ferried us from Chelsea, Callum boomed 'Fuckwit Indians!' when the young man at the AI counter politely regretted the availability of business class seats. The boy gaped at him in subdued fascination.

After two decades in Sydney – starting off as a theatre backstage hand, graduating to beating durries for a Russell Crowe action thriller, followed by two years of doing radio and the 'tiniest chicks ever' in Thailand and a three-year stint as assistant director in London – this 6'1", blonde, blue-eyed stud crash-landed in NYC as our production manager. Everybody loves Callum. He's been our backbone on the one major production we had last year, a horror romance shot in Jaipur and Bangalore. Post a hectic twenty-day schedule and a rollicking affair with a ferocious Rajput costume designer, Callum declared India to be a place of deep shit with an epic heart.

Given the sort of warmth he felt for my motherland, I took his outburst with a pinch of salt. Besides, he was equally capable of standing atop the Eiffel Tower and yelling 'Fuckwit Frenchies!' or facing the barrel of a Taliban gun in the midst of Kabul and merrily cussing the 'Fuckwit Moslems!' But when he realized that British Airways and Jet weren't viable options we could threaten India's national airline with, given the urgency of my departure, he enveloped the young man in a bear hug, heaping fulsome praise on 'his mightyness Tendoolkar', flirted mercilessly with his lady superior and succeeded in convincing them that I couldn't possibly stoop to economy.

Of course I could. I did.

Shaan is back with his mother. Sona has decided to spend the night next to me, curled up in a blanket, monkey cap and ear muffs on. The biryani was passable, though the basmati was undercooked and the deep-fried onions better omitted. The chicken tikka was stringy. I get them to arrange a fruit–cheese platter with what they have in the kitchen – papaya, apples, tangerines and Gouda. Need to get this thing read before we land.

An hour passes. The platter I had specially got made remains untouched.

The script kicks serious ass but has left me exhausted. I feel contemplative and need a smoke. Need to think of the past.

I came to NYC thirteen months ago on a mission to acquire, expand and redefine showbiz for Mumbai-based Daha Films. No, the name isn't Middle Eastern or Masai, and it does not refer to animal sacrifice. It is Sanskrit and means 'blazing'.

Expectedly, the city and I fell passionately in love. That's the secret to a life of uninterrupted success in NY – romancing the city till she gives in.

As soon as we landed in NYC, my colleague Vik and I set up swanky shop at 45th and Madison. I took a couple of weeks to wrap up wooing and poaching a pool of overpaid and egocentric staff.

– Adrina Costa, fifty-two-year-old Italian executive producer fresh off a tiff with Fox.

– Riyaz Rangoonwala, ripped from a famous Indian American film-maker's inner coterie.

– Ashleigh Pincer, part-time Broadway dancer and full-time Indophile hired to take calls and add some glamour to the front desk. 'Bawliwood! Dude, scrawl me up,' she'd squealed.

– David Kwong, eccentric script doctor who had single-handedly tied all the dangerous loose ends on Ang Lee's latest before it lurched into a multimillion-dollar production schedule. Suddenly, he was the next newest, biggest oddity, and everyone had to have a piece of him. He claimed to have accepted our obscenely generous offer because he thought that 'Shekhar Kapur's *Slumdog Millionaire* made Hollywood eat elephant poo'. A day after David signed the papers, my boss – Motabhai for the rest of the world – called from Mumbai to congratulate me. The grapevine was abuzz that we'd bagged Dan even as a big fat American film studio was propositioning him. My colleagues think the CEO's signature moong dal pakoras with imli chutney and slivers of fried radish had a strong part to play in Daha's Conquest of Kwong.

– Asmita Shetty and Raoul Pandit. Hardcore corporate rats. IIT, IIM, Ivy League thoroughbreds and bona fide second-generation immigrant success stories with brownstone houses and happy families. These guys nurtured brands for breakfast and gobbled competitors for dinner. At our penultimate brunch at Aquagrill, I soothed their Bollywood phobias, making their hidden love for the homeland surge at just the right moment. Daha is on the verge of signing its finest deal-making devils on.

The future is there, out of India. But I wonder why I am on a flight to Mumbai.

'Are we flying over Pakistan?' Sona's first question after she opens her eyes.

'Not yet. Good morning.'

'Where are we, then? Eyeraq?'

'Would you like breakfast?'

'Coco puffs. Tell me about Pakistan.'

'Why?'

'School praject.'

'What about it?'

She sighs, looks out of the window at the fluffy clouds. 'When did things screw up between ya guys?'

I look into her heart-shaped, angelic face.

'Indyah and Pakistan?' she persists.

'That's a long story. Let's get some breakfast first, okay?'

'Are ya making a film in Bombay?'

'What makes you think I make films?'

'Yar reading a film. My ant Sheila is friends with Aashi Kappu's mom.'

'The actress?'

'Duh!'

Sona's mum gets up, stretches her limbs. 'Thanks very much. I'll take her now.'

'She can stay. No sweat.'

'I don't get that often. Wallah, your girlfriend's a lucky girl,' she says, scooping up the little Pelican in her arms and proceeding to the bathroom.

I smile politely. It's time to get back to the reading. I dive into the remaining thirty pages without any interruption. Then, I go back and rocket through the entire script – all 126 pages of it. The English translation sucks. But the story soars above the barrier of language. It's gut-wrenching, a knockout.

All ambient sounds and thoughts get drowned out. The past, though, is on a nagging spree.

Sho Ramakrishnan. She always knew how to grab a man by his balls!

3

Shaking Like the Jujubes

SHOBHNA

'... It's so free. You can do anything you want, be anyone. This really is a city of dreams, no?'

It's a worthless shithole, so why don't you be The Girl That Shuts The Fuck Up, and do a good job of ripping the hair off my epidermis!

The dainty girl waxing my arms, fresh off the train from Manipur, is bubbling over with Mum-fatuation. While she trills about how tedious, dull and narrow-minded the folks in the hills can get, I'm thinking of ways in which to redirect this Himalayan Orchid back to oxygenated civilization.

The spa is a squat little place in one of the obscure lanes of Andheri, home to the Mumbai film industry, a putrid dump. Andheri is where the bad roads, the work and the potloads of dirty money live. Nobody sips sangria at 4 p.m. in Andheri and slinks out for protests later during the day – that happens in Bandra and southwards from there.

I personally would rather be in Abbottabad than in Andheri. At least Abbottabad is unabashedly what it is – a squalid hellhole – and doesn't try to hide its ugliness by sewing in tacky sequins at the borders. And you get the best jujubes here, at Mohan Karkaria's store in the back alleys of Versova. I picked up 500 grams and was in the vicinity of the spa. Can you blame a woman for getting a mani-pedi while the world is falling apart around her?

Ebullient owner of the spa waddles over in her Juicy Coutures with a 'Long time no see, loueve. How's Danny? Give him my loueve'. The Orchid is done with my arms and gets a-plucking, asking if she may pretty please divide the unibrow. I hiss. The lady owner clasps my hand and insists I indulge in the latest detoxifying manicure and some nail art.

'So, long time, ya, babeh? You stopped coming here now you become a star, haan? What you doing these days?'

Answer her. The juicy duck is asking you what you're doing.

'Films.'

She inches closer with a blob of translucent balm on her finger to soothe my stinging eyebrows. 'Ah, I always knew you'd make it. Brainy beauty, haan. Who are you with?'

You'll know soon enough. I keep mum, pretending to be busy with what The Orchid is doing.

'My brother-in-law Raju works as a casting agent for YuShiMa. You know the stud from Mexico is doing her next film, na? Raju says the Mexie's had a thingie wingie with her mummy, and now he's doing her. And her film. So multi-handed this Gen Zee, no? His auntie comes to us for Botox. You should meet her, yaar.'

YuShiMa is Yugita Shital Makara, rising scion of a loaded Bollywood family. The steaming young chica delivered a smash hit with her debut as a producer. Her Singapore-returned, sashimi-loving publicist is terribly anal that the press address her client with the bizarre geisha-esque acronym. The press will call her King Kong, as long as the free brunches and goodie bags keep landing where they should.

Phone squeaks. It's him. Triple S. He's just been initiated into the infectious world of texting and is going berserk hurling cryptic messages at me. This one reads 'Sevan'. That's it. But I know Triple S well enough by now. I dash back a reply saying we can't meet at 7 p.m. and postpone the much-dreaded Udayan–Triple S face-off till the weekend.

Noticing the spa owner trilling on her fuschia cell phone, I extricate my eyebrow from Orchid's firm but gentle grasp, hand her the required cash, and slide towards the door.

'Hey, Sho, did you hear of the RAA thing?' The spa owner asks.

'Yeah.'

'Strange, na? How can such a big man go like, just … you know?'

'Yeah.'

'What you think? YuShiMa gave his supari or what?'

'Yeah?'

'You film-wallahs! Always so much drama, na?'

'Yeah. Got to go. Bye.'

'Bye, sweetie. I'll tell Raju you dropped by, haan. Oh, how is Rosy?'

'Roja. She's great. I'll tell her you said hi.'

I get back just in time. Roja is catching up on local gossip with the watchman and Luchchi. She's starving, so we go upstairs and I make her her favourite – cheese French toast with a full cup of chopped coriander and one pepper-cheese cube. Then I check the bedroom. All's well. For now.

I make myself some filter coffee and settle down to watch *Lie to Me*. It's our favourite show. What's not to love about the adventures of a firm of face-reading applied psychologists working on criminal cases and FBI investigations? Roja, the impossible romantic, bets that Foster and Wildman will get together by the end of this season.

Let's pretend this is a regular evening, mommy and her little girl with food and telly.

The 'Quit Fucking Bombay' protests are threatening to divert attention from us. This was unprecedented. When it happened, I thought the little buggers would create a ripple online, bag a couple of 'youth of India rises against local fundamentalists' headlines in some obscure international newspaper, and the buzz would die in a few days. Now they are in Azad Maidan and hogging all the press.

Damn, stupid vigilantes!

It's 7.15 now and Roja has dozed off for a bit on the settee, her legs folded in, just like she used to when she was a baby. Everything's under control; she can wake up later. It's going to be a long night. I empty half the jujubes into the china bowl and consider spiking them with poison. Two more calls each from Bala and Triple S. A couple of other calls from journos I know and ... *hell* ... a text message from Veepee. He wants to know if I'm available for a weekend panel discussion on 'Youth against Local Goondaism'. For a second there, I almost want to call him and spill the beans.

If only I had balls. Big, bouncing balls of fire!

It's a chronic condition called Mars in Cancer, a planetary placement that shacks up the yang planet of aggression uncomfortably with the emotional ying crab, creating the most unlikeliest of couplings. Amma reads horoscopes and she has had a lifelong grouse against this placement in my birth chart, along with Appa's Venus in who-the-fuck-cares-what.

'It's like a soldier living in his mommy's house,' she says

when she is on my case. 'You will never go for the kill, na, chinna? Such a waste of that intelligent Virgo Sun and dashing Aries Moon.' It appears Pablo Picasso had his Mars wallowing in Cancer too. He didn't do so bad ...

Reality calling! Time to shower, and give a hurried thought to wardrobe options. Blue skinny jeans and black tee. Negative. Halter neck fuchsia churidar kurta. Negative. Beige-green Calcutta cotton sari. *Seriously, hurry up, da!* Green mulmul shift over black tights and black kitten heels. *Done!*

9.38 p.m. No shit, it's Bala at the door. Miss ten heartbeats in a row, until I realize my otherwise stoic colleague is on the verge of tears. So it's easy to stall him at the door without arousing suspicion.

'What do we do, Sho? What do we do?' he wails and wails, perhaps expecting to be invited in for a hug. Then he checks me out.

'Where are you going? We have an SOS at office. The presscon is barely more than a day away.'

'I have to pick up a ... relative. From the ... um ... Dadar Station.'

He squints. I look at the floor, then directly into his eyes. For a second, everything returns – his bravado, the pugnaciousness, the defiance.

'We're cancelling the presscon.'

No! Don't you dare rain on my parade, Bala. I grab him by his shoulders and shake him. 'Bala, he'll be back. Trust me. Trust me.' All you have to do with Bala is repeat simple words in a reassuring pattern. That hypnotizes him into submission.

'Right. We need you for the SOS.'

'I'll be there by eleven tonight.'

'Right. Be careful of those protestors. They've moved to Shivaji Park. Dadar is a mess.'

I shove him out. It'll take at least thirty minutes to get to the airport. One last check into Roja's bedroom, a double coat of gloss, and I rush out. Ditch car for auto-rickshaw. By 10 p.m., we're stuck under the Andheri flyover in a stubborn traffic jam. There appears to be a minor law enforcement situation ahead.

'Yeh kya ho gaya hai na Bombay ko, madam?' The rickshaw-wallah philosophizes with the wisdom of an aged grizzly bear. Wearing a goatee and spectacles – plastic, blue-framed ones – he couldn't be over twenty. Catching me admiring his style quotient through the rear view mirror, Blue Glasses swings his head 180 degrees with a dazzling smile and uproots his earplugs. I have his full attention and opinion.

'Madam, Bombay ki to lag gayi saali.'

Story of our lives, bro.

Here's how it pans out over the last decade. The city has always had a laissez faire attitude towards immigrants. Anyone from anywhere was always welcome to crash-land at the Gateway of India and try his luck at money-making, acting, selling peanuts, opening restaurants, smuggling, drugs, whoring, terrorizing, cutting diamonds, cleaning gutters ... you get the drift. All is chummy until the 'original' Mumbaikar – the Marathi Manoos, aka whining son of soil, wakes up from profound slumber and discovers he's nibbling on leftovers, as second-class citizen of adored homeland. Leveraging the issue politically, sons of soil spawn a roaring fistful of self-righteous parties whose agenda is to be loud and obnoxious and abuse and thrash anyone who as much as winks at their money. Crafty Cousins, especially from the North, aren't amused. Whipped by the Manoos at railway stations, hissed at and chased from Virar to Horniman Circle, Crafty Cousins – emboldened by secular slogans from the Centre – hit back with self-righteous glee. From the ensuing free-for-all fracas emerges a brand new party that redefines the paradigms of public nuisance – MaMi, aka Maharashtra Mitra. Friends of Maharashtra.

In April this year, the dean of Mumbai's oldest medical college was the guest of honour at a decaf-and-vegan burgers affair at Harvard where a reporter asked his views on 'regional fundamentalism tearing the cosmopolitan fabric of Bombay'. The good professor, in no uncertain terms, painted all homeboy outfits as a pesky crop of brain-dead carrots. Enraged at the slur on their international image, the goons at MaMi descended upon the medical college, growled ferociously at everyone, distributed pamphlets in Marathi and smashed up the labs, leading to a huge uproar. Other homeboy parties jumped into the fray. The police went on high alert, after MaMi smashed a coffee shop miles away from the medical college. The good professor – a very likeable Bengali–Muslim man – took the matter to Delhi and had the big guys publicly spank MaMi's bottom for being naughty. After they were made to cough up damages, the MaMi goons sulked en masse at their headquarters – the thirteenth floor of Worli's most expensive commercial tower. MaMi's HQ – a tad avant garde by right wing fundamentalist standards, but suitably ghoulish – was rumoured to be a virtually impenetrable saffron fortress, equipped with high-tech security software and stuffed animal heads.

'Saale gadhe … hatao!'

A miniature bust of Bachelor God Hanuman bobs violently from its perch on the rickshaw's dashboard. The air is extraordinarily muggy for this time of the night and year. Something a clichéd writer would describe as 'pregnant with the unbearable suspense of doom'. All around and across the packed flyover, people are hurling questions and abuses in equal measure. 'Arre rani, methi ka tadka,' a woman riding pillion on a scooter coos into her phone, while the scooter driver spits fountains of paan all over the road. In another rickshaw, a teenage boy has his hands all over his girlfriend, who in turn is tugging at his tush; their driver looks bored. Goth Goddess in a Honda City rolls down her window and screams into my face, 'Man, the suburbs suck. Are the protestors here?'

I ignore the woman.

An SUV edges up front, which releases the gridlock. Before anyone can react, Blue Glasses squeezes between two cars, curses three fellow rickshaw-wallahs, almost flies off his seat to kick two pedestrians in their shins and steamrolls us to the front of the first-gear pack of jackals. He is very pleased.

'Push, phusss,' he mutters, looking up at the silhouette of a billboard. It's a saffron-and-gilt edged confidence vote from the MaMi for the MaMi. No photograph. Very large Devnagari font framing the party symbol – something resembling an albino wild jackal. Appropriate.

'What side you on?' Blue Glasses turns around to look at me.

I don't get it.

'You are on which side? Their or here?'

'The ... um ... good side.' *Random shit.*

He looks pleased.

Another call from Veepee. And a text from a rival channel. A fundamentalist Islamic group in Jammu has banned all sorts of pant-wearing activities for women in the region. In protest, the channel is sending a bunch of celebrity women to Jammu, wearing a vintage lace studio pants collection from a topcat French fashion label. Full travel and stay sponsored with hair and make-up. Would I like to join them?

Time to switch off the phone.

4

Back to the Future

UDAYAN

Almost a year into Daha, NYC began to feel somewhat like home.

In the first week of August, Callum expressed an urgent need for a team night out to celebrate the anniversary of the setting up of the Daha office in NYC. Raoul had got the PR people to send out customized Dean & Deluca hampers and did a press splash on a yacht out on the Hudson. But the occasion required a more intimate celebration. Thus, that Saturday night, the Daha team found itself at a decrepit block in the Lower East Side. Like any NYC club worth its rep, this one looked like a recently abandoned factory from the outside. They said Jude Law was one of the partners. The little place inside was a riot, a colourful throwback to Moulin Rouge. Antique wood cabinets, naughty wallpaper, a mirror-backed bar, a row of jewel-dripping chandeliers with the last one suggestively dangling a rope right above a little stage. The little place was stuffed to the gills with merry, drunk, painted faces. The show that night included a ventriloquist midget from Argentina and a shrilly Texas chick who stripped to '*Like a Virgin*'. It was good fun.

The girls and Callum disappeared into one of the private velvet booths upstairs. Raoul and his fiancée were networking out of sheer habit. I chilled at the bar over a fennel vodka and a shot of absinthe until the tallest, most beautiful drag queen snuggled over and drew me into dazzling conversation. 'Baby, your peepers are as green as the Ganges.' She came closer, her ebony skin glistening, tasselled bright blue gown shimmying and exposing toned legs longer than a giraffe's. Then she placed an exquisite hand at the precise spot on my thigh and moved it, applying the right amount of pressure.

'Tell me Oodayahn. What do you feel right now?'

I felt something then. After the longest time.

Not an erection.

'I want to pee.'

It was an epiphany.

I was relaxed. I was happy.

Relaxed, happy and far away from Mumbai.

'I want to pee.'

Waiting for Shaan to emerge from the loo, I discover Sona's trailed us. She wants to know which movie I'm making in India. If any help is required, her family contacts with Aashi Kappu are available for me to me tap into. I appreciate her generosity and explain that I'm not making a film on this particular visit.

'Ya, thinking about yar girlfriend.'

'How do you know I have a girlfriend?'

'Because ya thinking about yar girlfriend.'

Monmoyee Bhattacharya. We met at an upscale networking party for South East Asians. She sat near the water fountain on the terrace, hands neatly folded on her knees, engaged in deep conversation with her coterie. Our eyes met as soon as I entered and went back to each other over the course of the night. A common actor friend introduced us over dinner. I learnt she was an art curator and worked with an established gallery in Chelsea. A few days later, the common actor friend dropped in at work and made overt attempts to set us up, reasoning that 'your value systems are so synchronized'. I had no idea what that meant and told her I didn't appreciate her hooking me up with random gorgeous women.

The offspring of a Bengali father and an American Irish mother, she'd studied and worked in Madrid and Paris, and had returned to NYC two years back. There was the unmistakable European air about her, but only the refinement, not the snootiness. By her own admission, she had her mother's fair skin and petite frame and her father's hazel eyes. She was warm and feminine. And independent. After fifteen years of mating in the urban corporate battlefield, in Raoul's words, 'we men had been made to forget that post-mod women could just be good ol' girls'.

I wasn't actively in the market for a serious relationship. Neither was I scoping the scene out for a casual partner. But the setting just happened to be ripe for romance. Daha was shining bright; we had a fine team (with some minor roadblocks) and some terrific projects lined up. *The Times* had done a Sunday story on 'fresh Indian blood redefining Bollywood' and we featured at number two, albeit with exaggerated numbers and outlandish projections. But that's the way this business works, and Motabhai was over the moon. His faith in me was paying off. He was looking golden to his board of star-struck investors in Abu Dhabi, Johannesburg and back home. Monee glided into my life at this convenient stage. We surprised each other. After the longest time, my love life and sex life took off in perfect synchrony.

I took her for Navratri dinner with the brood to Rajan Kaka's place at Queens. Kaka and family were mildly annoyed that I hadn't paid them even a single obligatory visit since I moved to NYC and loudly attributed it to the fact that I had turned into an ungrateful, wannabe-Upper West Side desi boy. But one look at Monee in her beige chiffon sari and they warmed up faster than the samosas ordered in from Mina's. I was thrown into the kitchen to supervise the dhokla that the cook had abandoned in the steamer.

Fifteen minutes later, Kaki strolled in with a bourbon to say, 'You bachcha log look like Amitabh and Jaya. Chhotu and lambu. Such a lovely couple!'

I had to calm her down. 'She's just a friend, Kaki.'

'Arre, friendship is overrated. Bengali girls make the best wives. Look at you. Forty years. Now when will you have kids?'

'I'm thirty-nine. We'll see where it goes, Kaki. Kashmiri mirch?'

We garnished and joined the others on the porch. The boys were mesmerized by Monee by then. My niece Sheetal's 'fall boyfriend' turned out to be a television actor who earnestly hovered around me and we began talking. Then we shifted to the futon inside, munching on dhokla and samosa-chat, and watching the Patels, Doshis and the singularly lissome Bhattacharya bond. We talked shop and had a long conversation. Yes, were looking to hear from the guys at Cannes about Callum's horror love story, which had turned out to be a sleeper hit in London and Germany. If they accepted it, it would be another large feather in our cap. Daha was also sitting on a Hollywood–Bollywood co-production which was being pitched to a huge superstar from Mumbai. Impressed by this glut of information, Sheetal's boyfriend handed me his card and noticed my eyes fixed on Monee. Like most out-of-work actors accustomed to dramatizing trivial events, he shook my hand, lowered his voice and whispered, 'She's the one, bro.'

At 11.30 p.m. this Tuesday at my condo, Monee made broccoli–lentil soup before we made love. She didn't pull any shocks in bed that night. I didn't want any. At 12.05, we lay in bed, naked and wrapped up in two bed sheets, my legs between hers, my hands on her slender hips. I admired her breasts and wanted them again. She propped herself on my chest and spoke about her new pet project – art therapy with autistic children at a Hispanic community centre in Secaucus. She was genuinely excited. Perhaps Monmoyee Bhattacharya was 'the one' – the most correct ever. I got inside her and heard a beep. It was my phone, bringing an unexpected email from India.

Two days later, I was on a plane to Mumbai.

'Is Cashmir the only problem between y'all?'

'It's complicated.'

'Like how?'

She won't give up. We're at the baggage claim where everyone's pushing. You know you're in Mumbai when the pushing begins. The local time is 11.10 p.m. We're on time, but the guys at the immigration counter are holding up a long line.

'Did ya like that story?' Sona's eyes are on my black briefcase, a gift from Monee.

'Yes.'

'Love story?'

'No.'

'Ya make it into a movie?'

'I don't know.'

'Ya like never give a straight answer.'

Sona's mum pulls up with Shaan. 'I'm sorry. She can be a handful.'

'No sweat. Can I drop you guys somewhere?'

'But ya friend's come.'

Across the terminal barricade, wearing a green dress, and trying not to look terrified, is Sho.

5

Bringing Home Hobos

SHOBHNA

Why is he carrying a fat Hobo?

'Sho?'

But why is he carrying a fat Hobo? The bag is an aberration. A wussy abomination on a manly man.

'Shobhna.'

'Hey.'

'What are you doing here?'

I've come to check on you, in case you decide to run back from the airport. 'Surprise! Are these your children?'

The little boy must be five, blue tee, blue jeans and droopy eyes. The girl must be eight or nine, wearing a printed white blouse, brown tights, and shooting poisonous darts with her eyes at me. I see they belong to his co-passengers – an ugly gent in a tight leather jacket and his really tiny wife – who are struggling with three baggage trolleys. He introduces me as his friend, the couple as his friends, the kids as his friends. Everyone's a friend of Udayan Doshi.

His green eyes flicker. 'But what are you doing here?'

That's right. Keep repeating inane questions. That should drive the awkwardness right out of the park.

A hug as smooth as silk. He says he'd arranged for a cab. Besides, how did I know what flight he was arriving on? I remind him of the text he'd dashed off the day before. He burbles thickly. Udayan was never a burbler, but people change. Two years ago, I wouldn't have pinned myself as the sort of person who pounced unexpectedly on old friends at airports either.

For the longest time, we look at Udayan's 'friends'. The parents have spotted a bunch of relatives and there's much hugging, backslapping and pulling of cheeks. Our awkwardness surges and we ache to crawl over and hide in the comforting folds of The Great Indian Family. After bundling her brood into an SUV, the tiny mom comes over to thank Udayan. The girl sticks her head out of the window to wave. Udayan waves back and blows her a kiss.

Still has a way with the little people. What's with the Hobo, though?

He looks good, in a pair of beige trousers with a white-and-grey semi-formal shirt. And moccasins. Conservative ones. The man would sooner chop off his feet than wear sneakers. He checks his iPhone to track the cab he's booked. I check my BlackBerry for nothing in particular. There are a couple of messages, invites to parties I've long stopped going to, and a follow-up call from Veepee.

'What the hell are you doing here? You should be home.'

'I … just wanted to make sure you're coming.'

'Fine. I'm coming home with you.'

Yes, please!

'No, let's start afresh tomorrow.'

'Don't be ridiculous. Let's go.'

'No, really. Everything is under control.' *He's tired. He's probably counting to ten. He may just slap me. No sweat, that's what friends are for.*

He scans my face for signs of alien abduction having lead to irreparable cranial damage. To the crowd on the right, we spot a smartly dressed driver holding out a placard that reads 'Udayan Doshi'.

'Samaan itna hi hai. Aur hum do log. Chalo.'

Uday's connect with the plebeians is as bang on as his connect with kids. After seeing the Hobo, I half-dreaded a New York twang. The car swerves past people and gates, into the wide stretch of road that's almost always a traffic nightmare. We have some time to talk but fill the minutes with the silence of discomfiture. I wonder what he's thinking. He must wonder what I'm thinking.

He must want to thwack me.

'How is Roja?'

I know he's fuming. I know he wants to come to my apartment pronto and get on with it. He has a hundred questions stacked in alphabetical order in his freakishly well-organized mind. He's probably still considering thwacking me. Hard. *Something he should have done two years ago ...*

But Uday will not launch into a full-frontal assault. That is not his style. It wasn't Gandhi's style either. Sneaky buggers, both.

I fight back tears; I must spill it all out. The bisexuality dream starring Rohini. The calls from Veepee to appear on his stupid panel. The 'Quit Fucking Bombay' protests that have gone out of hand. The miserable year that refuses to end. The frustration, the betrayal. I want to tell him about Triple S, about Sunny and MM. I want to discuss *The Dhaal*. And the ramifications of what I've dragged him into.

Instead, I ask to be dropped off at a rickshaw stand after

the flyover so they can turn left and head uninterrupted to Worli. Udayan insists they'll drop me off at my building. I haven't told him about the RAA SOS meeting yet. Hell no. I'm a big girl and can handle a fifteen-minute rickshaw ride after midnight. He insists. The driver insists. Perhaps, they've sensed the slight quiver in my voice.

'I'm all right. I'll go.'

He pats my hand. I hate it when people do that.

'This is ridiculous,' he says, and lets go of my hand and pats his idiotic Hobo.

Sensing an impending argument, the driver halts by the edge of the road. Udayan gesticulates that we step out. It's still muggy and the traffic is just about beginning to disintegrate. Udayan has a little paunch now, but it's negated by his height and posture.

'I wasn't expecting you.'

'Did you read it?'

'Hmmm ... this is ridiculous. I shouldn't be encouraging you ...'

'Trust me, you're not.'

'If anything happens to him, Shobhna.'

I know he's doing mental cartwheels. I know his nerves are getting frayed on the inside.

'I think it would be better if I drop in first thing tomorrow.'

I second that. Go, sleep.

'Umm. I have to attend an SOS meeting at RAA.'

'Can you handle it?'

'Yes.'

He hails me a rickshaw, biting his lip furiously. Sticks his head in before I'm off.

'Stay safe. If you need something, call.'

Three minutes before the rickshaw pulls up at RAA's seven-storeyed office, it strikes me. That wasn't a Hobo. It was a vegan briefcase designed by a Matt & Nat in New York. I've seen them online.

A freak vegan briefcase on Uday?

That's top on my mind? I need one of those jujubes.

6

Reaching Out, Holding Back

Udayan

'Char paanch bus phod diye.'

Mumbai is dulling around the edges. It's breathtakingly ugly. As always, on the streets, in the air, there's an unmistakable crackle and energy. Like something revolutionary will break through the monotony of money and glamour and sweat and stink. The thing is, it doesn't. Everything's just the way it has always been in here. Only, this year, the monsoon has played truant, recording the lowest rainfall in over a decade. The newspapers say its 1,111 mm.

Will it rain during Ganpati Visarjan on Friday? I don't care.

Rajesh is driving to Sho's house in Andheri. I just spoke to Motabhai, announcing my abrupt arrival in the city. He was convinced by the urgency of my move.

The CEO and CFO of GMine are in town for just one day. Getting a foot in the door for a distribution deal with them is essential to get our dark horse – Callum's horror romance – to gallop to a virgin African territory. Till now, GMine had been swimming in Africa's hottest diamond deposits. Now, they're branching into movie distribution. Tomorrow, it'll be production. Everyone's scrambling to grab a bit of the diamond dust.

The press had 'leaked' that they're meeting a top Bollywood star–producer before flying back to Durbán the next morning. It's a given that this private dinner will be a flashy seduction ritual with catering from the city's top chefs, high-tech gifts, and a parade of stunning women and beefy men. The mention of diamonds has that effect on people. The stakes look higher than they actually are.

Motabhai is worried our strategy may be a bit low-key. I'm not. In fact, I've just finished a brunch meeting with the two gentlemen at their hotel. Daha is smaller compared to other Bollywood empires, but we have a solid financial foundation, from a business they recognize and trust. They seem happy with our numbers and buoyed by inside information from their American informers about our operations there. And I've subtly waved the family trump card, the jewellery business. If they hadn't turned out to be the conservatives they were, I would have swung Plan B into action – a decadent lusty lunch at the Taj Ballroom. But it didn't come to that.

Of course, Motabhai doesn't know GMine is not the only reason I dashed to Mumbai. The coitus-interrupting email that forced me on the next flight to India was neither from him, nor from GMine. It was from Shobhna.

Subject: SOS

Hi,

Trust all's well. Situation developed in Mumbai. Only you can help. Details in attachment. Trash after reading.

Thanks,

Shobhna

In bed with Monee wasn't the perfect timing for Sho's mail. With a beautiful woman on top of you, especially one you are developing feelings for, you want to be reaching out to grab the bedpost, not the—

'Bachchan ka kutta!'

Rajesh brakes, almost crashing us into a BMW Z3 Roadster. I make apologetic hand gestures while he casually holds up traffic to ogle at 'Amitabachchan's' pet. The blondish Piranha Great Dane looks a lot like his owner.

We're a few kilometres away now. A bus looms large in front, with a sign asking 'Aapne humari biryani khayi kya?' with ten phone numbers to call 'Gift-a-Biryani'. In the horizon, a billboard for Diesel has a brunette at a bar with a dude wearing blue briefs. Two kids pee beneath the billboard, under a poster – 'Quit Fucking Bombay: Reclaim your freedom at St. Blair's Auditorium, Bandra' – on the makeshift wall.

After leaving Monee's apartment on Wednesday morning, I dialled Sho's mobile number in India. She explained the situation in precisely seven sentences, her voice unusually calm. I needed to head to my condo and get ready for work, but I asked her to hang on for a few minutes and that I'd call her back. I grabbed a coffee from the end of the block and reflected for a moment as the morning wave of commuters marched steadily past me. I had a couple of options. I could walk back to Monee's apartment, say I forgot to kiss her, have breakfast sex and forget all about the call. Or I could call someone in Mumbai and have them fire Sho's ass off to the Arabian Sea. Or I could just go home, shower, and get to office.

I called her back. She picked it up at first ring and laid out her POA with the deluded detachment of a rookie terrorist. At the end of her rational plea for my cooperation, she threw the clincher. Even with the distance between us, I could feel her eyes narrow down to lethal slits. 'Udayan, you *know* you *want* to help.'

It was the deranged self-confidence of an extremist. Like a Peruvian leader drawing his brethren to the blood-soaked Shining Path. It was the last-ditch crutch of romanticism that desperate losers latch on to. I didn't need it. I was too old, too intelligent, too successful and flush with the love of a gorgeous – and very sensible – woman.

So I cabbed home, took a long cold shower and called Adrina to book me the fastest air ticket to Mumbai. Of course, for the do-or-die meeting with GMine.

'Ye MaMi ke, maa ke … bhosdi cha …'

With that volley of expletives from Rajesh, I'm shaken out of my reverie. A mob in Juhu this early in the day is very unusual. We're locked in at a popular junction where three of the city's glitziest colleges sit cheek by jowl. They're mostly college kids, holding placards that say 'Quit Fucking Bombay' and 'Give Us Our City Back' and 'Down with Fascism'. They're carrying iPads and clicking pictures of themselves. In the periphery is a crew filming the protest and at least ten cops waving their lathis theatrically in the air. Another gaggle of cops is yelling at another bunch of kids who've put up a projection screen that is displaying the rally on the walls of one of the colleges, to focus individually on the protestors spread out on the road. Through the window, someone throws in a couple of pamphlets announcing a Krav Maga workshop with student discounts and a free drink at a sister-concern pub. A kid in blue denims and black tee slaps the bonnet of our car, looks at me and comes up to the window.

'Dude, back up, huh. This can get ugly, ya.'

It doesn't look like it'll get ugly. He's carrying a poster that says: 'The world will not be destroyed by those who do evil, but by those who watch them and do nothing – Albert Einstein'.

Rajesh cuts a close U-turn, cursing under his breath, and turns towards Andheri, Mumbai's cinema district. We're waylaid again, at the JP Road (or DN Road, I don't remember which) signal, thanks to the erection of a mammoth cloth banner – next to a billboard announcing a David Guetta night at south Mumbai – under what looks like the phantom construction site of a flyover. Next to the banner, they've managed to squeeze in a Ganpati pandal, from inside which a majestic idol wearing a hot pink silk dhoti casts two wise doe eyes out at the pandemonium around him.

'Ye Metro kab chalega, sir.'

It's a statement, not a question. While the Delhi Metro has been up and purring smoothly for over six years, Mumbai has been stumbling and struggling to get an underground rail network working, even as its efficient western and central rail systems get choked beyond capacity. The city's tolerance for inefficiency borders on the grotesque even as it pats itself on the back as the country's entrepreneurial capital.

We're right under Sho's building now. The panipuri-wallah trading in front of the apartment complex recognizes me and runs over before I can run up. I recall him being called 'Master Pandey'. He wears thick, dirty spectacles and reads every inch of newsprint before using it to wrap his chaat. Breaking into a paan-stained grin, he insists I say hello. He's ecstatic to know that I've been in NYC all this while, inquires about my family, and quickly pitches a business proposition. His neighbour's niece stays somewhere in the States, he doesn't know where, and she says the chaat there is disgusting. 'Shobha Madam' calls for a couple of plates every week; I can cross-check with her on quality. He's already begun assembling a plate for me.

Rajesh is salivating in the car, ready to pounce on a driver's discounted plate as soon as I hit the elevator. Except for black tea and a piece of toast at the breakfast meeting, I haven't had anything to eat after lunch the afternoon before. He holds out the first puri, his fingernails clogged with dirt.

'Kha lo beta. Jahanon mein naam hoga tumra.'

I remember, he's always used that turn of phrase. Roughly translated: 'You'll make a name in the worlds.'

'Are you insane?'

'Am I insane?' She licks her parched lips.

'Hah, are *you* calling *me* insane?'

'Yes I'm calling *you* insane. So shoot me,' she glowers.

Her apartment is mostly the same. The glass-topped table, the cane chairs and the green sofa. The shoe rack from Sri Lanka. The Rottweiler ceramic basket and 'Thunder Thighs' shot glasses. A framed photograph of Sho and Roja as a baby. The same television set. New orange curtains.

'This is illegal.'

'The thought did cross my little mind,' she retorts.

'I'm not here for your sapphires of sarcasm, Sho.'

I don't want another argument. We just concluded a thundering session some fifteen minutes ago, and nobody won. I had gone over the situation all of the night before, even during the spurts of consciousness between the two hours of sleep I managed to grab. I thought about the situation from all perspectives, without bias, and came to the same conclusion that I'd come to after that unexpected mail in NYC. After every ten minutes post that mail, I tried convincing myself that all of it is a joke. But it isn't.

The woman is on edge.

'Let the man go, mundan. Free him,' I say, fighting to stay calm.

'The word is mundam! You still haven't learnt, have you? Let him go? Or what?'

'You could have found another place!'

'U-huh! Like what? My godown in south Mumbai or my farmhouse at Karjat?'

I realize I need to put an end to this stupidity. And quick.

She springs up and jams her fists into my chest.

'You drop this right now, Sho. Or I'll call the police.'

'Call them. I dare you.' Her body is pressed against mine.

'Look, I know it's the frustration. It's gotten to you. Come with me to New York.'

'What? To be your concubine?'

'To work at Daha. We need someone like you.'

'No, you don't.'

She's right, we don't. There are enough self-destructive psychos in the team. But this doesn't take away from her brilliance. She's got one eye on the bedroom and the other on my phone, lest I dial 100 or send a smoke signal to the CBI that is waiting on call outside the building.

'Did you read it? *The Dhaal?*' she asks.

Silence.

It's the question we've been dreading, the answer to which unlocks the potential of my involvement in the retarded scheme of events Sho's set in motion. It's best to be straightforward.

'Yes.'

'So?'

'It's good.'

'Look me in the eyes and tell me this isn't the most mind-blowing script you've read in a long, long time?'

'It's good.'

She smirks and rolls her saucer eyes like a doll.

'Return to earth. There are a gazillion outstanding scripts floating between here and LA. All great scripts don't get made into movies. You know that better than I do.'

She bludgeons her fists into my chest. 'It is *the* best script in the world.'

'Listen to yourself. Extremist!'

'Let's do coffee.'

Vintage Sho. Abysmal sense of focus. Reaches a precipice she can't jump off and makes a sharp turnabout. Either that, or she's killing time. Deflecting attention. Very clever.

I smooth my shirt and peek into Roja's bedroom – for the third time in the past thirty minutes.

'Stop checking! He's alive!' Sho yells from the kitchen. 'And Roja is at the doctor's.'

'Now?'

'Yes.'

She's whisking up a storm in the kitchen. Two spoons of Nescafe with ten drops of water and a Sugar Free pellet until the mix is a camel-coloured paste. Then she pours a combination of hot milk and water into the mix until it froths up. There's a bamboo steamer on top of the refrigerator, with onions in it. There are around seven fridge magnets sticking to it, including a lace bra and shoes and a lion and one with Bruce Lee saying something about overcoming limitations of the body and mind.

'Do you want something to eat?'

'No.'

'Paruppu usili? Eggs?'

'Sho!'

'You'll get ulcers. We can't afford you getting ulcers. Everybody has to eat … Fuck, you're hurting me!'

I am willing to break her arm, if that is what it takes. Her chocolate skin glows in contrast to my hands that are grabbing her shoulders. We stand head to head, almost the same height. Thick, bright rays of intelligence break through those outrageously expressive – pugnacious for now – eyes. But – and I confirm this by snatching both her hands – she isn't shaking or trembling. She isn't panicking. Which can only mean one thing: she's made up her mind.

'Should I take you to a doctor?'

'I'm not a lunatic, Uday. Let go of me.'

I do. She calmly picks up a bowl and a beater, and cracks some eggs. I watch her for a minute. There's still time to sort this out smooth. No lumps. No press. No embarrassment for anyone concerned. It would take an hour, perhaps another day to soothe all the fractured egos. By Friday, I could be back in NYC.

She's got the eggs and milk in a pan. The kitchen is tidy.

'You should have called me earlier.'

Out comes skimmed milk from a carton. And salt. Cumin powder follows. Then she goes back to the fridge for a tiny splash of pale lager. Good girl. I taught her that.

'I'll get soya keema and veg pulao for dinner. Will you eat here, please? I'm calling Triple S.'

'Oh, a picnic?'

She splutters for a split second, voice crumbling, a hint of tears so faint, it sounds like a wheeze. I reach out to hold her but she recovers instantly. Instead of a hug, she hands me my share of the runny eggs in a soup bowl, garnished with torn coriander.

'You're scared ...'

'*Make* me scared,' comes the retort.

The eggs are perfectly soft and creamy. I have to pick out the coriander leaves; she still hasn't learnt to chop them finely. I should not be sitting here eating scrambled eggs, trying to get this woman of steel to acknowledge her fear. I should be getting people out of this mess, catching a quick wink, and rushing south for Motabhai's evening durbar.

'Here's a question for you, Uday.'

She's scoping me, coldly.

'You could have blown the whistle from Manhattan. Why did you come all the way here?'

'Bunged it with work stuff.'

'Po da! Bull ...' She puts her bowl aside and assumes the evangelist position. Down on one knee, both her hands on my knees, blazing brown eyes looking straight into mine.

'This is our retribution, Uday.'

'What retribution?'

'If you thought this was crazy, you wouldn't be here, because you know you can't change my mind.'

'This is not about *me*, Shobhna. This is about *your* life and how you're wasting it.'

She grabs my right hand, places her fist into my palm and pumps our hands up and down, vigorously.

'This is about all of us. You, me, Triple S, Sunny, AK—'

'What *us*? The Democracy of the Demented? Listen to yourself, lady. You need a psychiatrist.'

'You need a life.'

'I have a life, Sho. The sort of life you people dream of!'

Silence.

She's a provocateur, forcing demons out of people.

'Sho, you can't get away with this.'

'I can't *live* like this.'

'You want to make a statement? There are other ways to make a statement.'

'Like what? Another final fucking draft?'

She is crouching. For a second, I think she's going to stick her head into my crotch, but she pulls herself up and stands straight, hands on hips. It's time for truce.

'Okay, I'll do it. Daha will do it. Anything you guys want. Just not this way.'

'Wee late in the day, huh, Mahatma Doshi?'

'I'm not going to apologize for the past.'

'I'm not asking you to.'

'Let this go. I'll make your movie.'

'No. I don't want your charity. We'll beat everyone on our own.'

'Go smash your life, Sho! I can't help you any more.'

Her cell phone rings. It rings a lot. She mostly ignores it. Now, however, she picks it up and speaks in broken Hindi. After two minutes, she hangs up and smiles at me.

'Deep in shit, Doshi. Can't turn back now.'

'Sho, you have a good future. You're a brilliant—'

'You're changing the top—'

I almost throw the bowl of egg on her face.

Just like that, wiping away years of recovery, we're back to where we were.

7

How Shobhna Ramakrishnan Met Udayan Doshi

All great incomplete love stories are best narrated in third person.

By May 2008, Shobhna was inching towards completing a year and a half in Mumbai. Not that she celebrated or even acknowledged the occasion. Her life was in limbo.

Back from Edinburgh during the Christmas of 2006, she'd landed a job at *X'Quisite* publications as assistant editor of their lifestyle glossy for the swish set. It was at her parents' modest bungalow in Basavanagudi, Bangalore, that Sho had met the publisher's daughter, the occasion being the famous New Year katta party. The dinner-do over bisi bele baath, home-made wine and Sho's amma–appa's motley group of architect-, doctor- and kanjeevaram-clad artist-friends, had erroneously imparted an air of free-spiritedness to the publishing scion who was otherwise all Chanel and Giuseppe Zanotti. A month later, Sho found herself in Mumbai, in *X'Quisite*'s beige-wallpapered office with alabaster-skinned girls in six-inch heels and dainty boys in slim ties and billowing jodhpur pants. They fell for Sho. Everything from her huge, sparkling kohl-eyes to her obvious intelligence and her idiosyncratic wit thrilled the twenty-somethings to bits. She found a cubbyhole in Breach Candy to live in, which meant that her professional and social life were restricted to the most 'Bombay' part of the metropolis. On the personal front, an accomplished half-Indian–half-Czechoslovakian fashion photographer had dangled a casual proposition for her to pick up or pass up. All was bling-bling-dahling until the thirteenth day of her twelfth month at work. In the midst of a brainstorming session on autumn–winter trends, Sho excused herself, rushed to the washroom and retched. Her mind was a fiend. She was attractive, bright, and determined to ruin her own great future. She was ready to resign from *X'Quisite*. Just like that. On the basis of an uncontrollable puke.

That's what her grandmother said happened to people who were too smart for their own good. Like Pallavi Periamma, awesome mathematician, now spending her days as an unwed, unloved old 'buffalo' teaching number-crazed nerds at the University of Wisconsin. Paati made sure she drilled Pallavi Periamma's tragic tale into Sho's mind, suspecting the girl might follow on the heels of her mad aunt.

The *X'Quisite* retching was her Sign To Move On.

She took a month to put in her papers – to indignant protests from her adoring fans – and escaped to Bangalore to introspect. On offer were four fabulous jobs. The most interesting was editing an American travel magazine, set to launch a dedicated Indian edition. She met the top guns and they approved of each other. Accepting their offer meant she would be working for a brand she believed in. Given a decade, who knows she could be Mark Twain-ing somewhere in her micro castle at Machu Picchu as the grand dame of intrepid lifestyle. It could have been her aha-moment. That is until her headhunter called by-the-by with a new vacancy 'which I don't know if you'd be keen on'. RAA films was scanning the market for a senior creative development associate – creative.

RAA Films was a six-decade old relic, a thumping success of a family enterprise, founded by Ramrakha Khan, a man whose barrel-moustached charisma lay framed in life-size gilt-edged portraits in all cabins and corridors of the company's office. Old Man Khan, an immigrant from Lahore, started life in Bombay as a nihari-kulcha vendor. The six women in his family cooked in their little shanty – at the Bharatiya Railway Mazdoor Sangh quarters – donated by a relative. The dozen menfolk, including four little boys, ran around grabbing lunch orders. By 1950, Old Man Khan was the proud owner of Bombay's first and last nihari-kulcha speciality restaurant in Amaan Gully in Juhu. Within the next two years, the family allotted franchises and pretty soon Old Man Khan became Bombay's Nihari King. It was only time before the city's Hindu Brahmin hotel owners' lobby sensed danger and pulled some political strings. Old Man Khan's franchisees were raided overnight and threatened to either shut shop or switch to peddling puri–bhaji. His family was harassed. It was an unfortunate time for Old Man Khan; cruel wags rechristened him Nihari Ghost. In the midst of the mess, one of their many Hindu patrons stepped in with a timely business diversification plan. Adding biryani, paya, kebabs, keema pao, veg pilaf, dal fry and kheer to his menu, Old Man Khan began a catering business and sent packed food to film studios. This way he could stay out of the public eye and continue to earn fancy profits. The Khan women were nifty vixens in the kitchen. Their business spread roots to Kolhapur, Pune, even Madras. In 1958, Old Man Khan's star-struck second cousin coerced him into producing a Muslim social drama. It had the usual elements of a despairing poet, a pure-as-lotus nautch girl and two sets of militant parents. The film was a grand flop. But childless Old Man Khan felt fatherly affection towards his second cousin, and so gave in to his request to produce another film – a musical romance with a second-grade actor and an unknown, wispy heroine. Old Man Khan was a hands-off producer. But the one time he chose to visit his set, the crew was filming a crucial scene where the lead pair confesses its love in the middle of a sugarcane field. The patriarch, always pragmatic and progressive for his times, balked. He felt that the couple looked like frigid scarecrows. 'Are they dying of cancer? Show me the passion,' he thundered mid-scene. Then he called the director aside and commanded him to get the lovers to stand atop a haystack, embrace in an oops-didn't-mean-to slow-motion moment, and tumble down before breaking into a song and dance. Old Man Khan's utterly romantic approach to courtship gave Hindi cinema one of its top ten iconic clichés. The film turned out to be a sleeper hit.

Ramrakha Amina and Associates went on to produce the most successful romantic dramas of the 1960s and '70s. In the mid-eighties, Old Man Khan passed away and the reins of the company fell, by default, into the hands of his alcoholic second cousin, who ended up diminishing the bottom line of the enterprise substantially. In 1990, the cousin handed full control to his London-returned third son, Afzal Khan. AK was a cherubic pink-cheeked, violet-eyed bon vivant with a fetish for aesthetically assembled food and an instinctive nose for blockbuster scripts, who happily began running RAA like his personal fiefdom.

After 2001, he began the painfully slow corporatization of RAA. Slow, because AK remained unconvinced that MBA upstarts in suits should run his company. But the noughties, more than any other decade, promised to be all about appearances. Most of the other A-list family-run film corporations were suiting up and hopping on to the stock exchange with a fair amount of success. AK had to acquiesce.

The first person Sho met at RAA was its affable CEO, Vasant Bala, an IIT and London School of Economics alumnus. 'I'm going to say you're perfect for RAA, Shobhna. We're looking beyond Bollywood, beneath the masala, above the big stars. A couple of American tie-ups this year and we roll out two big co-productions by the end of the year. We're also in talks with an Iranian film-maker, a Cannes discovery, and a couple of exciting voices from Korea. And we're sitting on a break-out animation project. I've looked at your career graph and its diversity excites me. Your outputs at *The Asian Today* and *X'Quisite* were diametrically different, but both are powerful. You have a distinctive voice, an international perspective with an Indian touch.'

Coming from some other corporate rodent, it would have sounded like a truck of shit. But Tam-Bram Bala had injected his stirring call-to-arms with sensible facts. RAA had a concrete past, a very promising future, and was in able hands. Sho was charged. All that remained was to meet the man-who-owned-the-spaceship, Mr Afzal Khan.

AK's office was a Zen studio – 350 square feet of white stone and steel, with non-flowering plants at the large French window. There was a massive glossy black-and-grey rug sprawled in the middle of the room. The bookshelf was one of those super-light Japanese wonders of architecture that appeared to be suspended in mid-air without any support, and held city guides, film guides and Russian novels. His table held a Mac and a big silver bowl of what looked like steamed tofu and alfalfa sprouts.

A part of the wall slid softly as AK stepped out of his private bathroom. He was apple-cheeked, fair, well-groomed and paternal, and offered Sho a choice between jasmine, orange and chamomile tea. She chose chamomile, which arrived ceremoniously in the prettiest tangerine china.

'I hear you've written a screenplay yourself?'

'Hasn't everyone?'

He smiled warmly. 'Would you like to share what it's about?'

'It's a romantic thriller set in the seventies.'

'I like that. You give me a one-page synopsis.'

The interview proceeded silkily thereafter, but Sho struggled to concentrate. Her script, all 126 outfuckingstanding pages of it, was a classified document, a secret between her and her Vaio. She'd managed to complete it in two months and hadn't bothered to promote it. Life had got too entangled at *X'Quisite* and, besides, she'd heard horror stories of people who wasted years dragging their masterpieces from one production house to the other until they lost everything, including their marbles. Now, this pink-cheeked Rennaisance Man had brought her heart's desire out in the open.

She took the job and shifted to Andheri. RAA was a generous employer; so she gifted herself a sunny, glorious two-bedroom affair that towered unapologetically over a cacophonic basti. The British Raj hangover of Breach Candy was shaken off as soon as she shifted to Ivory Towers. More than any other city suburb, the deep end of Andheri was loud, filthy, smoky and uncivil. Surprisingly, despite her sense of aesthetics protesting, Sho felt more at home in Andheri than she ever did at tony Breach Candy. Breach Candy was Bombay. Andheri was all Mumbai. Posh people lived inside tall buildings, with modular kitchens and fancy security alarms. But step outside and you collided with hairy men in striped tees smoking beedis and women who cooked dried fish curries in spectacularly clean baby-kitchens. Teens cussed at the top of their voices and played cricket every waking hour. At approximately 9 p.m. on her first night there, Sho was introduced to the local deejay's oeuvre – '*I see-ee, I see-eee your hump, I wan-nnna see you ju-ump*'. Before her eardrums could recover, he smoothly scratched to a Hindi song that translated as '*I am your parrot, you are my mynah*'.

The new job started off on a high note. AK personally led her to her office – a small but passionately decorated red-and-green space. Lording over it was an 18 x 30 inch, framed black-and-white photograph of a handsome lion, blow-dried mane flying in the wind, cognac eyes making love to the sky. AK was an art aficionado and had planted pieces from his personal collection in every room in the office.

'It's a limited edition from Omar Simon's work in the Masai Mara,' he boomed. 'Do you like it?'

She had no idea if Omar was the lion or the shutterbug, but she felt privileged. More so when she saw the *Kamasutra*-inspired mortification hanging in Bala's room. On day five, she bashed out a synopsis of her script and delivered it to AK's office. That was the last she saw of it or heard any further on the subject. To make up, AK airlifted her into his social circle, making her part of his distinguished entourage. On any given day, AK's Zen durbar held at least five people. The day Sho was initiated into AK's social project, the cohorts were Bala, Rahul from computer graphics, Rehan from marketing and an unidentified gentleman in kurta–pyjama and chappals.

They arranged themselves in AK's Bentley and the mysterious kurta–pyjama–chappals man's BMW, and sped to one of the city's swankiest preview theatres. Before Sho could visit the ladies' room to pretty up a bit, AK beckoned her to his side. In front of them, gurgling merrily on his Marlboro, was Ronnie M. You could say Ronnie was AK's slightly dim-witted rival, the Malfoy to his Potter. But in Bollywood, as everywhere else, there are no permanent friendships and no lasting enmities. It turned out AK and Ronnie were single malt buddies and hung out at the Otters' Club every second Sunday evening. The current occasion was a hush-hush industry preview of Ronnie's son's directorial debut. The heir apparent hunched close to his father, curly mop held together by one of those multicoloured headbands that were in vogue amongst metrosexual gents. A manbag warmed his bum. He looked like he'd come prepared to scoot at short notice, should the pronouncement over his debut be anything less than spectacular. AK presented Sho like a proud hen showing off its chick; Bala, displaying a smile that could put a protractor to shame, was snuggled in his other arm. Ronnie and son, and a bespectacled girl in a bandage dress, smiled at her warmly. All of them could well have joined hands, swung hips and shimmied in a circle to '*We are family*'. The industry was a notoriously happy and hospitable place. Everyone smiled, kissed, shook hands and sang Christmas carols with strangers.

They almost had you believing you belonged.

To her own distress, Sho began to look forward to these amusing socio-political field trips. If summoned, she'd bound into the durbar, delirious with curiosity; where was Papa taking his brood today? If not summoned, she'd sulk and write odious remarks on the script at hand. Sometimes, she'd call in a writer on a whim. When the poor sod arrived, hope glinting in his weary eyes, she's sit him down and treat him real bad, tell him he was a hack and his script was the pits.

Not that it was untrue, but to say it to his face was being ferociously cruel. After he left, possibly to lie prostrate on the railway tracks, she'd feel better. It was a bizarre, convoluted, empty power trip, unlike the equally empty but simpler one she'd enjoyed at *X'Quisite*. She was turning into a hard lump of seething coldness.

And then it happened – like all epic events, utterly unexpected.

It was a routine durbar call. AK was at the window, whispering to his potted plants. The head of publicity Priyanka and her assistant were busy on their phones. By the desk, an office boy was replenishing the large glass bowl with what Sho had first thought was steamed tofu, but had turned out to be sugarless giant jujubes – great for your blood pressure – from Cairo. In the middle of the room, the kurta–pyjama–chappals man was conversing with a man in a white linen shirt, who had his broad back to her. Seventy-two-year-old, raven-haired Dalmiyaji, whom Sho would always remember as Kurta–Pyjama–Chappals, was one of RAA's oldest associates, their distributor in the Middle East. His right palm was in the hands of the man in the linen shirt – who was examining a large green ring on KPC's forefinger – and with his left hand, he sucked on a jujube. Since AK appeared to be in silent union with his greens and the girls were creating a racket, Sho gravitated towards the two men.

'You can't get a Columbian emerald this size in India, even if you pay in crores, Dalmiyaji. The maal is just not available. This is beautiful, but it's Indian.'

'So they cheated me?'

'Give me the number of your agent. I'll speak to him.'

'Never mind, jaan.' Kurta–Pyjama–Chappals called everyone jaan.

'No, Daly. The trade is based on ethics. They can't get away with this.'

'Bloody bitch won't bend!'

That last endearment was from Priyanka, chain-smoking, secretly schmaltzy girl driven to extreme cussing by extraordinary work pressure. Sho often found her yelling at the toilets in the ladies' room. RAA's latest release, a satire on sodomy practices in rural India, directed by the wife of a prominent actor, was causing much grief. The actor, a luminary on the RAA's roster, had muscled in the weird project, much to AK's annoyance, but Bala had let it slide in, reasoning that it would get them to look intelligent to international agents. But the film opened to empty theatres. It wasn't cutting ice with foreign critics either. The girls were desperately drumming up a scandal to keep the accursed picture afloat. They'd arranged a faux pow-wow with an international NGO – NGO would accuse the director of gross insensitivity to the honourable image of rural Indian boys; director would riposte with all the right noises about artistic freedom, wriggling in a dig about how Austin-financed NGOs shouldn't be lecturing Ambala on how it laundered its dirty linen; prime-time television would trip over the poison. But the star wife-cum-director turned out to be an uncompromising moralist. She took her satire very seriously and was hurting ever since she heard they thought her film was too stupid for anyone to genuinely object to. So she dug in her heels. The bitch, like Priyanka said, refused to bend.

'Where's Bala?' AK asked his basil pot.

'In Delhi,' Sho replied.

'Doing what?'

'Inking the animation deal.'

AK plucked out a leaf and chewed on it.

'This is the problem with you fearsome little sparks,' he continued to address the basil. 'You can't finish what you start. You think you're taking risks, but it's the risks who're taking you.'

The doggerel escaped Priyanka. 'So what do we do now? Drop?'

The room filled with silence. Then, like two coordinated rays of sunshine, Sho and Linen Shirt spoke at the same time.

'No.'

It was simple. Priyanka's girls would go ahead with the NGO plan, without the director's permission. Instead of a two-sided pre-planned televised stunt, they'd do a one-sided pre-planned televised stunt. The director would be indignant and feel cheated. But that's the way the world worked. She'd made a bad film; what's worse, she'd made an unsuccessful bad film. It was preordained. Those who had invested money took charge and tried to cut losses, the director got to gasp on prime-time television.

As soon as their thoughts collided, Linen Shirt turned around. He was just a little taller than Sho, with great posture. He had a body some seven to eight muscles short of ripping, which made it all the more appealing. He wore flat-front beige trousers and brown moccasins. Accessory-wise, he sported an understated watch. He was fair, with a neat mop of curly brown hair. And those green peepers! None of that shifty, icy, grey–green–blue stuff, holding secrets that would destroy you if you found out. They were smiling, unflinching eyes, the shade of a calm eternal ocean, profound, yet penetrable. No ordinary green, they were aquamarine eyes.

It was a blockbuster moment. Every person in the room couldn't help but be acutely aware of it, including the two perplexed perpetrators. Sho and Udayan shook hands and faced each other like gladiators in Arena Amour, making no sudden or overt moves, but maintaining eye contact. Kurta–Pyjama–Chappals sat between them; AK stopped chewing on the basil; Priyanka weaned herself off her phone; her girls, relieved at the break, bared their pearlies and giggled discreetly; the office boy flitted in and out of the cabin under ridiculous pretexts; up above, the doors of heaven parted and celestial beings rushed from their afternoon siesta to peer down.

For Sho, the moment recorded a double whammy. It woke her up from the stupor that she'd fallen into post her first day at RAA, the one in which she'd morphed into a masochistic avatar of powerless script-developer-dominatrix. It wasn't the second coming, but it served the purpose of stirring her awake. And, of course, she'd met Aquamarine Eyes.

After a full-minute freeze-frame, AK spoke first.

'Udayan, this is Shobhna Ramakrishnan. She heads our script department and is *the* writer to watch out for. Shobhna, meet Udayan Doshi, senior VP, programming and international relations at Zenith.'

Zenith was the number one television channel in India, a joint venture between a Sydney-based media conglomerate and a couple of top corporate players in the country.

The Doshis, family friends of the Khans, were one of Mumbai's biggest jeweller clans. Young Udayan grew up in a sea-facing castle in Worli. After a distinguished Ivy League career in business, finance and marketing, he'd twirled his magic wand on the family business for eight years, during which time he'd not only established Akshara & Co. as India's first multi-brand jewellery retail giant and exclusive authorized sightholder for the world's largest gemstone trading companies, but also propelled himself to the enviable position of chief puppeteer. Then, handing over the nitty gritties into the hands of a line-up of able managers, and much to the alleged consternation of his father, he turned his attention to a latent passion – media. The word was barely out when Zenith snapped him up. It seemed he was already setting the wheels into motion to haul Indian television into the post-reality-show era. Business A-listers knew him as an atrociously sharp, ethical and surprisingly modest Young Turk. Given his low-key persona and lack of the propensity to swagger like a stuffed cockerel, Udayan Doshi was a bit of an enigma.

AK diligently unfurled Sho's less dazzling but more colourful resume. He rambled as far as portraying her as the avatar of Elaine May in India, minus the string of psychoanalysts.

When Sho and Udayan left AK's cabin that afternoon – not together – all six of the excited spectators could only guess what happened next. Did the handsome couple exchange numbers and plan a movie date that very evening? Did they play cool and enigmatic and leave it all to kismet? Did they scramble to their laptops to Facebook each other? Or, most likely, did they rush to one of their homes and tumble uncontrollably into bed? Who knew! But one news byte was corroborated by all six. It spread thick and fast though the unofficial gossip channels in RAA. Shobhna Ramakrishnan and Udayan Doshi were incontestably an item. B-town's official it couple of 2009–10.

8
Vexing the Ex

SHOBHNA

'You kidnapped Khansaab.'

Udayan likes to be direct. And repetitive. Only a select group of AK's family friends call him Khansaab.

'Correction: I had him kidnapped.'

It's uncomfortable to have an ex-amour sitting on your bed. Especially while he's barefoot in lotus pose, investigating the circumstances under which you had your boss kidnapped. Udayan never sits on a bed or sofa with his shoes. Like a devout Hindu in a temple, he carefully removes his shoes and socks, carries them to a safe place where nobody is likely to trip on them, folds the socks and places them on the shoes as against stuffing them in like most men do. This painstaking attention to detail is, for someone like my friend Benji – a keen observer of human behaviour – a dead giveaway. When Benji first met Udayan, he ran to his laptop and mailed me a blogger's post on fifty famous people with OCD. The list includes the likes of Martin Scorsese, David Beckham, Donald Trump and Charles Dickens. It's the only one of Benji's relentless fifteen-a-day email forwards that I've stored.

Uday frowns. Perhaps it's the heat. Roja is allergic to air conditioning, and I can live with a fan on full. Uday's worry lines have become more pronounced. He checks his stodgy Baume et Mercier for the time and arranges his body beautiful in pose no. seven – injured chin on bent knee, the other foot placed down the bed, on the floor. The tide has ebbed. No more fist clenching, or dramatic one-liners. We've been going over the situation for two hours – six scrambled eggs, two cups of chai and one packet of honey–oat cookies down. Amidst all the hurly-burly, Uday hadn't forgotten to issue exacting instructions on how his chai ought to be prepared. No milk, no artificial sweeteners, no caramelly shade.

Yes Saddam, I remember.

He presses his forefingers to his temple. I know what he's doing; he's willing a bompu moment. When we were together, Zenith had an annual retreat in Shibuya, Tokyo, where Uday tripped on a Zen master. After spending two days with him, the monk announced that his Indian student had an instinct for the more advanced practice of Zen – daijo. But Uday stuck to the more elementary, and more important, practical implementation of Zen – bompu. Since then, bompu has served as Uday's shtick.

'Wake Khansaab. I'm taking him with me.'

'But how can you take him? Before that, we need to speak with him. *You* need to speak with him.'

'How do I speak with him if he's drugged? How can we keep him here for so long? Unconscious!'

'The effect wears off in about two days.'

'And your grand plan is to bury him like a mummy in Roja's room? Isn't the presscon tomorrow? This is ridiculous! Are we supposed to just chat here, waiting for the drugs to wear off?'

'They'll wear down his resistance. He'll be open to … umm … suggestions. The presscon is tomorrow afternoon. We have between tonight and noon tomorrow. MM is ready with AK's suit and car.'

'Sho, he's a Pathan. He'll kill you.'

'Then we'll just have to inject him again.'

Uday has the temerity of a Spanish bull and the charisma of a bullfighter. This is a man who, at the age of twenty-eight, stood up in a room of the jewellery trade's richest daddies and humbly declared that Akshara & Co. would not sign the Indian Exporters' Guild agreement that sought to lock in the prices of diamond roughs. He is no peacenik bunny. If Uday had flown to India with the intention of blowing the lid off our kidnapping of AK, he would have done it long ago. And if he's read *The Dhaal*, there's no going back.

'Call him.'

'Who?'

'This asshole you're messing up your life for.'

Four years flash by in a second.

'We're not sleeping together.'

'Do I care?'

Oh, you do.

'He's not an asshole. Triple S is the greatest writer the world will know … soon.'

'So where is he?'

I've told Udayan several times in the past two hours that Triple S had to rush to Pune on an emergency and will be back in the night and so Udayan can meet him the next day.

'So he's jumped.'

'Da, he *hasn't* jumped.'

And then, for the umpteenth time, Udayan sums up my own event for me, just to convince himself it has actually happened. 'Shobhna, you have kidnapped Khansaab with the help of two small-town goons and drugged him. He's lying in your house for the past two days, while you have been busy visiting spas and airports. The word is out. They know he's not in Khandala.'

'Who's "they"?'

He waves his hand and checks a text on his phone.

'Motabhai?'

'*Everyone!* You have Mumbai's most illustrious film producer in your bedroom.'

How strong is our bompu today?

'Look. Even if this freak plan is a success and you get Khansaab to buy this … this script, you know damned well he could nix it even after it goes into production. What are you hoping to accomplish here?'

'I don't hope. I will.'

'Who do you think you are? Renegade Ramakrishnan? Che Guevara of starving writers?' He frowns deeply and looks at me like Paati used to when I ate her murukkus raw off the terrace. '… After everything Khaansaab's done for you!'

Uday is putting on my orange bamboo house slippers. He doesn't know his flip-flops are still lying in the cabinet outside. I know he'd rather use the toilet in Roja's room. It's bigger and has little potted plants, and the larger pot with a customized blue–grey seat. I've given it a premium scrubbing and installed fancy new handwash and napkins. Also replaced my lemony air-freshner with AK's favourite – lavender. But Uday had dashed into the bedroom within seconds of stepping into the apartment and had felt acutely uncomfortable seeing AK prostrate in Roja's huge bed. It's a nice place for a kidnappee to be. The bedroom has received a premium scrubbing and dusting as well. I've drawn the curtains and lit lavender incense sticks on the computer desk. Roja's favourite stuffed doll, Dora, is on the bed. She doesn't mind sharing it with AK. '*Goodnight Moon*' is playing on loop on the laptop. AK had mentioned that it was his favourite song: 'There's a shark in the pool/ And a witch in the tree/ A crazy old neighbour and he's been watching me.'

I had to gently remove the duvet to show Uday that I hadn't chopped off AKs extremities or got one of my goons do horrific sexual things to the old man. Nevertheless, the sight of the rosy-cheeked Pathan sleeping like a baby had disturbed Uday and he hasn't set foot in the room again.

He takes a call while in the loo. It appears to be Danish, Motabhai's personal assistant. By Uday's stilted monosyllables, I figure they're discussing 'Khansaab's mysterious disappearance'. Uday emerges from the loo and heads straight for his shoes, then to the door.

'I have to go.'

'Did you tell Danish?'

'That you've kidnapped Khansaab? No.'

He opens the front door, and leans on the frame, all manly and sarcastic. 'What's Bala doing?'

Bala has finally stopped hounding me. After confounding and pissing off Uday the previous night, I had taken the rickshaw straight to RAA for the late-night SOS and put up a stellar performance. They bought it. They were at the end of their tether. Calls had been made to AK's relatives in London, Amsterdam, Amritsar and Mumbai. The only person from his family to attend the SOS was a nephew, a mousy software engineer from Pune. Expectedly, the rest of his red-blooded Pathan family didn't give a twat. A ferocious bunch of his friends and close aides turned up, though, led by Kurta–Pyjama–Chappals. Finally, the issue I'd expected to come up much earlier was brought to the table – seeking police help. That was when MM stepped in, like a wise old wizard with an invisible long shining white beard. MM said that AK had explicitly instructed him to avoid the police like the plague. The gathering – grouchy, worried, hungry, sleepy – fell upon poor MM, almost ripping him apart. But people like MM are made of sterner stuff. He wouldn't budge. He said he didn't know anything and that all he knew was that AK had told him to not allow anyone to make a single move until the presscon ended. Bala, finally mustering some sort of autonomy, and without the slightest trace of irony, pronounced the situation to be very 'filmi'. By then, it was past 1 a.m. MM had the last word, and with much wringing of hands, it was decided to let things stand the way they did, until the press conference.

Uday is at the window, looking down five floors, shaking his head. 'What's MuPo doing here?'

I almost leap down the ledge. There's a blue-and-white Mumbai Police van parked next to next to Master Pandey's set-up. 'You tell me. They're talking to *your* driver.'

One of the men in khaki is gulping down a panipuri, a rifle casually slung over his shoulder. The other is chatting with a bunch of people, including the watchman and a lanky man in a white uniform who is gesticulating wildly.

'What virus is your driver spreading?'

'There's a situation.'

Aw c'mon, are you giving up on me again?

He's on the phone, frowning deeply. Down below, the MuPo is kicking up a storm. 'What the hell is a MaMi?' he seems exasperated.

'Maharashtra Mitra Sanghatana. Political party. Fundamentalist homeboys and all. Why?'

'They've murdered someone. There might be a curfew.'

'It's all right. Happens every other day.'

'Sho, there might be a *curfew* in the city.'

'Oh!'

'That was Danish. I have a meeting in town at five with Motabhai.'

'Okay, yeah. Go. Be careful about the curfew situation.'

'Where is this writer of yours? What do we do without him?'

'I can't reach him.'

He points his iPhone at my BlackBerry. 'Who the fuck's been calling you constantly?'

'Umm … Andrea.'

'*Who?*'

'Andrea Rai. From *X'Quisite*. They're sending a bunch of celebrity women to Jammu, to protest against a ban on ladies' pants. They want a token liberal Hindu celeb type. Andrea wants me to wear her clothes.'

'You're messing the presscon tomorrow and going to Jammu, wearing pants?'

'Of course I'm *not* going.'

He has grabbed my phone. 'Who's Veepee? Vignesh Pandya?'

'Yeah, he wants me on a panel.'

'What panel?'

'On fundamentalism corrupting the cosmopolitan spirit of Bombay. They're airing it at prime time, tomorrow.'

'Amazing.'

'They've got a conflict and peace-building expert from Sierra Leone on the panel.'

'Sierra Leone, the place with the bloodbath?'

'Yeah.'

'They think Mumbai will become another Sierra Leone?'

'It's close.'

He's back to leaning on the door frame. 'Unbelievable! This city is living an alternate reality. That's what this city is doing.'

Ask me, I'll tell you. I live in this mucky madhouse!

'Fine. Here's what. Ask your man to meet me first thing tomorrow morning. I'll take a call after seeing him.'

Yessir.

He disappears out of sight as I gnaw on the 'your man' dig. Five seconds later, he strides back. 'Shobhna. Why is Roja still at the doctor's?'

'It's her biannual examination. The doctor's in Parel. Takes half a day.'

'Don't you dare leave her alone with Khansaab again.'

'I'll tell her you said hi.'

He steps in and shuts the door behind him.

'If you want my help, you do as I say!' The thread of dark green inside the aquamarine eyes flickers. Dangerously. 'You are not leaving Roja alone here, or anywhere, with AK.'

'She manages very well.'

He expounds on his theory. 'She's only three!'

'What do you care? She's not yours any more. She's *my* responsibility.'

'And what do you know about responsibility?'

As if on cue, the elevator creaks and Roja bounds in. For a split second, she cocks her head to one side and sniffs. Soon enough, her front paws are on Uday's shoulder, and she's knocked him over flat on his back. The pansy vegan purse that he's held on to all afternoon slips from his hands.

9

The Red-hot Ghost of Yasser Arafat

Roja was Udayan's gift to Shobhna at the zenith of their relationship. In hindsight, the arrival of the chubby two-month-old Great Dane in their lives was a subtle signal of impending doom.

When Udayan walked out of AK's office after meeting her for the first time in the autumn of 2009, he was pleasantly aroused. Beautiful, intelligent, sensual women weren't an anomaly in his life. But at the ripe age of thirty-five, he was a veteran at the love game and, like the bulk of his generation, was weary of it. A love interest on the horizon didn't send him into a hormonal tizzy. Ditto for Sho. They were closely and discreetly trailed – on orders from the boss – by Martand Murkute, AK's faithful driver. The pious, pigeon-like fifty-seven-year-old Murkute admirably escorted Sho to the reception lobby, where Udayan was glued to his cell phone. They smiled and spoke, while MM leered at them and hung around until the duo decided they'd relocate to Rashomon for a late-afternoon snack.

The most pretentious new hangout in the suburbs,

Rashomon offered Japanese bites on a conveyor belt from 4 p.m. to 7 p.m., because it seemed the Japanese did not eat after sunset. The stares that adored them in AK's cabin followed them to Rashomon and beyond. They quickly realized that public adoration was an inevitable intruder in this game of two. Usually, Udayan's personality dominated those of his women, and Sho's individuality didn't make her the best of partners since the partners always ended up seeming dimmer in comparison. But when together, they exuded an exemplary star aura. They'd go vegetable shopping or to a party and strangers would smile at them. Jaded couples would sigh in envy and awkward young lovers would marvel at their seamless union.

Neither could be accused of sentimentality or prudishness. That weekend, they made love at Sho's apartment. Udayan's pre-coital ritual of removing his shoes, socks and clothes, and neatly folding them did not turn off Sho in the least. She waited until he dispensed with his OCD oddities, and completely took charge of the proceedings. Sho's monk-like silence, punctured by husky moans, turned him on. Immensely. She, in turn, melted like golden butter under the intense heat of his masculinity. They came together like chocolate and champagne. If they hadn't talked late into the night, it could have been labelled porn.

Significantly, they never held hands, even in private. In public, they never, ever, played cute.

Udayan was in the midst of a massive campaign by his family to get him married. Things weren't lovely with his father. Bhai Doshi was still sore that Udayan had chosen to take a *sabbatical* from the family profession to dabble in media. Things hadn't rotted beyond repair, because Bhai believed that anything Udayan did besides jewellery would always be a temporary distraction. Of all his children (two boys and two girls), Udayan had inherited and exhibited Bhai's famous focus and drive from a young age. But unlike Bhai, Udayan was multi-faceted. And he was capable of polishing each facet to its optimum when its time came. Smarting from Uday's rejection of the business he had taken such pains to set up, he'd instigated the Doshi family to find an appropriate bride for his prodigal son. They'd roused the entire community to a frenzy, sourcing fair Gujarati maidens from Amdavad to Atlanta. Gujaratis rule the world; the shortlist included some of the most accomplished, clever and companionable women. If you ignored Udayan's grandma – a silver-haired hag who stayed with a string of servants and poor relatives in Gokarna, Karnataka, and was very anal regarding astrologers and the girth of her to-be grand-daughter-in-law's hips, the Doshis weren't stodgy. Udayan was about to go on a third date with the svelte Archana Patel, Mumbai head of India's largest luxury and lifestyle PR firm, when Shobhna happened to him. He liked Archana, who had great legs and had a 'clean cutlery' fetish. She was charming, efficient, punctual and, like him, loved kids. She would have made an ideal wife and daughter-in-law. But that piece of flawlessly crafted femininity was pitted against a force of nature called Shobhna Ramakrishnan.

For a full month, he saw them both. Archana for strictly matrimonial purposes, for lunches and at her company events. Sho, because there was something breathtakingly mysterious about her.

He'd bought fully-furnished digs at Goregaon near the Zenith headquarters, but largely lived out of the Doshis' castle at Worli. Then he began spending more time at Sho's sunny apartment. Three nights a week, he'd pick her up post 9 p.m. from RAA. He'd make them dinner, they'd watch a bit of TV, perhaps play Brainvita. Then they would make love, copious quantities of it. Later in the night, they would lounge peacefully to the soft soulful strains of Illayaraja's '*I met Bach at My House*', a gift from Rohini, until they dozed off. Udayan got himself a copy of the album and often played it in his car.

Sho had mixed feelings about marriage then, and she did not feel her womb crying out yet. Like Udayan, she was a Sterling Gold Member of the world's largest matrimonial site, and had gone through the drill – from sex-fiends to namby-pambys, to men who actually managed to look better than their profile photos but dived into shit as soon as they opened their mouths. Udayan was the first whiff of a full-blown non-psycho male specimen she'd had for a long while. Her last significant relationship – the shutterbug at *X'Quisite* didn't count – was in the spring of 2006 with a Pakistani art teacher at Cardiff. That time round, she had spent a better part of her time working on her laptop at his rented apartment off the campus, while he lectured or held workshops. He guzzled beer and wrote soulful shaayari when she attended creative writing classes. But by the end of summer term, she'd grown weary of his drinking and skirt-chasing. What would get her goat would be when he'd throw beer cans at his pet hamster Sir Khomeini when pissed with his own friends. The day he unveiled his painting of Sir Khomeini wearing a lilac lace sari torn to shreds and covered in purple blood, she handed the custody of the rodent to a kind classmate and ended the relationship.

Finally, Sho and Udayan got to a point where Udayan had to speak – separately – to Archana and Bhai, telling them about his commitment to Sho. Archana remembered Sho fondly, gave him a half-hearted scolding about leading her on, shook hands, hugged, and promised to be friends forever. Udayan was banished from her Twitter and Facebook lists that very night. Bhai threw a fit and summoned the entire clan at Doshi House to shame the prince who had gone too far.

'Tu ena thi lagan karish?' Bhai boomed.

'Hamda nahin.'

'To kyaare? At forty-five, when you get arthritis and lose hair?'

'Not now, Bhai.'

Udayan's older brother and his celebrity hairstylist wife interjected, 'Does the girl want to marry you?'

'Not immediately.'

'Then what do you want to do immediately? Abandon her the way you abandoned the family business?'

Bhai went on a theatrical hunger strike, proving once and for all that the family shared a bloodline with Mahatma Gandhi. He grunted all over about what Udayan's mother would have said if she were alive. It was agonizing. The taciturn septuagenarian had never resorted to blackmail using his dead wife's mention since she passed away in 1999. To put an end to the silliness, Udayan arranged for Bhai to meet Sho, over gourmet khichdi at the city's most upscale vegetarian restaurant. To soften the edges, Udayan invited his elder sister, who came with her two-year-old daughter. Sho and Bhai were on their best behaviour. Things started looking up.

That Diwali, Sho went to Bangalore. It was a busy time for Amma and Appa. The Reddys next door were back from a Cuban holiday and had bought cigars and a set of dominoes for what they crowed was a substantial discount. That loot and their tropical island tales largely dominated the festivities. 'Manana Manana Chinna' the Ramakrishnan seniors chuckled when she told them about Udayan. But Sho knew that as soon as her flight to Mumbai took off the next day, they dumped the cigars in the bin and drove straight to the Ghati

Subramanya Temple near Doddaballapur with fifty-one coconuts and five kilos of sweets. Amma actually wept a bit behind the daughter's back. So he was a Gujraathi deekra, but educated all over the world. This boy sounded interesting. Back from the venerated shrine, they abducted Rohini for an interrogation.

'What did he sound like?'

'Very husband material.'

'How does he earn?'

'He's Gujraathi, da!'

'Does he smoke?'

'No.'

'Does he read books?'

'Sounds like the type. I'll mail you the list, okay?'

'Any painting or music? Artistic hobby?'

'Dunno.'

'Carrom?'

'Sari, naanu bhartini. Aha, but Appa, he cooks.'

Appa melted into a puddle of dosai batter.

Having convinced both sets of parents, Udayan and Sho brought out their relationship like vintage bubbly. AK had been sending feelers to the couple for over a month that they visit him. The minute he saw them together in his office, he knew they'd be together. After the Bhai–Sho orientation, Bhai called AK for the low-down on the girl, but was told to fog off. All AK said was that the children were very lucky. So the minute they formalized themselves, the grateful young couple accepted his invitation for a party at The Four Seasons.

Food and booze flowed. Girls in towel wraps and ladies in gorgeous chadors gossiped over wine and amuse-bouches. Hedge-fund managers flirted with starlets. Producers sat by the bar and pretended to be important. B-list actors stood at the heels of the A-list actors, laughing loudly at their fart jokes. AK wore his grey double-breasted Milanese suit and sat in a corner with Kurta–Pyjama–Chappals and a couple of his buddies, nursing his Johnny Walker Blue. As soon as Udayan and Sho entered, and before people could start admiring them, they were whisked to an ante-chamber. A special feast was laid out for them. After introductions with his buds, AK hustled the rest out and observed the couple with much affection. 'You look so happy,' he purred. 'Don't you ever get married.' They'd always be grateful to AK for his unsolicited advice.

Between the film and television industries, the couple received a dozen invitations every week, but socialized selectively. Sho hated the charade of dressing up, doing her hair and driving in murderous traffic just to kiss air and ass. She'd done her time at *X'Quisite*. Udayan wasn't a big fan of nights out either. So they wore their fancy costumes only for special events. Like Zenith's Christmas party. Radiant in a pale pink khadi silk sari, she worked the room on her own while Udayan talked ratings with his team from Singapore. Zenith's hallways were abuzz for a whole week discussing how Euro-chic the couple was – independent, charming and so dashing together. The going rate was Rs 50,000 – would they outlive 2009?

On 31 December 2009, Udayan arrived at Sho's apartment with a blonde in a basket. He wasn't much of a gift-giver, which was just as well because neither was she. Given his easy access to jaw-dropping jewellery, he had asked her outright if she would like pretty baubles. She had declined. He had let it be at that. But he knew she had a soft spot for big dogs. The first choice was a Golden Retriever, until he remembered how she'd cooed – and she wasn't a cooer – at pictures of Cynthia the receptionist's Doberman. For Udayan, all tall dogs were the same, Doberman or …

'A Great Fugging Dane?'

'The breeder says she's a bundle of intelligence, strength and sensitivity.'

'But I have *you*.'

'Hah!' He placed the D&G basket near the settee and produced a folder.

'Diet instructions. Exercise routine. Vet suggestions.'

The pup peeped out with a baleful expression.

'This is a big dog, da. It's not fair to keep her in this little apartment.'

'You have an extra bedroom that's getting wasted.'

'So you gift me the Michael Jordan of dogs?'

'She has great pedigree.'

Udayan tried to put the Dane back into her basket, but – surprising, given her chubbiness – she sprung out of his hands and landed on the glossy black rug they often made love on. The rug was gift from AK.

They couldn't agree on a name for her, so they stalled. But with the advent of the puppy in their life, Shobhna and Udayan tumbled into the trials and tribulations of parenthood. They were in their mid-thirties; the time was ripe. Amma, Appa and Bhai were sniping at their heels. All family involved had interpreted the arrival of the Great Dane as a proposal in canine disguise. Why else would a cat lover give his dog-loving girlfriend a Great Dane?

News spread around Ivory Towers that the rich, handsome man who had an ongoing affair with S. Ramakrishnan from 502 had gifted her a giant bitch. This meant he wasn't a south Mumbai playboy, but a decent human being who had plans of marrying the Maverick Madrasi. Housewives smiled at them and children walked up to ogle at the friendly little canine. In one pet stroke, Uday and Sho attained the bourgeois acceptability they weren't exactly looking for.

After two months of playing Mummy and Daddy to Nameless Puppy, the couple decided they needed a break. They travelled together – a first – to Dubai for the Valentine's Day weekend, where Uday had a work thing. Neither felt inclined to make wildly mushy gestures of epic romance. So, while Uday met up at The Atlantis with a few of Bhai's business associates, Sho turned into a mall rat. They didn't make love for two nights and barely spoke during the day, which wasn't unusual. What was unusual was the deathly silence that accompanied breakfast on 14 February. It wasn't a comfortable silence. After close to a year of being together, it seemed they had finally run out of conversation. That morning, Uday poked his sunny side up. Sho got into a friendly discussion with the lanky blonde Spaniard who was waiting on them. He and his girlfriend were taking a week off to trek in Jordan. He bubbled over with enthusiasm, and swept Sho into his sea of youthful wanderlust, recounting tales of his travels real and imaginary, with such fervour that Uday was forced to look up from his eggs.

On 16 February, Uday and Sho found themselves at Queen Alia Airport, waiting for their guide Hamid. The Spaniard – whose girlfriend worked in housekeeping at The Atlantis too – had left the former *it* couple with a niggling sense of ennui. They feared turning into a hotel hopping, white linen pants couple that brunched on frozen Daiquiris and made love by rote. Before the feeling turned into the elephant in the room, they plunged into an impulsive Jordanian sojourn. An itinerary that consisted of church-hopping at Bethany, bathing in the Dead Sea, skipping the tourist trap at Petra and rekindling their romance at Wadi Rum. Hamid was pleased; a last-minute booking meant that he quoted a plump premium and – unlike Indian customers who haggled till the cows came home – the well-heeled couple had agreed and the credit card payment had come through overnight.

That five-day Jordanian adventure somewhat stirred their relationship from the tedium it had fallen into. It started ominously. Uday caught a cold and the Dead Sea salt residue left Sho's sensitive skin chaffed and bleeding at places. Nevertheless, they broke the sexual dry spell and shagged relentlessly. When they weren't, they ate and drank and went for walks. On the way back from Bethany on Day 3, they stopped at Hamid's family home where they helped his sisters-in-law cook a mean maklouba (upside-down chicken). There was much merrymaking, more walking and more hours of sex. By the time they arrived at their night camp at Wadi Rum, they were exhausted. Floating on her back in the Dead Sea had left Sho – a non-swimmer – buoyed and exhilarated. Uday's cold, however, had escalated into something of a flu. The last time Uday had felt even vaguely sick was during his school days. Almost like he'd discovered a long-lost treasure, Uday revelled in his escalating delirium. Sho plied him with cold packs and the meds that Hamid supplied. Combined with his own spectacular immunity, this left Uday with enough physical strength to jump up and down the Land Cruiser that roared through the softly billowing sands and surreal, sky-scraping rock formations. Hearing of 'Lawrence's dripping well' at Wadi Shelaala, he insisted on undertaking the forty-minute hike to stick his head into the icy spring water, much to the amusement of Mahfouz, the teenage Bedouin boy accompanying them. Halfway down from the green oasis, Mahfouz sat them down to partake of the hot mint tea from his stinking leather-lined flask. Uday drank, laughed and coughed all the way back to the camp. The next day, their last in Jordan, instead of barbecuing by the beach at Aqaba, Uday insisted – once again, in uncharacteristic prima donna fashion – that they drive to Jebel Burdah. Before they left, he demanded two crates of Coke – which Hamid produced instantly – and sat at the back of the Land Cruiser, ripping apart the cans and dunking slabs of taboon into them. By the time it was noon and they touched down upon the white sands of Um Alouan, he was asleep. To shield herself from the blazing sun, Sho had Mahfouz tie her red cotton Chanderi dupatta around her head in traditional Jordanian style. With her aviators covering the remainder of her face, and another vermillion dupatta wrapped around her blouse and cargos, she dragged her heels farther and farther until the Land Cruiser was a dot in the distance. When she returned, exhausted and sweating, but exhilarated, Uday was leaning against the Cruiser, staring wordlessly at her. Six hours later, over their last dinner in Jordan, while ripping apart more pieces of taboon, Uday told her he had seen the ghost of Yasser Arafat. The ghost was tall and beautiful and mysterious and dressed in red. Perhaps it was the colour of the ghosts of dead Arabic rebels, Udayan concluded along with Mahfouz. Mahfouz winked at Sho.

Around 1 a.m., Sho woke up to find Uday butt naked, curled up in a foetal position, his blanket thrown to the side of the tent. His body felt hot but was soft to her touch. She brought back his blanket and noticed the sweetest smile on his face. He looked peaceful, almost otherworldly, like a 5'10", muscular, naked fairy. Sho pulled her mattress close to his. He grabbed her hand and opened his eyes. Still smiling, he said he loved her and pressed her palms to his chest. She stared into the liquid green pools that were his eyes and said she loved him too. They spooned blissfully, the heat from his body warming hers, until it was time to leave for the airport.

Back in Mumbai, and years later, even after he grew old and had the leisure to dust and polish his memories to a shine, all Uday would admit to recalling – at least in public – about that trip would be the red-hot ghost of Yasser Arafat. Even when Sho tried telling him that the red apparition on white sand was her and not the ghost of the deceased PLO leader, he stuck to his guns. 'I remember what I saw,' he persevered. 'I also remember I said I love you.' She didn't want to argue with that. It was the one and only time they had said those three words to each other.

By the end of February 2010, the nameless puppy got a name. Roja – red in Spanish, rose in Tamil – named after the Spanish waiter at The Atlantis. Uday and Sho could never be accused of sentimentality. But they would never forget Roja.

Sho would also never forget that Uday – albeit in an unusually feverish state of mind – imagined her to be the ghost of a revolutionary. Or terrorist. Whichever way he saw it.

10

On the Precipice of Reason

Udayan

'What was the MuPo asking?'

'They dropped by for some chaat.'

'The MuPo don't "drop by" in this area.'

Rajesh smirks at me in the rear-view mirror. 'You know this area very well, sir?'

Drivers have a seventh sense.

'What's happened in Worli?' I inquire.

'Murder. MaMi ne to baja daali.'

'MaMi … it is a political party, right? Kya hai yeh, exactly?'

He is aghast. How do I not know? MaMi is on foreign channels – in America too! I apologize, saying I must have missed them. To make up for lost time, Rajesh profiles MaMi, all the way from Juhu to Bandra.

According to Rajesh, it is a very 'high funda' local political party. From being a virtual nobody in 2006, it had come to a point where the party had lost the Bombay Municipal Corporation elections just by a whisker the previous year. It is 'fast friends' with the saffron biggies in Delhi. 'High funda' MaMi has an office in Worli atop a thirteen-storey tower, where its functionaries are rumoured to be carrying on their work on computers and expensive phones and other large, imported machines. It has two back offices in Girgaum and Koparkhairane as well. Unlike other parties, MaMi is not known by one leader but by small 'mitra mandals' or 'MaMi gangs'. The organization is very popular in the interiors of Maharashtra and one cannot move around freely and speak what one wants in places like Latur and Jalgaon without obtaining prior permission from the party. In Mumbai, MaMi is slowly turning out to be the protector of the underdogs, the working class and the natives of Mumbai.

'So they are thugs. Goondas.'

'If that is what you want to call them,' he shrugs.

Apparently, earlier this year, the principal of Mumbai's biggest medical college said very bad things about MaMi at a 'foreign location'. MaMi boys tried talking to him, through phone and email, that such slandering was not good for the image of the country. It seemed – and this information was classified – that they had got wind of the principal's son's 'lafdas' and a land-grabbing history in his hometown of Indore, and so 'politely' offered a deal according to which they would keep the damning information to themselves if the principal didn't make further insulting statements. They didn't even ask for an apology! When the principal refused to cooperate, they smashed up the chemistry lab in his college to teach him a lesson.

'So, they are blackmailers. And they destroy public property.'

'How else do you expect them to make an impact?'

To make further impact, it appears that MaMi stopped hounding the medical college, and attacked a 'high-funda hotel'. The 'hotel' he mentions rings a bell; it's an upscale

Mediterranean fine dining restaurant on Marine Drive. The owners – a pair of Parsi siblings – run two more restobars in town and a French bistro in the suburbs. MaMi made several calls to the owners, inquiring about the 'illegal and immoral activities' of the establishment. When the owners did not 'cooperate', MaMi raided the hotel and smashed their bar and a sofa.

This hooliganism is what the protest mobs are up against. I ask Rajesh if he is pro-MaMi.

'They are my people. I will stand by my people.' He wipes the sweat off his face with a dirty brown washcloth.

'Are you from Mumbai?' I ask him.

'Rourkela.'

'Whom did they murder?'

'I think it is one of the Parsi owners of a restaurant.'

'What happened?'

'They smashed his own bottle on his head. Also shot him, I think.'

Danish's call again. Motabhai is driving to Napean Sea Road for our evening durbar, and is trapped at the Bandra–Worli Sea Link. There's some sort of law-and-order situation at the Worli end of the sea link. MaMi has clashed with the protestors and the MuPo has had to intervene. The incoming evening traffic has made it all even more troublesome. Danish advises I stay put in Andheri, but we've almost reached Bandra. He also clarifies that there is no bandh as of now, but the situation is tense. I ask Rajesh to take the Mahim Causeway.

Rajesh is in a jolly mood. He tunes in to a local FM channel.

I scroll down on my phone to realize that the MaMi news is all over the Internet. Twitter's choked. The GMine guys haven't reverted yet. The phone rings with a happy Callum at the other end – our first ad film for a designer innerwear brand, which premiered on Fox while I was flying to Mumbai, is a resounding hit on screen and has gone viral with a vengeance. Motabhai was a bit concerned that Daha was launching itself in the lucrative ad-film space with a chaddi–banian ad, shot by the insane Indian-born, NY-based Lara De. The ten-day shoot at Aspen with an almost-naked Italian Greek god astride a bull, during which she held the entire office to ransom, is finally paying off. We had been worried about the numbers – the twenty-seconder cost us as much as any big-budget Bollywood film.

'But the shit's hit the roof in Bombay. Your local goons are cutting in on our online space,' he says.

'No big deal, mate. Local politics.'

I dial Motabhai and convey the good news. I don't have to. All Motabhai cares about is whether Daha is making money, not in the details of how the cash flows in.

'Axe-lant, Uday. Very goo ...'

I've lost him to a low network zone. Before I can call him again, it's Monee on the line. She wants to know if there's a problem in Mumbai. Her cousins have texted something vague. I tell her all's well, just the usual. She asks about the GMine meeting and tells me that Kaka's daughter-in-law has called her for a drink at the Village after work. Should she go? Of course, my family is hers. She pauses, always thinking before she speaks, in that soft, soothing manner.

'Sweets, is everything all right?'

I nod. And though she cannot see, she understands. It's good to hear her voice.

Another pause, from my side. 'I'll call you later, babe. Love you. Stay safe.'

She kisses her phone and hangs up. No fuss. No drama. Before I can take a moment to breathe, it's Danish again.

'Mr Doshi, this call is to inform you that Mr Patel just called myself. He regretted that your conversation had to be terminated. There appears to be a hint of … violence involved that has kept Mr Patel and other commuters stranded for over an hour, as we speak.' Though he speaks like a nineteenth-century telephone operator, Danish is the world's most conscientious secretary.

'Yes. Is he okay? Is he out?'

'They have managed to drive onwards … yes.'

'… across the bridge?'

'I would like to believe so. May I ask your whereabouts at this moment, Mr Doshi?'

'Bandra. We're taking the Causeway.'

'A very good decision. Mr Patel has suggested you take it … easy, Mr Doshi. The situation could get out of hand at any point of time.'

Perceptive!

Once I'm done speaking over the phone, Rajesh switches off the radio and informs me that the MuPo and MaMi have a bilateral hands-off policy. If MaMi, he smirks, wants to show these college-going kids from Bandra and Breach Candy who is boss, then MaMi will do it. In return, MaMi's minions – notoriously rough with the state administration and the janta – stay out of MuPo's daily grind. He adjusts the rear view at various angles, then clears his throat to catch my attention and resume his defence of MaMi. The traffic looks ominous.

Murderers. Madmen. The city is teeming with idiots on puerile missions. Political goondas, failed writers. They're all the same.

Here's how I'm trying to make sense of the situation:

Sho, during her unhappy days at RAA, discovers a writing protégé – someone she code-names Triple S. The two idiots kidnap AK just four days before RAA is to announce the launch of its official Bollywood remake of an iconic Hollywood blockbuster, slated to set the box office in India ablaze. Their plan is to weaken AK's resistance with illegal drugs, and on the day of the press conference, get him to do a volte face and instead announce the launch of a new film scripted by a first-time, unknown, small-town writer – the mysterious Triple S. His screenplay is a fantasy–thriller with a working-title – *The Dhaal*. At the presscon, with the national media present, they plan to get AK to announce that RAA will produce *The Dhaal*, claiming that it will be a blockbuster and a breakout global hit for RAA, which is still Bollywood-oriented. Understandably, it is the sort of melodrama that the press will lap up. Sho was banking on the very janta-friendly battle of an artistic David taking on the commercial might of Goliath.

The presscon is on 5 September. Tomorrow. Which is why they've named it Strike at Thirty-Six – ostensibly because it is five days after 31 August.

'We are fully fucked!'

Given the turn of events on the Sea Link, the only other connect between Mumbai's western suburbs and main island – Mahim Causeway – is clogged. This would take at least an hour.

'You want a film, sir?' Rajesh asks as he attacks a box of DVDs in impotent resentment at the jam.

No more films. 'Not now.'

Daha and RAA are considered rivals, though, technically, we are not. RAA rules the Bollywood playground; Daha never intended to compete with them for that target audience. We utilize the large resource base of Motabhai's investors, a majority of them Indian, to make original content that will appeal to a global audience, including, but not exclusively, Indian. When I heard that Bala had acquired rights to the sci-fi Hollywood cult hit, I wasn't jealous. They'll make it with an Indian crew, and it is likely to become an international joke, even if it's a blockbuster at home. Indians can't make sci-fi. But Khansaab considers every film company in the world his arch rival. I know he's viewing their latest acquisition – that goes by the name *Yogi* – as RAA's hostile takeover of all the major Hollywood studios. He is also a beloved family friend. Attempting to sabotage his prestigious presscon is not only a ridiculous plan, it's plain … ungrateful.

The little twist in this tale of monumental idiocy? Mystery man Triple S's script – *The Dhaal*. All 126 badly translated pages of it.

An awesome game changer.

A total knockout!

'Aye! Kamla ka hamla!' Rajesh exclaims and grimaces in the middle of his high-pitched monologue on the phone.

A eunuch is pressing her face to the rear window closest to me. She can't be over thirty. A beautiful face, deep brown with two dozen pockmarks, but great bone structure. She hasn't pulled up her sari and isn't clapping her hands in my face or screaming. She just sticks to the window with a gentle smile. I give her a hundred-rupee note. She blesses me and moves on.

'You believe in this hijda-blessing nonsense, sir?'

Right now, I don't know what I believe in. Across the street, a young boy with a newly sprouted moustache, in jeans and tee, sits on a wooden stool, while an older man measures his moustache with a wooden ruler. There is no trace of any shaving equipment nearby. What are they doing, and why are they doing it in the midst of a street that's clogged with smoke, dust and wheels? Perhaps it might help to stop thinking entirely and focus on soothing memories of Monee. No such luck. Before we can get out of the maddening traffic jam, a walkie-talkie taps on my window. It's a cop.

'Is your name Gharpuré?

'No.'

'Ey babdya, adnav Gharpuré kai?' he barks at Rajesh.

'No.'

The cop is in his fifties, with a barrel chest, slight paunch, fading khaki uniform and Ray-Ban aviators. He checks our IDs, shoots some questions about what I do in New York, and asks his lanky hawaldar to fiddle in the dicky. None of the dozens of other vehicles around is being stopped.

'Mr Doshi, what are you now doing in Mumbai?' he shouts politely above the din, raising his palm to indicate that the interrogation is limited. I need not step out.

'I have my family and business here,' I answer in chaste Marathi.

'Girlfriend? Wife?'

'Girlfriend. In New York.'

'Her name is Gharpuré?' He's not clowning.

'No, sir. Is there a curfew?'

'Does this look like a curfew?'

It takes us another thirty minutes to reach Worli. By the time we pull into the driveway at Doshi House, my head is about to burst. Strike at Thirty-Six. Sho in a mental asylum. *The Dhaal* winning a Palme D'Or at Cannes for best feature film. Khansaab on Roja's bed. Monee's calming voice. GMine. And who the fuck is Gharpuré?

'Mama, I've been direct messaging on Facebook!'

It's Neelu. She arrived this morning from Boston, via Pondicherry. With the rest of the clan out to seek Sai Baba's blessings, she's twiddling her thumbs and so suggests that I take her out for dinner if it isn't inconvenient. How do you refuse when your favourite niece meets you after a year and asks you to take her out? She hugs me; a sharp pain cuts through my spine as her gigantic wooden bangle gnashes against it. It's been months since I've felt that gym injury.

'Are you super tired?' Neelu follows me inside, letting loose a steady stream of questions on the weather, food, family and curfew. No matter how tired I am, I can see what she wants. I can't disappoint her. Everyone, including the drivers and the household help, has vamoosed to Shirdi. It's just us. As the only and ardent carnivores in the Doshi family, we have a tradition to uphold – late-night fried bombil and shark masala at Saayba, followed by tender coconut ice-cream at Naturals.

'Can I shower first?' I interrupt.

While I'm showering, I miss a call from Sho, so I call her back.

'He's up,' she declares.

'Now?'

'He's babbling.'

'What is he saying?'

'Something incoherent.'

'Tell me his exact words.'

'Kaafir kaafir, beta kaafir. Munni jao. Hurr.'

The kidnappee sounds as demented as the kidnapper.

Sho has Khansaab on 'barbies' – soporific red capsules of sodium pentothal that she bought wholesale from a woman she knows from *X'Quisite*. This is what she told me during the call from Manhattan, when I asked her how the hell she intended to capture the big Pathan. Barbies, short for barbiturates, are sedatives used to depress the nervous system, and are used by psychologists to 'open up' patients with deep-seated issues. Sho said they've been used by MuPo on the perpetrators of the Mumbai train blasts. Anyhow, I got the meds seconded by Priya, a pharmacist friend from faraway, whom I trusted not to ask the obvious questions. Priya said they were safe unless used in excess or diluted in water or alcohol. Before I'd left for the airport, I got Sho on con call with Priya and made sure we were on the same – and very strict – page, as far as the dosage and precautions went.

I'd rushed into Roja's bedroom this afternoon, desperate to get a word with Khansaab. But for the four hours I was there, he slept blissfully. He felt neither hot nor cold to the touch and was breathing normally. His eyes were neither red nor watery. These were signs, according to Priya, that he was safe. Since he was snoozing, I'd killed time trying to knock sense into his kidnapper. And now that I'd left and reached the main island, he was awake and ready to be spoken to!

'Neelu is here from Boston. I have to take her out for dinner.'

Deep pause.

'So you're going to—'

'Yes, the usual. Sho, I'm not going to help you.'

Her voice cracks. 'But, he's awake. You *have* to talk to him!'

'I don't *have* to do anything. I'm tired.'

'You can't quit! Not now!'

Shit that blows.

I tell her I'm calling Bala first thing in the morning, hang up, and fall on the bed. It's only a few seconds until Neelu's voice echoes from the living room: 'Chalo, Mama.'

A breath of fresh air should do the trick. Monee would have

dragged me out for a quick spin to shake off the tiredness as well.

Twenty minutes later, Neelu and I are speeding down the Mahim Causeway again, this time on Hetal's Kinetic Activa, a surprisingly fast, un-geared blue scooter. It was the only vehicle at home, much faster than the chauffeured car. I feel my mind begin to relax. It is much cooler now, and the wind is soothing. Mumbai is not as stinky at night as it is by day. Besides, the festivities are on in full swing. Except for the benevolent, looming idols of the elephant god Ganesha – some as tall as twenty-five feet – everything about this festival has become a cacophonic, garish joke. With a quick stop to top up the tank, we reach in forty minutes, at 10.45. Saayba, which used to be a takeaway pigeonhole, is cramped. Now it's a mess to get into, but they've amped it with Formica tables, benches and an air conditioner. But, as it has always been, drivers of die-hard Saayba fans, from Colaba to Thane, are jostling at the kerb for their takeaways. Neelu had her first bombil fry here at the age of seven with me. As soon as we spot the board, she bounds off her seat.

'Should we eat in or would you rather not park the scooter here?'

She's dressed in brown shorts. There's some sort of multilayered billowing top and coloured stockings too. She's grown taller and really worked on toning her arms. I would like to believe it is thanks to me tutoring her at a gym session a year ago. She's still lanky, though. But that million-dollar smile's gotten wider. Even as a baby, Neelu was pure sunshine.

'Go in and check.'

The scooter doesn't have a side stand and needs to be hauled back in the manner of a good old Bajaj Chetak. She runs back in a couple of minutes, her long arms flailing.

'Chalo, I got one half of a table.'

Nobody appears to care where I park, so I stick the scooter by the masjid, behind a Pajero. Neelu is standing on the pavement, very jumpy.

'Mama, you won't guess. Look who ...'

Sitting on the edge of one of the crowded benches, Sho is sipping on a solkadi.

Two years ago, sitting just like that, in another place, with another sort of drink, she'd thrown away everything we had.

11

The Beginning of an End

Shobhna and Udayan's zigzag train to Matrimony Junction was chugging along – slow but determined – when it received a quick and fatal blow. Udayan quit Zenith.

It was *Loo-tere* that did it. Zenith's new reality show revealing the bathroom secrets of stars was the lowest point in his career as well as in the history of Indian television. Udayan had sacrificed his family prestige and the gloss of the gems-and-jewellery trade because he wanted to explore his creativity. Something, he realized quickly, was never going to happen at Zenith. In the spring of 2009, when his creative director fluffed his chest and laid out the loo show concept, Udayan's endurance struck rock bottom.

The heavens opened up prematurely on Mumbai on the twenty-first of May, when Sho, along with the rest of the city, read in a leading tabloid that Zenith's handsome VP was plotting to leave and start a film company of his own. She called sick at work (both AK and Bala were in Singapore for an awards ceremony) and sat at home the whole day, staring out at the pouring rain, Roja by her side. The tiniest knot began to form inside her gut.

Udayan spilled the beans at breakfast the next day. The new partner was a Bimal Roy-loving NRI from Johannesburg, Bhavin Bhansali, fondly known in trade circles as Motabhai. Apparently, he'd been scoping Udayan for over six months and was convinced that he'd be the right man to lead the charge. Their aim was to build the first Indian-owned film company that would make movies for a global audience. After that, Sho stopped listening to what Udayan was saying. After what seemed like an eternity, she heard something to the effect of 'I think we should get married'.

She must have indicated in the affirmative, because he kissed her, wet and hard.

After he left, she rushed to her bed and flopped upon it. They'd been together for a little less than two years. And it had been over two years since she began working at RAA. She wondered why she hadn't seen it coming. The two most important aspects of her existence had collided. One was the most successful. The other, the most inexorable failure. She clutched at the M word for support and fell powerlessly into a deep dungeon of intense depression.

Shobhna was miserable at RAA. She met actors, directors and producers. Everyone made her feel part of the big, shiny Bollywood family. AK engulfed her into his fold with paternal protectiveness and the legendary Pathan generosity. She sat in the meetings that green-lighted high-profile projects. She had an all-seasons pass to all of RAA's sets. Six days out of seven, they spent at least four working hours daily in languid 'meetings' in AK's cabin or one of the three lush conference rooms at RAA. At least twice a week, they had some major event to attend, en masse. It could be anything from a shoot to a film premier, a music recording or some celebrity's pre-nup party. The few hours in a day that she spent in her own office, lorded over by the framed photograph of the lion she'd named Istanbul, she read scripts. Of the ten-odd scripts that were mailed, posted and fervently hand-delivered to RAA every day, Sho dismissed nine as standard stuff. After some time, she stopped reading them. When they gave her an assistant, she passed on the gunk to him. The interesting ones she took straight to AK, who routed her to Bala, with whom she spent hours discussing the script and potential cast. Sometimes, they called in the writer, who often doubled as director and held exhaustive meetings that mostly led the unsuspecting sod up the garden path. It was cruel and draining.

The singular reason why she continued dragging her feet through the iridescent corridors of RAA was her baby. Her own script.

She was taken aback when AK mentioned it during their first meeting. Did she envision a career as one of Mumbai's highest-paid and most respected screenwriters? Did she fancy her words uttered aloud on a large screen so that millions could acknowledge her visionary genius? Did she see offers from American and Chinese film-makers – to script a quirky, cryptic tale that would break the barriers between the East and West – on the horizon? Like hell, she did. She was hooked. She never heard from AK after she handed her carefully crafted synopsis to him. Whenever she asked for his feedback, he called for some more jasmine tea or introduced her to a hot actor. She got caught up in all the fun, the activity, the glamour. But it took just four-five months for the jamboree to get tiresome. The film industry was a cult of the demented and deluded. It didn't matter whether you were a snotty cinephile praying at the altar of the Duplass brothers and Krzysztof Kieslowski or you pelvic-thrusted to Bollywood item numbers. To be successful in cinema, you had to ooze it from every pore of your body, until you bled and hurt. That, of course, didn't ensure success. It simply ensured that you could survive the inevitable failure.

Udayan was the most stabilizing, balancing force in her life in Mumbai. And now, during the premature monsoon of 2010, he was joining the film industry and starting a new company that would make wonderful global films. Stung with this development, she sat on their bed all day and watched as her mind split into two, like a schizo on steroids: of course she would show him her script. He would love it and would promptly crank it up to pre-production level. She could even direct it. After all, she was going to be his wife. Surely he wasn't above a little nepotism!

No, she couldn't do it! It was beneath her talent and her upbringing. She would do the right thing and be Mrs Shobhna Ramakrishnan Doshi. The options were limitless. She could write a book, a worldwide bestseller on her Bollywood sojourn which they'd turn into a syndicated TV show. Udayan and she would be the ultimate 'it' couple.

Dang, no!

She wanted what she didn't have: that her script be made into a film. Desperately. Like thousands in the city, and several millions in the world, she wanted to show the film industry that she was above them. She wanted to prove to AK – that generous, paternal, patronising Pathan – that writers, not producers, made outstanding films. Hang on there; what if Uday didn't like her script? Why wouldn't he! Didn't she have confidence in her talent? The knot in her stomach tightened further. She had to pop pills to get some rest.

Things took a turn for the worse on their monthly dine-and-whine of The Thirties Club at the Singhals' apartment up Pali Hill. Apart from Sho and Benji, there were four married couples, friends for over two decades. One of the men sold soaps to rural India, while two handled investment portfolios and one was an architect. The women wore cropped white linen pants, had two beautiful children each and one of them did all that while running a bank. For the longest time, Benji – the forty-one-year-old environmentalist from San Francisco – and Sho were the only single ones. For a brief while, they had regressed to the debauched nightlife of their twenties, until Uday came along.

That night, they were lounging in Salim's beautiful study where, on popular demand, Uday had to reveal the deets about his new cinematic venture. Anita and Salim had cooked Uday's favourite Macanese egg tarts and potato gratin. Sho felt dizzy and went to the balcony to get some air, where she was accosted by the wee ones. The older children had taken Roja for a walk. All the offspring of The Thirties Club members knew by then that Shobhna Aunty didn't appreciate extended contact with kids. They had a mutual agreement: they'd kiss, hug briefly and high five, and she'd ask about the latest on Spongebob Squarepants, and that was that. That night, though, the youngest of the bunch, three-year-old Karan, was in a rebellious mood. He brought out his dad's new tablet phone and insisted on showing her pictures of their latest family vacation in London. She saw a few, gently pushed him away, and returned to the study where Uday was waxing eloquent on how his new company would be looking at exciting new global cinema. She squirmed as Karan jumped on her lap and stuck the tablet into her face. He was a cherubic child, with curly hair and dimpled cheeks. Not too heavy.

Karan's father intervened. 'C'mon, champ. Don't disturb aunty.' Everyone else in the room offered to see the pictures. Karan giggled and pulled Sho's cheeks. Everyone smiled. Kids could be so cute. Sho told Karan, gently but firmly, to scram. She told him thrice, in English and Hindi. He didn't listen. Instead, he playfully slapped her cheek with his gentle baby hand. She slapped him right back, pretty hard, and ejected him out of her lap. Karan's eyes widened and he burst into tears.

Uday dropped her and Roja to the car, said he'd take a cab and asked her point blank if she didn't want to marry him. If she did, what could possibly be the explanation for her exasperating behaviour? She sucked in her breath and let it out: she had a script to show him, and she was scared shitless that he'd hate it.

He almost laughed. 'That's it? That's what all this drama has been about? Give it to me tomorrow, okay?' He kissed her on the forehead, like a parent comforting a child. Daddy would take care of everything. She edited it feverishly all night, and gave him a printout next evening. He came home the day after.

'It's fabulous. I couldn't put it down. Simple plot, but there's a lot of complexity and depth to the characters. It's ... poetic.'

She knew he was born to be a global film producer.

'Have you shown this to someone else?'

'No.'

'Great. We'll do it.'

'Okay.'

'Really good stuff.'

'Thanks.'

'Super.'

'Yo.'

That was it. She didn't hear about it from him again. She didn't ask. It was that doomed passive aggressive Mars in Cancer that Sho's amma dreaded. A desire so intense, it shuffled and shifted and throttled the life out of Sho, but refused to take a full frontal approach. Sho, who always prided herself on her easy-going personality that was not given to typically feminine manipulations and emotional hypnosis, was falling prey to her image. Another month passed by. Uday went to Johannesburg for a week to finish the formalities on the new company.

During that week, Bhai tracked her down to ask her the same question that Udayan had. Did she not want to marry his son? Why, then, was she so woebegone and uncommunicative? She assured him that she was over the moon and to prove it, she called Appa right then to invite the Ramakrishnans to Mumbai for a traditional meet-and-greet. She felt much better after that call. The claustrophobia melted away. All went smoothly, even after Udayan returned from Jo'burg with his new partner. Once back, he asked her if she preferred the name Divine Lotus or Daha. She didn't care for either.

The final blow fell unexpectedly on the ides of October. Sho was frowning over a pink cupcake and a mug of questionable brown fluid called Jamaican Blue Mountain at a coffee shop in Andheri, Roja lying next to her. It was one of the few places that always welcomed Roja without freaking out as if Godzilla had padded in. She had an hour to kill before Appa's and Rohini's flight landed. Bhai had arranged for an elaborate dinner the next evening, with the entire Doshi clan in attendance. Amma said there was a crucial meeting with a new client, but Sho knew it was just one of her silly superstitions – she didn't want to meet the Doshis till the wedding was finalized. But that didn't mean Amma wouldn't call Appa after every five minutes for a blow-by-blow account of dinner at the Doshis'. Around 7.30 p.m., Uday walked in with Archana Patel. They were deep in conversation and didn't notice her. Sho didn't go up to them and twisted and turned conspicuously in her chair instead – until Roja trotted up to Uday. She had to follow her, more pissed off than surprised. They'd agreed to meet at 9 p.m. at the airport. Uday had seemed excited about meeting Appa.

'Hey, I thought you had a meeting,' she said.

'This is the meeting.'

'At Beans & Booze?'

'Archana's managing a press event for us.'

Sho thought – aloud – that it was awfully pre-emptive on part of the Divine Lotus slash Daha to enlist a PR girl when they hadn't even starting approving scripts. Or – and the thought struck her like a thunderbolt – *had* they?

Uday excused them and led Sho back to her table. Roja followed.

'Have you been drinking?'

'You know I don't drink.' She crossed her arms and slumped into her low-slung chair.

That meant Uday had to raise his voice. Both of them were riled.

'All this is about your script, right?'

'How perceptive!'

'Your fiancée's written a script?' Archana had come over to see what the matter was.

Sho glared at her toned legs, Udayan at Sho.

'What do you want me to do, Sho? Announce it as Daha's first project?'

'Oh, that'll be great. A professional and personal collaboration,' Archana trilled.

'It's a great script,' Uday nodded at Archana.

'Have you even read it?' Sho pouted. Even as her rational self fought it, she found herself behaving increasingly like a spoilt brat with delusions of entitlement.

'Let's talk about this later.'

'Ah, so you're ashamed of me.'

Uday frowned. He rarely did. 'Sho. It's a great story, but ...'

The classic professional 'but' rebuttal. Sho had heard it from a lot of people, including AK. At the best of times, a 'but' pretended that it cared for you but then quickly kicked you where it hurt most. Coming from Uday, this particular 'but' pierced through Sho like a poison-tipped arrow.

'Maybe I should leave you guys alone?' Archana said, without making any attempt to.

Uday gestured for her to wait. Like the uncharacteristic fever that had gripped him in Jordan, an unfamiliar belligerence began to build around his facial muscles. Simmering in her own resentment, Sho fatally failed to notice this. Perhaps he was disappointed with her 'princess-in-waiting' avatar. Perhaps, like Sho's amma had discovered that week, his notoriously steadfast and patient Mars in Taurus – hidden behind a peacemaking Libran Sun – was beginning to fray at the edges.

'Why don't you just have the balls to say it isn't good enough?'

'Fine. It isn't good enough!'

She could never explain why, and never forgive herself for it, but Sho picked up her mug and flung the remaining Jamaican Blue Mountain on Uday.

As if on cue, Roja growled and sunk her fangs into Sho's right arm. She'd never bit anyone and would never do it in the future.

That was the last time Uday and Sho saw each other. Until now, almost two years later.

12

Shit Hits the Roof

SHOBHNA

Aquamarine eyes on fire. Udayan is livid. If it weren't for the beige Hobo permanently pinned to his side like a baby roo to its mommy, he would look ferociously virile.

His pet niece, Nalini, is grinning at me like a loony bird. Sweet kid. We'd met at a Doshi Diwali do, just after Udayan had whispered in my ear to check on a situation in the ladies' room. Nalini's first period. I remember her being completely un-traumatized. She'd merely asked for a splash of my Burberry and we'd hugged.

'Hey, di!'

Pretty chummy, for Uncle's ex-girlfriend.

'Nalu …'

'Neelu.' She sidles closer to me.

Two tables away, talking rapidly to a waiter and eyes firing green darts at us, Uday looms like the Rock of Gibraltar. Within the approximately 500 sq. feet area, families and blue-collared single men silently share tables, polishing off stainless steel plates of fish, chicken curry and rice. And amboli – the chubby Maharashtrian dosa. Service is supersonic. Someone's arguing with Uday, who has positioned himself as an obstacle to the waiters: does he want to sit or go? A large bony woman – with a perfectly round face, in a brown-and-blue salwar-kameez and orange gajra in her hair – pokes Uday in his ribs. She's holding two ambolis in her bare hands. The dosas are hot and she's fat, and Uday is forced to sit down diagonally opposite me to let her pass. He's squeezed in next to two teenage boys who are dressed in Ed Hardy tees bought off the roadside.

'Lady, stop stalking me!'

Neelu must wonder why Uncle is hissing at his ex-girlfriend.

We need Udayan. Triple S and I need Udayan. I have to beg and beseech him. Soft talk. Sweet talk.

'Damn, da, you know you want to do it!' *Go, psycho Alpha girl!*

Against my wishes, I'm thumping my fists on the Formica table. 'You've read *The Dhaal*. You know it kicks major ass. That's why you came home. That's why you're here. This is why we wanted to do cinema. If you wanted to make money, you would be selling rubies and diamonds and gold. I would be blogging about terrorists wearing palazzo pants and kitten heels. *The Dhaal* is the real deal. We're in our thirties, da. If not now, when? When do we do something that really changes the world?'

The teenagers and Neelu are gawking.

'*The Dhaal* is an outstanding script. But it will not change the world. What you're saying is that it will change *your* world.'

'But this isn't about just *me* anymore. Look at you, Uday. You're restless. There's something that the big life in the Big Apple isn't giving you. You want something—'

'I want you to get lost.'

The teenagers stare deep down into their curries. One of them dips his face into the curry bowl and begins making loud smacking noises. The other one has a large unidentified animal tattoo on his arm with an inscription in Devnagari that reads 'dirty'. Neelu looks embarrassed for me and starts fiddling with her phone.

'I won't.'

'Shut up, Sho.'

'Yeah? Make me!'

Right then, Saayba is plunged into darkness.

'Sheet, yaar!'

'Sagoti sambhalo. Sagoti sambhal re ...'

Clang!

Power blackouts *never* happen in Mumbai, at least not in the western suburbs. This must be a sign. I crank up my volume, not for effect, but because he needs to hear me above the din. Bang! I think Uday's fist hit the table. Something small and wet lands on my hand. The teenage boys cough theatrically. I lick the wetness off my hand – lemon pickle – and grope for him. He whacks my palm and grabs my wrist. Really hard.

'You don't have lifetime access to me. I owe you nothing!'

The power returns.

'Mama, she's crying.' Neelu's high pitched voice rises above the din. I think Neelu is guerrilla-taping us on her phone.

Someone dumps a large white plastic bag on the table. Uday slips two hundred-rupee notes into the little steel bowl, takes a pinch of the supari and walks out, without touching the parcel of food.

This isn't the sort of place where you hide your tears under your aviators post sunset. A waiter hoots in my ear: do I want anything else, or do I want to pay and sod off? Orange Gajra, who had seated herself on an adjoining table, gets up, deposits my handbag in my hands and stands by in case I fall apart. From what I can make of it, she was with the teenagers who were sitting with us, but sat apart because of the rush. The beige Bottega Veneta is sticky. In my haste to corner Uday, I had spilled half a glass of solkadi on the last designer item I own. It is unlikely to be replaced with anything as fancy. I have lost all interest in the glamour of brands.

Done with her videotaping, Neelu holds the parcel in her arms. Her face is awash with apology. 'I've never seen Mama so rude.'

On my other side, Orange Gajra is pushing her cloth clutch into the crook of my arm.

'Neelu! Ahi aav!' Uday hollers.

'Heck! He's going to make us go back home,' she whines.

'I've got Sunny's Pajero. You can … sit in it. And eat that before it gets cold,' I say in desperation.

'Mama, let's go eat in Sunny's Pajero!'

Uday glances back in exasperation while still walking forward. 'Who the fuck is Sunny?'

'I'll explain that later,' I snap back, shouting to counter the ambient noise.

As Neelu and I scramble to join him, we see that Uday is spewing fire at the entrance. A burly fellow in red kurta and jeans has sauntered up and struck up a conversation with him. Orange Gajra is paying for my solkadi. I try to interject, but she thumps my shoulder in dismissal. She's figured we've had a lovers' tiff and is showing sympathy. In that single minute, two more guys have surrounded Uday at the entrance. He's listening to them intently. Then he shakes his head. And frowns. One of the men smiles and touches him on the shoulder. Uday snaps as smoothly as a thread of silk. Before anyone realizes, he's yanked the man's arm.

'Holy fuck!' That's Neelu.

We have to muscle through the crowd. The arm yankeee is not fatally wounded, just in shock. Red Kurta's cronies are trying to calm Uday down. The teen boys from our table have joined the crowd that's surged to the spot.

'What happened?' Neelu screeches.

'We were only talking. He's our friend.'

'I don't fucking know them!' Uday bellows.

'Bas kya, Gharpuré Saab?'

Uday leaps up and is restrained by the 'dirty' tattoo youngster. His terribly-styled oily Mohawk sways as he tries to reign Uday in.

'Shobhna Madam, you tell Gharpuré Saab.'

They know my name! Who are these men?

'Hey, you!' shouts Neelu and pounces on a blue scooter which one of the smiling lumpen sods is wheeling in. Lumpen No. 1 tells me we need to get a move on it; we have to go with them. Orange Gajra is neighing like a fat mare to my right, mouthing curses in Marathi, perhaps Konkani, and waving at Dirty Tattoo, who lets go of Uday, but trains his eyes, hawk-like, on him. The teenagers have clearly sided with the lumpens.

Usually a reincarnation of the crowd-pleasing Gandhiji, Uday is playing it all wrong. He's frowning and cursing in Gujarati and de-endearing himself rapidly. The crowd doesn't like him. It is with the lumpens. Stumped, but ready to give the situation her all, Neelu still has a firm grip on the scooter. Suddenly, Red Kurta whips out a Swiss knife.

Yikes! Tacky.

'Enough hua, madam. You just tell Gharpuré Saab ...'

Who the dickshit is Gharpuré?

'You tell him or ...' Red Kurta growls menacingly.

'Or? Or? Nahin toh? Nahin toh?' Uday's breaking the last shackles of the Mahatma inside him. 'Saale!'

Shit, no!

He grabs Red Kurta's collar and punches him in the stomach. The goon lurches, springing back like a jack-in-the-box to extract revenge. At the same time that Neelu abandons her scooter and rushes forth, arms flailing, the other Ed Hardy teenager tries to stop her, but she kicks him. He squeals, calls her a bad name and grabs her shoulder, thereby driving Uday's machismo even further up his ass. Before he does something foolish and gets us into more trouble, I swing my Bottega at the youngster and pull Neelu away from him, seeing which, another chap from the lumpens hobbles forth on a wooden crutch and jabs it at my thigh.

Blackout. Again.

The moon casts an eerie milky shadow. A sudden hush descends upon the warring parties as eyes adjust to the ghostly shadows. Somewhere, a child begins to cry.

My cell rings. Shit, is it Sunny? Is AK awake? Is it bloody Andrea pushing her French studio pants up my crotch? Neelu's hand is still in my other hand. The kid is freakishly strong. My BlackBerry drops to the ground, but before I can bend down, someone grabs my shoulders and pushes me into the crowd. Seems people are figuring out whom to shove and smack in the dark. I kick out and try to free myself when I realize it's Uday.

'Stop pushing her,' he barks.

'No, bugger! I'm pulling,' I retort, and pull Neelu even closer.

He lets go of my shoulders and snatches Neelu's hand from mine. Suddenly, I feel something wet on my hand. Again.

'Dogs! **** dogs!'

Gujarati cusswords are so filthy.

The wet thing doesn't feel like lemon pickle now. Yet, it's familiar.

Ah, blood.

In the next fifteen minutes, we find ourselves in Sunny's Pajero. Uday, Neelu and I are at the back. Once we reach the damned Pajero, it is apparent the goons have full control over the situation and the vehicle. Three of the goons are squashed up front; one of them driving like a nightmare, the other tending to his bleeding fingers, the third not sure how to fuss over his friend's bleeding finger in the cramped space. The louts have donated us big, brown, sweat-stained handkerchiefs to tie up our cuts – on my left arm and Uday's right. Uday has thrown his handkerchief away. I'd rather live, so I've tied mine to my arm. Behind us, resting his long legs on the spare tyre, and romancing girlfriends on his cell phone, is Dirty Tattoo who it seems is with the goons, after all. The other teenager has vanished after the fracas at the restaurant.

Nobody else is talking, partially because Dirty Tattoo is so loud, but also because nobody wants to fight anymore and 'accidentally' cut up any more people. Neelu – seated cross-legged, buffer-like between Uday and me – tears opens the food parcel from Saayba and begins to nibble on the famous fried Bombay duck. There's a prawn pickle and another fiery red condiment as well. She offers the spread to us, but I'm vegetarian and Uday is pissed – so amped up, he could explode. He has tightened his fists and sunk them in his cheeks and is polishing the simmering rageholic in him to a shine. Neelu devours the pickle, smacks her lips and adjusts her layered top.

During the blackout fracas, the Swiss knife–bearing red kurta guy accidentally – and very neatly – snipped one of the spaghetti straps off her tank top with his knife. I don't think it was a calculated attempt to outrage her modesty, else he wouldn't have lopped off a portion of his own finger alongside. Besides, she's wearing a tube below the tank and a shrug over it, so there was no indecent exposure. I bow-tied the broken strap and all was fine. Like at our first meeting, Neelu remained unfazed. The ruffians fussed like mother hens over Red Kurta's bleeding finger, then hustled us towards Sunny's Pajero, which I'd parked behind the masjid. I handed them the key because the limping lumpen who had jabbed my thigh earlier had begun to jab my stomach and that hurt like hell. As soon as I gave him the keys, he stopped jabbing me and began poking Dirty Tattoo. The toughs bickered for a while amongst themselves. Uday, now invoking his inner Hulk, refused to get into the Pajero. Nobody jabbed him. Nobody danced knives in front of him. Like teenage groupies at the altar of Robert Pattinson, they 'saab, please corporate'-ed him into the vehicle, where he eventually lapsed into a thundering silence, rapidly texting on his phone until it ran out of battery. A minute ago, he had flung it on the seat and is now venting on Neelu's yellow phone, pansy eco-friendly Hobo held between his knees.

We're speeding on the Western Express Highway now.

'I said no bloody tweeting!' Uday admonishes his niece.

'No. You didn't.' She grins.

He grimaces, snatches her phone and puts it under his bum. Within a second, Dirty Tattoo cackles like a jackal from his back perch. Uday swings back, snatches the lad's phone – presumably in mid-coochie-coo with girlfriend – and keeps that under his other bum.

'I said shut the fuck up.'

Recovering instantly from the shock, Dirty Tattoo gives us a rakish smile, stretches his legs further and strikes a mock rapper pose. 'Shit the phuck. Shit the phuck, Bappa. Shut the phuckkkah.' Dirty Tattoo is oozing mirth.

Limping Lumpen at the front giggles and wipes streams of facial sweat with the back of his hand.

Uday drops his head between his knees. Desperate bompu requirement.

'Let him be,' Neelu whispers on my shoulder, reeking of fried semolina and white flesh. 'He thinks he owes me one, because my parents are divorced.' I tell her my jabbed thigh hurts where she's poking her elbow. She eases out her elbow and drops a crumpled aluminium foil wrap in my lap. 'Mama thinks he's responsible for everyone in the world.'

Has this loony Doshi bird been tweeting about our colourful experiences since Saayba? As if this evening needed to get any more bizarre.

We're whizzing past Santacruz.

Is this an interrogation? An encounter? Am I – the kidnapper – being kidnapped? Has AK's family unleashed detectives upon us?

That is impossible. AK's right-hand man in Mumbai – MM – is aligned with us. The rest of the Khan family-who-matter, essentially Ammi who controls the purse strings and AK's brother Rahat, are settled in Amritsar and London, respectively. Has Bala or any of RAA's top brass ganged up with MuPo? Knowing the jokers, and especially post the midnight SOS, I think not.

Phone. It's Sunshine Sunny again. He probably wants to know when I'm coming back. I text him asking if all is okay and that I'll call him soonest. Unlike Triple S, Sunny is comfortable with texting. He replies within a second, assuring me all is okay, the old man is dozing again. Also – his next text message states casually – the disappearance of AK is on national television. Since 9 p.m.

Finally! If the 'Quit Fucking Bombay' morons hadn't stolen our thunder, we'd have been on air eight hours ago.

Vile Parle is a middle-class suburb between Santacruz and Andheri. As far as I know, it's not a particularly hot spot for interrogations or underworld shootouts. The Pajero turns into Hanuman Road, a bustling thoroughfare saturated with vada-pav stalls, biscuit factories, white-collar offices and family restaurants.

Sunny texts again – WHERE MY PAJERO. I WANT TO CALL. YOU CALL. OR I CALL. Before I can text him back, his Pajero screeches to a halt. We've stopped at a nice residential area, and are asked to alight. Nightmare Driver growls at Red Kurta to take us into the house while he parks. Lumpen No. 2 whistles loud and two more toughs come running out of the darkness. Dirty Tattoo, after extricating his phone from Uday's seat, comes up front. They form a human circle, and struggle to get Uday, Neelu and me to civilly stand in it and walk ahead. The entire group stumbles forward. This is really silly; we're a little off the main road, there's nobody around and it's highly unlikely that any of us will make a dramatic run for it. Uday grabs Neelu's hand to keep her between us. I am thankful. I'm pretty sure he is itching to strike me hard.

'Give your jackit,' growls Red Kurta.

They bind my hands with Neelu's using the full sleeves of my mulmul shrug. Once the shrug is off, I realize it is for the better. It was sweltering, despite the breeze.

'What is this?' Uday barks.

'Vile Parle.'

'I know it's Vile Parle. What are we doing here?'

'Saab, thoda more corporate, okay?' Red Kurta has returned

and is leading our human chain. For additional effect, he produces another weapon from his arsenal, a little black revolver. It looks genuine.

'Give me your phone,' Uday looks ahead, addressing me.

'Go to hell.' *That feels good.*

Neelu sizes up the situation with the alacrity of a Doshi. 'Mama, seriously, what's the deal?'

'Ask your *di*. We're changing the world.'

'Di? What's the deal?'

'Shh, hang on. We'll get out of this.'

Uday snorts. My left hand, the untied one, touches his back. He winces.

We've walked around twenty feet to a swanky high-rise with a neon back-lit board proclaiming it to be Rajputana. There are at least a dozen armed security guards on duty, serious-looking fellows. Smart black uniforms with plain metal badges. No logo of any security agency. Dirty Tattoo breaks the human chain, brings out a card from his pocket and slides it into a slim slot on the left pillar by the wrought-iron gate. The gate splits. We shuffle ahead and the human chain dissolves so the guards can get a closer look at us. They ask for our cell phones, upon which Neelu clutches hers, grabs my waist and begins to mock-wail. Dirty Tattoo has a word with the guards. We can keep our phones, but we need to be frisked. Neelu and I are directed to an anteroom at the massive foyer of the building. Our hands are untied. I push the door and stick my head in, expecting some sort of female guard within. There is nothing in the room except a large plasma screen with a little machine attached to it, a chair and a white tube light. The machine's blinking red.

'Hand print, madam. Ek haath maaro, ho gaya.' Standing behind me, next to Neelu, Red Kurta brings out his revolver with a flourish. It's some sort of a hand-print recognition software. You place your palm on a groove on the machine and it records your print and face on the screen. The contraption beeps after a few seconds. I guess I've been granted permission to enter.

Neelu's eyes are shining with excitement as I exit and she enters.

Uday isn't around. This might be a good time to get in a word with Red Kurta.

'Bhaisaab, yeh kya ho raha hai?'

He looks me up and down – his gaze lingering a second too long at my chest, but I could be wrong – and smiles like a wise old geezard, with hoary secrets hidden inside his unkempt goatee.

'Sab Bappa ko maloom hai. Very hot, no? When rain comes?'

Interesting question, but that's completely beside the point.

In the distance, Dirty Tattoo has stuck his Mohawk into Uday's Hobo. He rummages a bit, looks up and they have a brief but peaceful conversation. Uday shakes his head a couple of times, and the Hobo is dutifully returned to him. Neelu and Uday join us and the group proceeds towards the elevators, three in a row. Outside the gate, a bunch of people is creating a ruckus. They're arguing with the guards in Hindi. I hear the words 'camera' and 'DCP'. The guards strike up a chorus of 'Saheb nahi, sahib nahi! Jao!' In the flurry of distorted human noises that follow, a high-pitched male voice bandies the C word. Dirty Tattoo slides his card into a slim slot, which blinks green, and the doors slide open. Inside, the elevator is cool and spacious, with a very cutting edge steel-and-chrome finish. The muzak sounds retro, sixties. A Marathi song. I catch the words 'Satyamev Jayate'. We alight on Level 21.

There appears to be only one apartment, at the end of a very long corridor. No guards, guns or dogs. Nothing except a tulsi plant in a huge pot outside the undecorated door. No nameplate. But there is an ominous block of sleek steel boxes and more slots on the column to the left of the door, above the tulsi. Red Kurta thrusts his face into a teeny aperture, which promptly displays an angry red spot. Dirty Tattoo shoves him aside and thrusts in his own face, the right way. The dot turns yellow, then purple, and displays a psychedelic image of his retina on a screen above. The door opens. A sprawling living room, partially lit by white tube lights embedded into the walls. Plain brown curtains, drawn. Striped rugs and thick bed sheets lined neatly towards the left of the hall. The walls – newly painted – are decorated with large framed photographs of a dour-faced, bald, elderly gentleman. In frames across the hall, the same gentleman is younger, wearing the typical Maharashtrian cap, still dour. The only pieces of furniture in the hall are a huge armchair in green-and-yellow stripes and what looks like a television set – covered with lilac lace – on a sleek stainless-steel shelf that appears to be suspended from the roof.

'Cool digs!' Neelu's excitement is reaching an audible crescendo.

A pot-bellied old woman in a crumpled, yellow-flower-print, nine-yard cotton sari emerges from the far end of the hall with a plastic bag and a large steel thali. She settles on one of the rugs, produces three bunches of dill and half a kilo of garlic from the bag, and ignoring us completely, begins to pluck and peel. There's a large, rustic, blue-ink tattoo on her hand that has 'Ma Mi Vee Vee' written in Devnagari script alongside a large lotus. I've seen this woman somewhere. From the brief look she throws me, I think she recognizes me too. But where? From inside the house, the echo of vessels banging against each other. Someone is screaming at someone. A male voice. It's very faint, but there is something very familiar and very discomfiting about it.

We're standing here – seven lumpens, Uday, Neelu and I – and nothing is happening. No instructions, no more security scan slots. Only deafening silence. A couple of the tube lights flicker. Uday asks Dirty Tattoo if he has a light on him. He smiles and produces a packet of 555 and a lighter. Uday – an avowed non-smoker – lights up, rests his hand on his hip and looks at me.

'Avenged now?'

How is this my fault? I don't even know who these psychos are! I want to go home to Sunny and AK and Roja.

'No smoking allowed here. Please.' A deep baritone booms from within the walls.

A solid, bespectacled man in his late thirties enters from the same place as the old woman. He is enveloped in the smell of sandalwood. He is almost as fair as Uday with grey–green eyes, and is in a spotless white kurta and churidaar with a fresh vermillion tika on his forehead. It's possible; in this other world in Vile Parle, pristine-looking men could be performing pooja at 12.30 in the night.

'Wait, I will get you an ashtray.' He disappears inside and returns with a tiny steel bowl, the kind that Luchchi drinks water out of. 'Come, my friend. You know smoking is injurious to health.'

Uday surrenders his ciggie to the bowl.

'Good. I'm Saurabh Mahajan. Come, sit.'

Silence.

Saurabh Mahajan. Chief of MaMi? 'MaMi?'

'MaMi?' Uday catches on.

'The goonda party? No shit!' Neelu is excited and skipping on her toes.

'Always good to meet a fan.' Saurabh smiles indulgently at Neelu, no trace of sarcasm or malice in his tone.

Emboldened, she whips out her yellow phone. Saurabh raises his palm, the practised, perfect hand wave of a political patriarch. 'No tweets, no photographs, no Facebook. You can do that at the press conference.'

What press conference. Our press conference?

The smooth, urban-Indian English accent has thrown us a googly. One expects the chief of MaMi to be a barking son-of-the-soil, drenched in vernacularism. This fellow is nice. He lives in a peculiar but interesting house. He is tall and handsome, well muscled. He speaks English, prays at midnight and appears to be anti-smoking. It wouldn't hurt to listen to what he has to say and get the fuck out of here.

'Come now, sit. We don't have time to waste, do we?'

It's been a long day. I plonk on the rug, as far away from the old woman as possible. Crossing his arms, Uday stodgily leans on the wall, near the television. Saurabh doesn't seem to mind.

'Can I use the washroom ...?' Peeing on the side of caution, '... Sir?' That is Neelu.

'No.' He smiles at his own joke. 'Relax, Nalini. Of course you can. Straight and to the left. Indian-style loo.'

Neelu's eyes widen. She shoots me a 'when you gotta go, you gotta go' look and disappears. Saurabh reposes in the armchair. The lumpens also begin to sit, but Saurabh yells at them in a torrent of Marathi, which has them galloping for the main door. 'Pushkie!' he booms, and Dirty Tattoo falls back, adjusting his Mohawk. The rest proceed towards the door.

After they've left, Dirty Tattoo sits down next to the old

woman and irritates her by trying to set the vegetables on fire with his lighter and shouting 'Dada kothay?' every two seconds. She curses and thwacks him repeatedly.

Deep inside the house, vessels bang. Again, that familiar voice. Is it that I've slept barely five hours in the past two days, or is that voice really ringing in my ears?

Wait ... gaah ... Is it? Could it? Could that? No, it can't be!

'So, how are you people doing?' asks the chief of MaMi.

'Great. What do you want from us?'

'I appreciate your forthrightness, Shobhna.'

The old woman coughs. Saurabh calls her 'Ajji' and asks if everything is all right. She grumbles, says something about garlic being sold at Rs 400 per kg and resumes attacking the pods viciously. Neelu is back, unhurt. She wants to survey the hall, but Uday pulls her beside him and clamps a protective arm over her shoulder. There's a big macho display of congealed blood on his right forearm where Red Kurta knifed him.

'Let's get you some Dettol and bandages. Sit.' Quite odd, coming from the MaMi chief.

'Thanks, I'm good.' Uday wishes to remain the king of sulk.

'I insist. I have to keep explaining to my boys that we can't hurt people. Please sit.'

Nice brand of irony.

Uday is not sitting. He's reached the end of his tether – from Shibuya to here, the bompu's maxed out. So have I, but my legs are wobbly, so I need to sit. Someone has to, very quickly, put a stop to this suave Maratha kingpin–Florence Nightingale doppelgänger. He's clapped his hands at Pushkie who's jumped up and sprinted inside.

'Saurabh, we need to know what's going on.'

'Of course. I'll come straight to the point.'

Pushkie emerges from the same spot that Saurabh did, bearing a white first-aid box. He hands it to Saurabh, who opens it and produces a bottle of Dettol and white gauze.

'Shobhna, you have kidnapped, drugged and kept Khansaab in your house. Later today, you plan to stage a siege at RAA's press conference at the Four Seasons. And you, Udayan, are in this too.'

Did Uday nod? Did our man just visibly nod?

Saurabh springs up from the armchair with the grace of a cheetah. Brandishing Dettol and bandage, he approaches Uday.

'It was a brilliant plan. Deceptively idiotic, idealistic, but intelligent.'

The familiar voice wafting from inside the house is now rattling in my ears like giant blades flapping in the darkest part of hell. Along with the voice, an olfactory rush of jasmine and sweet, wet coconut.

They're standing head to head, Uday and the MaMi kingpin. Saurabh's mopping the wound with motherly concern and precision, instructing Neelu to hold up the tee sleeve. Uday's looking straight at him, unflinching – I'd say it is a semi-erotic gaze, but that could be my bias, given my own bisexuality. I could also help with the bandaging, except that I can't feel my legs. Sticky, sweaty skinny jeans are sucking the life force from my thighs.

'Unfortunately, your idealism collided with reality.'

'Your plan coincided with the "Quit Fucking Bombay" movement. And your press conference coincided with an alleged murder.'

'I don't get it.'

I'm getting it. Piecemeal. The world is spinning. A voice is ringing at the back of my head. 'You peepul, you just giuve up!'

'The south Mumbai murder?' Uday pipes up.

'Alleged murder.'

'By one of your people?'

'Yes.'

'Is that the MuPo below?'

'That's the press. The police are here.'

'What does the murder have to do with us?'

Did he just say 'us'?

'The alleged murder. It has everything to do with you. And RAA. And Khansaab.'

'How?'

The voice is getting closer.

'Because it is going to upstage your hijacking of the RAA press conference.'

Ada Poya!

Two MuPo men emerge from the same spot that everyone has been entering and exiting from. Between them, a tall, dark, sulky young man.

The world's greatest scriptwriter. The Artist who would triumph over dirty commercialism. The Hot Bod. The Big Hope.

Saurabh thumps his back. 'Udayan, meet Sagar.'

Sagar Saraswati Sonawane.

Triple S.

Now with the chief of MaMi?

With them?

With us?

In either case ... arsehole!

13

Slumdog Slayer

'Is he backward class?'

Sagar and AK had got off to an ominous start.

It was fifteen months since Sho and Uday had parted ways in acrimony. Uday's exit from her life had brought Sho face-to-face with the nastiest of her inner demons. After two decades of dating hamster-slashing weirdos and intensely creative egomaniacs, she'd met the man of her dreams and successfully managed to screw it up.

Benji called it The Curse of the American Sitcom – a defence mechanism ingrained in single urban Indians past partying age, regardless of gender. 'We've lost the plot, baby,' he'd wail. 'Dysfunctionality is so last season. Europe has returned to romance, but we're still trailing the Yankees, scared of settling for love.' Benji could be cruelly ironical, considering that he himself was in a steady relationship with an American lawyer. But Sho saw his point.

Like mathematicians, writers live in very dangerous places inside their heads.

When Uday left Zenith for the movie business, Sho was

scared shitless. Struggling to get her script to see the light of day was emotionally draining to begin with, to have her lover and soon-to-be husband as a potential producer, or yet another rejecter, was gut-wrenching. To add terror to fear, for once in her life, it seemed love was overshadowing work. So she did what any self-respecting woman in love would have done – she threw love out with the cup of coffee.

Post-Uday, the script assumed gigantic proportions, scorning, rebuking her. She abhorred the peddling, the pitching, the egos, the psychos. The more she got embroiled in that circus, the more she craved a stable life with Uday, Roja and a lovely journalism career. Then, promptly, she hated herself for being an unstable, indecisive prick. Six months after Udayan left Mumbai, she met a funny, good-looking banker. They had two memorable dates and a romantic night at her place. The sex was fantastic and the momentum just right. In the intervening period between Udayan's departure and Arindam's entry, she had been vigorously courted by a rakish art house director, which didn't work out because in the throes of a sexting avalanche, she realized that his texts ate the vowels. Arindam, on the other hand, was perfect, linguistically and otherwise. Everything went great for two months. But on their fourth night home, Roja had a change of heart and went straight for Arindam's groin – in a very vicious fashion – chasing him from living room to bedroom, until he got rather vexed. Their fifth to seventh dates were spent at his pet-free Bandra pad. On the eighth date, just after dinner, Sho felt the first stirrings of something she'd never felt – maternal guilt at having abandoned Roja. The brief and passionate love story died a natural death.

One day, Sho was in the RAA toilet, where she had taken to attending the ranting sessions of the chain-smoking marketing head, Priyanka. They were sitting on the sparkly red platform, pumping the moisturiser dispensers and discussing Priyanka's perilous BP, when one of the peons banged on the door.

There was a huge ruckus in the lobby. Someone was hell-bent on meeting Shobhna Madam. Sho sighed and hollered for her assistant, Rohan. This was supposed to be *his* headache. The peon rushed forth and back to announce that Rohan wasn't in the office. Sho grunted. The peon scratched his chin impatiently. It was 2.45 p.m.; he was already late for lunch. The leech at the lobby refused to leave. Could she please have a word with him?

He was a short, small-town boy in a shiny purple shirt, skinny black jeans and black sneakers with purple laces. He spoke only Marathi and Hindi. His name was Sunny. He said he had the best script in the whole world for her to read. She told him they weren't listening to new scripts; he could leave his phone number at the reception. He said please. She said no. It went on for three minutes, until she threatened to have security throw him out. He said people had told him she was the only person in this industry who could recognize real talent.

It was a cheesy, fake and painfully ironic line that didn't do anything to soothe her fractured ego, but she wanted to get rid of him, so she asked for the script. He plucked out a spiral-bound bundle of handwritten foolscap papers from the back of his shiny shirt and handed them to her.

'It's in Marathi.'

'Here, take it back.'

'No, I got it translated into English for you.'

'What's it called?'

'*The Dhaal*.'

He left after begging her to read it. She didn't.

The next Saturday, she had a meeting with the enfant terrible-come-lately of the industry, a cocaine addict from Bhopal who'd burst into Mumbai six years back to shake up Bollywood with what had now become His trademark – a dark, gritty oeuvre. While Bollywood hired white agents and desperately threw in its monetary might to get its stars on red carpets abroad and to grab two-bit roles in Hollywood films, this curly-haired, allegedly smelly Rastafarian had swooped in from nowhere to become India's darling on the world cinema stage. He'd agreed to meet Sho on one of His film sets inside a seedy building near Grant Road. It was rumoured to be the story of an incestuous, abusive father–daughter relationship, with several scenes involving heavy S&M. Sho wanted Him to read her script.

He was seated on the edge of a filthy bathtub in the middle of a ramshackle room, filled with technicians buzzing around. An assistant director – Sho knew him; he was a UCLA grad who'd made a short film that had won a lot of obscure international film awards – knelt inside the tub, furiously rolling joints for Him. Italian opera oozed in the background.

'I read the script, Shobsie. I'm going to come clean to you. I don't love love stories.'

She knew that.

'But yours is poetic; it's sort of masochistic and sad and rodent.'

She had never thought of it that way.

'I don't like it anyway. But tell me, would you fuck yourself for cinema?'

A little girl, about five, ran up to Him and straddled His knee. He offered her a joint. She threw it away.

'Nayloochi, you tell this nice lady here if you think your Baaboochi fucks himself for cinema?'

She stuck her tongue out and tumbled into the tub.

On the way to the exit, He offered Sho a job as His first AD, adding immediately that He would loathe her if she took it up. He took off His thick black-rimmed glasses and peered at her, using the stems to clean the tobacco between His teeth.

'Cinema is a 75-mm fuck-fest, babe. I have jokers who feel honoured if they roll my grass and lick my dirty ass and they call it learning about cinema. I like you, Shobsie. Say hi to that chubby gigolo you work for, eh?'

Despo Script Guy was waiting for her outside the building, holding open the back door of a taxi. She pretended not to remember him and continued walking.

'Madam, I am Sunny ... *The Dhaal*.'

He hopped behind her all the way across dusty Lamington Road. Finally, she had to tell him that she didn't want to read his script, she didn't care, and he could go to hell. He stared at her, speechless for a second. Then he grabbed both her hands in his and knelt down, right in the middle of the busy thoroughfare. She tried shaking him off, but he was surprisingly strong. He said nothing, just pumped her palms and kept smiling. She said she would read it, if he let go.

'Mother promise?'

'Haan, mother promise.'

She didn't read it. She didn't even remember where she'd dumped it in the midst of the rotting library of screenplays, treatments and piles of crap in her office. All she thought of was whether she wanted to fuck herself for cinema. She didn't. She never had.

The following Friday, Sho was returning to Andheri after meeting Benji when Sunny grabbed her hand again, in the middle of swarming evening traffic outside the station. They were outside an Irani café. He beseeched her to 'Come in, no, please, please'. She was ready to attack in case he touched her again, but a tall, dark man emerged from the crowd inside the café and scowled deeply at Sunny and Sho.

'He is that one,' Sunny gesticulated wildly.

'Who?'

'Writer. Sagar.'

It turned out that the script that was being forced upon Sho was not written by her shiny-clothed stalker but by his friend, Sagar.

'Writer Sagar' was 6'1" with a dark cocoa complexion. He was wearing a cheap printed cotton bush shirt, brown trousers and blue Bata chappals. He wasn't handsome. Damaged by the sun, his skin was mottled, dry and angry. Like his scraggly stubble. But two things about him stood out. The nose. It was so straight and sharp, you could cut veggies on it. Surrounded by slim, suspecting black eyes and thin, mean lips, it dominated his scowling face. The other striking thing was his charisma. An undeniable crouching jaguar-hidden-jackal appeal.

He glowered at her.

'Who are you?' he frowned.

The English was smeared with a thick Marathi accent. Sho guessed it was semi-rural.

'What do you want?' came another query.

She was exasperated. Two men, one stalking her relentlessly and the other interrogating her while she was trying to go about minding her business. 'I don't want anything. This person, your Sunny, is following me everywhere with a script.'

'How you dare to read my screeept!'

'But she like it!' Sunny lied smoothly.

'Eeet does not matter. My writing is not for you peepul.'

He looked down at her like she was dirt, grabbed Sunny

resolutely and walked back to the Irani cafe. Sho hailed a rickshaw and, with a brisk change of plans, went to office instead of home. There, she asked for two coffees and an aspirin. It took her over an hour to locate the script, in longhand, blue ink on foolscap. The translation was ghastly, but she read it from end to end, without a break. The cell phone number at the end of the script was in Devnagari, as was the name. She dialled Sunny's number and asked him to bring the rude writer to RAA's office three days later. On Wednesday, Sunny showed up. Alone.

'Where's your friend?'

'Sagar? I don't know.'

Sho told him she was very busy and didn't have time for writers with inflated egos. She'd give them one last chance. He could get his friend for a meeting on Friday, or forget about the whole thing. It was then that Shani Bha, or Sunny, as he preferred to be called, launched into an impassioned defence of his best friend, Sagar Saraswati Sonawane. Sho found herself unable to interrupt him.

They were from a village called Pandare in Baramati, the heart of the sugar belt in Maharashtra, 300 kilometres from Mumbai. Sunny's family was relatively prosperous; they owned sugarcane plantations and a jaggery plant. The Sonawanes were poor. Very poor. When Sagar was five, his father – allegedly manic depressive – abandoned his mother and five kids. His mother worked at the sugarcane factory for Sunny's family, which is how the boys befriended each other. Sagar's mother – Sunny called her Akka – was a woman of steel who, though uneducated, managed the administration of the factory with a formidable reputation for being nobody's fool. Eventually, all of Sagar's siblings were sent off to Pune and Chiplun, where they stayed with relatives while they earned and got an education. Sagar chose to stay with his mother. A stroke of polio at the age of three had left him with a permanent limp in his left leg. When the children at school teased him relentlessly, Akka went and gave the teachers a dressing down, after which the teachers hated him too. But he was always good at languages – Marathi and Hindi – and earned an income on the side by giving tuitions to duds like Sunny himself. (At this point, Sho offered Sunny a cup of chai and biscuits, which he accepted.) Sagar was the only boy in the entire district to receive a scholarship to study in a prestigious English-language 10+2 college in Pune, but he refused since he wanted to stay with his mother who didn't want to move out of Baramati. At the age of fourteen, Sagar started a local theatre group and wrote and directed several plays. The group soon started travelling to nearby villages and became so popular that it was invited to Delhi to participate in one of the most prestigious amateur theatre festivals in the country. Sagar was offered a scholarship to the arts programme at JNU, but he refused. His theatre group worked with school dropouts and juveniles; he didn't want to abandon them. But when Sunny read the film script that Sagar had been working on for two years, he insisted he'd get it out of Baramati into the bigger world. But Sagar turned his offer down.

Sho thought she saw a hint of tears in Sunny's eyes.

'Let me get this straight. You are trying to sell his script against his wishes?'

'No! No sell-well. He will direct the movie himself.'

She considered throwing him out of her office for good. It was probably the best chance to do so. As she pondered, he pushed himself to the edge of his chair, threatening to fall on his knees again.

'Please, madam. Last chance. I will talk to him.'

'Can you get him here on Friday and make him behave himself?'

'Hundred per cent.'

'Wait. What is he doing here, in Mumbai?'

'Akka has a slipped disc operation. My father's friend is a doctor at JJ Hospital. We are staying at my aunt's house in Thane.'

Sunny returned on Friday, with Sagar. The brooding artiste was wearing the same shirt, brown trousers and chappals as before. He'd shaved, which made no difference to his belligerent expression. Sunny was in his favourite shiny lilac shirt with matching lilac laces on his shoes. Sho had instructed Rohan to entertain them in her office while she prepped AK. The Pathan was intrigued. It was the first time in three years that she'd insisted, almost begged him to meet a writer.

'Are you backward class?'

Sagar looked daggers at AK, Sunny at Sho, who was looking at Sagar. AK chewed on a jujube. Kurta–Pyjama–Chappals was typing furiously on AK's Macbook in his favourite corner. The faithful MM hovered by the table, speaking to AK's cook on his cell phone.

'Are you a Dalit?'

'Yes.'

'Dalit Panther.' AK muttered to himself, walking his fingers on the glass table-top.

The Dalit Panther was an activist organization founded in the seventies in Bombay by a fiery poet, writer and human rights activist. Sho didn't know what it was. Sagar didn't care because it was not functional anymore.

'So, you do theatre with *underprivileged* children.'

'Children.'

AK waved the white flag. 'Sho says your script is brilliant.'

'I know.'

Sunny compensated promptly: 'Thank you, sir.'

'Sho says your script will be the *Slumdog Millionaire* of 2013. If we make it.'

'I have not seen that film.'

'What sort of cinema do you like?'

'I do not see much cinaema.'

'Are you always like this?'

'Yaes.'

AK smiled his warm, paternal, dimpled smile and walked around the table to their side.

'How old are you?'

'Thirty.'

'I was exactly like you when I was that age.'

Sagar's arms remained crossed on his chest; his face expressionless.

'Have you thought of who you would like to direct this movie?'

'Me.'

'Do you have any experience directing?'

Sho interrupted to elaborate on Sagar's theatre group in Baramati. AK listened to the script writer's achievements with wide-eyed fascination. When Sho was done, he went close to Sagar and looked him in his eyes.

'Look, boy, I like you. You have spunk. And if Shobhna says so, I'm sure your script can be India's next *Slumdog Millionaire*. And we will make it. Yes, RAA will make it. But, boy, I'll tell you what I've learnt during my forty-five years in this industry ... Am I speaking too fast? Martand can translate what I say if you want.'

Martand smiled. AK smiled. Sagar's facial muscles twitched.

'No. I gate eet.'

AK placed his plump paw on Sagar's bony shoulder. His personalized musky perfume, alchemised and flown in from Morocco every month, filled the room.

'You're smart. But see, that doesn't work here. What works is being a nice person. Ask Shobhna. She's also written a script. It's a fabulous script. She knows it will get made when its time comes. She's laying the groundwork.'

Sagar looked at Sho, who was texting, pretending she hadn't heard what was said. AK returned to his chair.

'So, Sanjay—'

'Sagar. Sagar Saraswati Sonawane.'

'Sagar. The endless ocean ...'

'Sea.'

'Sagar the Sea. Welcome to the RAA family. Keep in touch with Shobhna. We'll keep working on the script. We can work on a monthly retainer ... I mean pagaar. Martand will explain everything to you.'

Everyone in the room felt a little whip cutting through the air when AK translated the word retainership to the very plebeian Indian word for salary. Even Kurta–Pyjama–Chappals looked up. 'Should we leave, jaan?' he interjected a little too quickly.

'Haanji. We have a meeting with the Oberois at the race course,' AK nodded.

With that, Sagar, Sunny and Sho left AK's office. She took them to an Udipi restaurant near RAA's office. Sunny buried his head inside his cup of tea, while Sagar's eyes spewed fire at Sho.

'Do you know how difficult it is to get a one-on-one with

the most influential producer in Mumbai? And all you do is sit there with your arms crossed, pissing people off with your attitude.'

'Ees eet my attitude or how dayer someone like me shood hauve an attitude?'

'Do you want me to leave?'

'Eet is yuar life.'

She couldn't.

That was when she saw them for the first and last time – half-a-dozen angry tears slithering out of the corners of Sagar's eyes. He neither hid them nor played them up. His nose went red and snotty. Sho tried looking away, but couldn't. Even with the tears and snot and ugly scowl, he was electric – straight and sharp, with long, lean muscles – not an ounce of fat, a compact chest and a tight butt. That body wasn't made in a gym. It was cut and burnt under the sun and had taken root in dry, parched earth. It sprouted way too much hair and smelled strange, and did things that … So, she turned to Sunny.

'I can't talk to him. I just …'

'Why don't your saheb's driver to talk to me? You know … we reejanal-taype peepul can koommunikate better.'

'What is with the chip on your shoulder?'

'What cheep?'

'Look, I'm doing this for you. Because your script is good. I'm doing you a favour. So maybe it's time you start …'

'Saala who came to you? You called us, no?'

Sho turned to Sunny and complained, 'You said he wasn't interested in selling the script. Now he wants to direct the film. What does that mean?'

'What the hail!'

Sho stood up, ready to leave, fighting the impulse to slap Sagar. Sunny came to the rescue.

'Madam, please. Sagar! Gapp bas na.' Sunny exhorted his friend to shut up.

'You're wasting your time, Sunny. Some people don't deserve to be helped.'

Sagar threw a hundred-rupee note on the table and hobbled out, saying, 'And the peepul who cannot get their scripts turned into films ... they only help others.'

After Sagar stormed off and Sunny followed him, Sho stayed back at the Udipi hotel, and went through two masala dosas, a khara bhaat and two filter coffees, with her mind looped hopelessly on *The Dhaal*. She had re-read it, four times. And was gobsmacked every time. It was a ripper of a story, even when she hadn't known the arsehole who wrote it. In one giant killer wave, *The Dhaal* had drowned her obsessions about her own script, her life and the sheer, impassive mediocrity of her existence.

The Dhaal was about a bunch of school kids in the fictional village of Rohu near Nagpur, on the border of Maharashtra. Eight- to sixteen-year-old boys and girls take lessons in math and history in a ramshackle wood-and brick-building. It is the only school in a radius of 250 kilometres. The fifty-odd children come from impoverished families, with tales of abuse, abandonment and physical and emotional dysfunctionalities. According to a government scheme, the students are promised a glass of milk each, every day, around mid-morning. These children barely get two square meals a day, so the milk is a big incentive for them to attend school. Bureaucrats from the nearest town create a minor press spectacle and leave. The milk doesn't show up on the first day. Neither the next day. Or the next. Not a single drop. A group of six rogue students – four boys and two girls – begin to raise a storm and create a hostile environment by starting fights, tearing precious textbooks and provoking the two underpaid teachers, driving them to tears. Twenty-one days later, the official vats of milk arrive at the school. The milk is rancid. A fracas ensues, in which the rebel group is made to drink the rancid milk. Overnight, one of them, already malnourished, dies. The next day, the remaining five children – lanky, rebellious twelve-year-olds procure a gun – cordon off the school building and threaten to shoot anyone who tries to enter it. That section, which reached up to page fifty, was enough to blow Sho's mind. As the plot unfolded further, *The Dhaal* – which is what the band of underage outlaws named themselves – became more and more like an amazing secret that Sho desperately wanted to keep to herself, but about which she desperately wanted to shout to the world. Every scene escalated the drama without missing a beat or tumbling into clichéd muck. The emotional build-up was complemented by the fantastical action sequences that flirted heavily with a dark and twisted fantasy world, something even children could identify with.

The Dhaal turned every cinematic cliché about impoverished Indian villagers and children on its head. It was a kickass combination of surrealism and activism and unexpected humour that miraculously climaxed on a feel-good emotional high note. Even as she read the screenplay for the nth time, Sho could see the pages rip onto the screen and tear into the imaginations and hearts of audiences worldwide. She knew it was a ticking bomb, which would burst and catapult India to the world stage. It would make *Slumdog Millionaire* eat shit … no irony intended.

She tried getting her ebullience across to AK the next day at Otters Club. They had brunch with Aashi Kappu and her German boyfriend-cum-manager. The twenty-seven-year-old ex-Miss World was on the verge of signing her third film with

RAA. Currently, she endorsed ten products and charged an average of three crores for each. Her boyfriend-cum-manager wanted to negotiate with AK, considering that she'd just been signed on to peddle a top Italian car brand, the first Indian to do so. Normally, Bala handled Kappu, but for this new remake of a Hollywood sci-fi blockbuster, AK wanted to negotiate with Kappu himself. She was asking for eight crores to play the monkey princess who leapt over treetops and mountains and fell in love with the emotionally damaged Golden Boy from Earth who would finally save her galaxy from annihilation. They were going to call the movie *Yogi*. AK wanted to bring the little bitch down to four crores.

Mid-meeting, Kappu and boyfriend called for a break; they had to get on an urgent con call with Rome from their suite upstairs. As soon as they left, Sho grabbed the opportunity to launch into a passionate plea for *The Dhaal*. AK licked tiny spoonfuls of his grapefruit yoghurt. He was getting irritated and decided to be forthright and nip the matter in the bud. He'd met the young man just to indulge Sho. RAA was not interested in making art house regional cinema. If she was so obstinate about pushing it, she could speak to Bala about edging the project into their new offshoot – RINDIE, short for RAA Indie. Sho almost spilled her iced tea over her new daffodil-yellow maxi dress. She knew as well as anyone else that RINDIE had secretly shut down after producing three highly-acclaimed films that struggled to recover their investment. One of them was a Marathi film that came achingly close to winning the Academy Award for the best foreign film in 2009. After RINDIE put RAA in the good books of the press and multiplexing public, AK made Bala kill it and pretend it was alive. But Sho had just had a word – rather argument – with Bala and knew that RINDIE was gone.

Sho leaned forward in her white wicker chair. 'C'mon, AK. You *must* do *something*.'

The heat was seeping through to AK's unflappable temperament, as was Kappu and her outrageous eight-crore demand. He was in no mood to coddle two prima donnas in one day.

'It's going to be a breakout film, AK!'

'Will it breakout at the box office?'

'Please AK! There's no guarantee to success.'

She knew it was untrue even as she said it. RAA's fat-cat projects had pre-set lucrative distribution and music/satellite sale deals, which made sure that the picture earned back its costs even before it hit the screens. These were run-of-the-mill formula films with the same song-and-dance sequences repeated in different locales and the same actors doing the same thing for increasing amounts of money for the same audience. *The Dhaal* was a potential sleeper hit, but also a potential dud at the box office, but it would definitely raise their creative stock and boost their rep as visionaries and risk-takers.

The Dhaal was a huge risk, one that RAA could easily afford to take, but AK didn't want to.

Sho writhed in frustration.

'Sho, how is Uday doing?'

'I don't know. We are not in touch. How is that of any concern here?'

'What about your own script?'

'It's not good enough. *The Dhaal* is light years ahead.'

AK finished licking the last of his grapefruit yoghurt. 'Can I be honest, beta?'

'Yeah.'

'I've observed you closely for more than three years now. You're like the daughter I never had.'

Sho smiled. His hollow, pink-cheeked paternalism had been rattling her bones for over a year. 'You give up too soon …'

'But what does that have to do with *The Dhaal?*'

'You're so talented, but really, what have you done with it? You had a great career in journalism, which you gave up for movies. Then you gave up Uday. Now you are giving up on your own script, for this silly, strange, little village …'

'It's not silly or strange, you know that!'

AK heaved his bulk out of his wicker chair and held Sho's hand. 'You're too emotional, Sho.'

'Again, AK, what does this have to do with *The Dhaal?*'

'That ghati boy cannot walk in here with some sort of talent and think that is enough. This is the world's largest film-producing industry. There are millions of people at our doors, desperate to do anything to get in, giving up careers, families, money, love … But only a few chosen ones get lucky.' Then he drove the final nail in the coffin. 'Writers don't run this business, Sho. Businessmen do. Nobody knows that better than you.'

By the time Kappu returned bathed in post-coital glow, Sho had stormed out of the club, MM – whom AK had dispatched with a peace message – in hot pursuit. But she didn't stop. She walked – fast and furious – to Bandra railway station and after the longest time, hopped into a local train to Andheri, unmindful that it was peak time, the hour of the Great (In) Human Squelching. Sandwiched between housewives, fisherwomen and college girls, unwittingly groped and pushed, Sho finally let out the impotent rage she'd bottled up for so long. Nobody paid attention to her guttural bawling, which gave her the freedom to fully express the intense frustrations of her powerless Mars in Cancer. When she reached home, at 9 p.m., she'd cried off the past five years to her satisfaction.

She called Sunny at eleven and asked him and Sagar to meet her at a coffee shop near her house the next morning. Sagar came along, clearly coerced and emotionally blackmailed by his childhood pal. Sho laid out her plan. The duo listened in disbelief. At the end of the narration, Sunny smiled. The boy had no moral compunctions; he was ready to champion genocide, as long as it got his friend's talent up centre stage. Sagar stared at her from the slits of his eyes that were ensconced behind a lush curtain of lashes, then hobbled out. His limp proved to be an asset; Sunny easily caught up and cajoled him back to the table. Seated again, he was direct.

'T'chaila, you are maintal or what?'

'Do you want to go back to Baramati and let your script rot?'

'Yes.'

'No. You're angry. You're giving up.'

'Maybe, *you* are angry. *You* are gieuing it up.'

She stirred her mocha and tried to peer through the two thick black curtains of eyelashes.

'Listen, what are you going to do with it? Make it into a naatak?'

'Whai not?'

'Oh come on! You know it's a visual epic. Are you going to screw it up just because of your ego? And because you're scared?'

'T'chaila!' he whispered and hobbled out again. This time, he wiggled out of Sunny's grasp.

Sho stayed back and mulled over her plan. She could, she considered, be sensible and just leave RAA, get the hell out of Mumbai, get back to a real job and get on with her life. It was *The Dhaal* that stopped her from running away, again. Blessedly, it was something outside her, so she could see it objectively.

Two days later, she almost begged Sunny for another meeting. Sagar chose a restaurant in Vashi. The girl who walked Roja thrice a week had taken the day off, so Sho bundled Roja into the car and drove an hour and a half to sector 19 in Vashi. The restaurant refused to accept dogs, so they had to relocate to a shack in Kopripada. It was a large, open-air stretch of a dhaba, where they served them chai and crisp, crackling medu vadas immediately. Looking at the quality of service, Sho guessed the dhaba owner knew the boys.

Sho smiled a lot and discussed *The Dhaal* at length, digging into the imaginary – or not – lives of the anti-heroes of the script. She wanted to know why Arun chose to ditch Sai, what finally happened to Khapri's parents, where Gowri learnt how to cork and fill a gun, and why the teachers became as inexplicably cruel as they did. Slowly, Sho drew Sagar into a discussion. Mostly in the form of arguments. Arun chose to ditch Sai because he always resented the fact that he was attracted to him. Khapri's parents died, Gowri learnt how to work the gun from her constable uncle, and the teachers were so cruel because that is what failure combined with poverty and low IQ does to people. At this point, Sagar turned away from Sho, took Roja's snout in his hands and began picking her teeth with a matchstick. Amazingly, she allowed him to do it, occasionally grabbing one of his long, artistic fingers between her fangs. It was early evening. The weather was pleasant. Sho looked at Sunny, who nodded encouragingly, even as he maintained the Bollywood-hero pose he'd assumed while sitting.

'You really don't want to do this, Sagar?'

'You are taking the story vhery literally. You cannot peek up a gun for euvrithing in the reeyal world.'

Done with the teeth, Sagar began to run his fingers over

Roja's coat, looking for nesting fleas. Sho was too involved with *The Dhaal* to object. Besides, Roja appeared to be enjoying it, even when he – unsmiling as always – knocked on her forehead like one knocks on a door.

'Do you know cheelren with autism? They giuve them cats to make them calm. But I think dogs are vhery good also.'

Wondering if Sagar was autistic as a child, Sho bashed away regardless. '*The Dhaal* needs a bigger stage than what you can give it. You know that.'

'Stage? Bluddy media circus. What you going to giuve me? One crore heets on Tweeter and a televishun programme? I will sing sad songs with my poor cheelren and salebreetys will clap? T'chaila, bakwaas.'

He spat sporadically, on Roja. Sho strove to keep herself together, and to overcome the overwhelming feeling that like before, her professional and personal life were on a collision course. But the two flirted mercilessly, even as she assumed a calm surface.

'Don't bluff me with that attitude. Every writer, artist, however arrogant, wants his work to be appreciated. By as many people as possible.'

'Will eet hauve heart of mutton?' His eyes were inscrutable, his body language schizophrenic – at once open and shut, defensive and interactive. Sho confirmed that though she herself was vegetarian, Roja loved kaleji. So he called over the boy – whom Roja had earlier growled at – who'd brought them samosas and asked him to get the stuff from the back of the shop. The boy returned in five minutes with a plastic bag, which Sagar emptied into his samosa plate and called the boy back for some 'rassa'. The fiery red watery gravy came in a tiffin box and was poured over the kaleji. Sagar set the plate on his bench. Roja fell over herself, neatly lopping up the pieces in single gulps. Noticing Sho's expression, Sagar smirked. 'Don't worry. Eet izh clean.'

'You think I'm exploiting you because I have issues with AK and I want to take revenge.'

'Yaes.'

'You're wrong.'

He picked up a piece of oily goat heart and pretended to chuck it into his mouth. Roja cocked her head and pointed the tips of her ears towards each other, a magic trick she'd taught herself. Sagar pulled her collar and stuck his tongue out at her, without the slightest hint of mirth. Rapt in silent concentration until then, Sunny suddenly leapt up to attend a phone call. The caller wanted to speak to Sagar, who listened intently, still looking only at Roja. Occasionally, he interrupted with a 'Pan, kaka' and 'nahi, nahi', following it up with a rasping 'Hmm … ho.' Eventually, he hung up and slammed the cell phone into Sunny's hands. Between a couple of 'saale harami's, he made sure Roja licked her plate clean.

'Halkat saale! Jeemy biskeet.'

'Huh?'

'If we kidnap that Khan and make a sceene at prais confrence … you think that is a freedom movement? Dalit Panther, t'chaila! You want me to be Jeemy biskeet, Tommy biskeet in front of a camera, wearing good clothes and eating pizzha and pashta and posing for dumb journaylists, but we will all steel be Jeemy biskeets, posing for dumb journyalist in morning and cleaning your sandaas in the evening.'

Roja propped up her front paws on Sagar's shoulders as he scratched her under the chin, whispering, 'Nako ga, gapp ga bai.' She was being routinely sprayed with his belligerent spit, but the happy canine was too involved with goofing around to notice it. In the throes of their man-upon-animal foreplay, Sho launched her final assault.

'Look, I understand. I am also a writer. Not as good as you. Or not where you come from. But I've learnt one thing from ... experience. Three things, actually. One: do you really know what you want? Two: will you let your ego ruin what you really want? And three: how far will you go to get what you really want?'

'Thair.' Sagar pointed to Sho's car parked around 200 metres ahead on the main road. 'I will go thair. We will race.' He relocated Roja's forepaws to the bench and placed her on the ground. Then he smacked her on the bum.

Roja outran the hobbling artiste that evening. And Sagar – henceforth Triple S – hopped on to the insane Strike at Thirty-Six bandwagon. That evening, very briefly, Sho sensed a kindred spirit in him, someone whose passion was led by deep-set emotion, whose arbitrary decisions to do apparently silly things were based on primal vengeful emotions. AK's condescending attitude was the excuse that Sho's and Sagar's convoluted idealism had been looking for.

She occasionally looked at his buff bod and wondered. But she knew it was *The Dhaal* and not something more carnal which inspired her. Besides, in the surly and sarcastic small-town artiste, she had found someone more than an unwilling co-conspirator.

She'd found a fellow provocateur. One as naïve as her.

14

Ambushing the Ambush

SHOBHNA

Uday is never condescending, unless he's being condescending to me.

'This is your Triple S?'

The dude writes a story on gun-toting, rebellious kids ... seriously, what was I expecting?

Triple S has grown a jungle on his face and is wearing his trademark attire. He looks tired and reeks of a strong sort of oil.

Uday extends his hand. Triple S doesn't do handshakes; he reciprocates by joining his palms into a namaskar. Everyone in the room – Saurabh, Pushkie, Neelu and the pot-bellied old woman – is looking from Sagar to Uday, back and forth. Only the two MuPo guys don't care, I suppose something should happen. Two tall, virile men, facing each other like gladiators. A diamond prince-turned-movie maven and a writer-turned-MaMi goon, if Saurabh was to be believed. They could erupt any minute, leap at each other. But they don't. They stand within pummelling distance, Uday's hands on his hips, Sagar's crossed on his chest.

Damn you, Uday, I know you're furious. So why don't you just wipe the inscrutable expression off your face, pin that hobbling, murdering rat to the floor and pound his brains out?

He won't. The men in my life are not spontaneous combustors, at the best and worst of times.

Saurabh beckons the MuPo couple, which leaves Triple S looking straight at Uday and me. The top three buttons of his shirt appear to have been ripped off. His curly black hair is messier than usual. The smell of the oil – possibly hibiscus – is overpowering, coupled with sweat. He looks tired.

All that lying and vandalizing and murdering must be so exhausting.

We stand like three constipated pressure cookers in a triangle, until Saurabh butts into the silence. 'So, Udayan, this is the first time you're meeting our resident Shakespeare?'

Suddenly, scarier thoughts explode in my head. 'Where the hell is Sunny? Where the hell is AK?'

'Sunny is fine, Shobhna. Khansaab is fine. So is your dog,' Saurabh says with a smile.

My mind is in a tizzy. Sagar? MaMi goon? Did he tip Saurabh off about not just Khansaab but Roja as well? *Vernacular prick! Not a hint of guilt in those black, black eyes. How could I not have seen this coming?*

Saurabh is herding the MuPo couple towards the exit. It's a good time to holler at his back. 'We are not making any deals with the devil!'

'By devil, you mean MaMi?' he sneers.

'Provincial, small-minded, arrogant, weak bullies.'

'That makes the two of us.' He's facing us again, smiling. Rolling back the sleeves of his kurta, he reveals a navy blue metallic watch, a bracelet of rudraksh beads and a couple of red threads on his left wrist. 'It's just that we people are politicians and you guys are artistes.'

Bleh!

'What is sauce for the political animal is not sauce for the suffering artiste?' he adds.

'Not murder!' I say.

'But of course kidnapping is fine.'

'Potatoes and tomatoes ...'

'... make a good curry,' he laughs.

Fruitcake despot alert!

Saurabh looks askance at Triple S, who wipes the sweat off his brow with the back of his palm. The air conditioning is pretty good. Before Saurabh can crack more cryptic ones, the pot-bellied old woman bursts into a monstrous coughing fit. Saurabh walks up to her, bends down on one knee, pats her back and pops a couple of unpeeled garlic pods into his mouth.

A guy in safari suit comes running up to him with what looks suspiciously like the eighteen-carat Vertu handset. Titanium plated, I think. Saurabh pats him on the back too, speaks in rapid-fire Marathi on the phone: 'Saheb, saheb, nakki, nakki, ata, ata ... Jayostute! Jai Hind! Jai Maharashtra.'

He returns the titanium phone to Safari Suit, shakes his head and directs his query at Uday. 'Udayan, do you think America is a meritocracy?'

'No.'

Uday's one-word answer is instantaneous, almost like he knew what the question was going to be. Black and white was never Uday's style. But people change.

'Ah, well, India doesn't believe in merit either. The fight belongs to everyone, right Shobhna?'

Whatever.

Having chomped gracefully on the garlic pods, he signals the safari-suited guard and Pushkie to follow him inside.

'I am going to give you a minute,' Saurabh says. 'Make that ten. You must sort out your issues quick. We start the pooja soon.'

'What pooja?'

'Ganpati visarjan.'

'Isn't visarjan on Friday?'

'We have a five-day Ganpati. The pooja is now. After that, all of us have a press conference to attend.'

Saurabh strides away out of sight, followed by Pushkie. There is an awkward silence in the room. The woman returns to her garlic peeling.

Is it rain I hear lashing at the windows? Epic moments like this are always marked by rain, aren't they?

After what seems like the longest time, someone speaks.

'Are you shagging him, S?'

'Neelu!'

She moves towards Triple S, bouncy as a baby ewe. 'Is he why you guys broke up?'

She must be thrilled. India is so much fun. Uncle and his ex with her new vile, hairy, younger murderer boyfriend who's sprung out from inside an unidentified apartment in suburban Mumbai. I'm sure this doesn't happen often in Boston. Triple S smirks, shakes his head and limps over to rest his hand on the armchair. Uday is watching him closely.

'T'chaila, this how you peepul always think,' Triple S waves dismissively at Neelu.

Uday lunges forward, his hands hitting Triple S's chest and toppling him over. The old woman looks up, coughs loudly, says, 'Hudd, hudd,' and throws a pod of garlic at Uday.

'Your godawesome Triple S is a MaMi goonda and he has just murdered someone. Did you know this?' Uday barks.

'No.'

'Seriously, Sho! *This* is what you called me all the way from New York for?'

'Oh, but you bunged it in with work, right?' *Did he just show me his middle finger? Yeah, up yours too, you naked foetal snorer!*

A loud bell and a deafening screeching sound. Around a dozen men in grey safari suits and big guns run out from where Saurabh and Pushkie just walked out. A man runs into the room from the front door, yelling, 'Dada, dada.' He's drunk. It's a lumpen from the earlier group, the one who'd stared at my chest. The men in safari suits push him aside and spread all over the room, a couple of them head out of the door. They're all big, burly men. There's much shouting for five minutes. Finally, Pushkie emerges from the front door. 'It's nothing. The drunk bloke only half-worked the retina identification. He forgot to close the door, which is why the alarm went off,' he says.

Drunk Guy plonks in the middle of the room and mutters, 'TV, TV.' Saurabh rushes out, followed by a petite girl dressed in jeans and a tee. He lifts the lace cover of the TV set, picks up a fancy-looking remote and aims it at the wall where the pot-bellied paatti is still plucking and peeling, oblivious to all the commotion. The white wall breaks open; it isn't actually a cement wall but some sort of a laminate. There's a massive plasma screen underneath. It comes alive to a racket of multiple voices on the leading news channel.

The time now is 1.10 a.m. It's a news channel, showing images of some sort of midnight candle vigil. The ticker at the bottom of the screen announces that the 'Quit Fucking Bombay' protestors have gheraoed the MaMi headquarters at Worli. The newsreader – very virulent – says something about the protestors demanding that the murderer of Homi Panthaki, owner of The Titty Tagine on Marine Drive, be handed to the police immediately. MaMi, the newsreader barks, has denied any involvement with the murder. There's a ticker at the bottom of the screen: BOLLYWOOD BIGGIE AFZAL KHAN STILL MISSING. BOLLYWOOD'S BIGGEST FILM YET TO BE ANNOUNCED TODAY AT FOUR SEASONS HOTEL, IN THE MIDST OF CONTROVERSY.

In the midst of controversy? Really?

The safari suits are bidding the MuPo couple goodbye. Pushkie has helped Triple S stand up. The girl in jeans and tee gestures to him to button up his shirt. He obeys. Then she turns to Saurabh and begins speaking in a very polished Marathi dialect and grave tone. She must be his executive assistant. The clothes are conservative high street and she's carrying an iPad and three phones in her hand. The words 'pan' – or 'but' in Marathi – and 'CM' are being thrown around much. After his first lunge, Uday has lapsed back into observing Triple S before lunging again … If he doesn't, I will.

Imagine spending thirty-five years of your life thinking you are a hugely evolved intellectual whilst in reality you've always been carrying a placard on your head that reads: 'Come make a fool of me'.

'Mama, really, what's happening?'

'We were involved in a kidnapping. Now, somehow, the kidnapping is connected to this murder.'

'Wow!'

'Will someone explain everything?'

Saurabh places a comforting hand on Uday's shoulder. 'I have to go meet the CM. I'll be back.' Having delivered another of his dazzling smiles, he rotates 180 degrees and disappears inside, trailed by six of the dozen safari suits. Uday tries to follow him, but one of the safari suits blocks his way.

'Come, let us talk,' the secretary lures all of us away from the gun-toting crowd. She has a surprisingly loud and raspy voice.

Her English accent is as peculiarly polished as her Marathi. Pushkie gets into an argument with Pot-bellied Paati.

'Sit,' Madam Secretary orders, promptly occupying the only piece of furniture in the room.

I am not in the mood to give in to Madam's commands. 'I demand to know what's happening. Right now. Or we're leaving.'

She snorts. 'Do you really think you can leave without our permission?'

Her denims are perhaps not high street. They're slim and fit her petite frame really well. The ochre tee is a plain V-neck, and there's a big, ugly diamond mangalsutra sitting upon it. Black suede ballerinas. Her hair is combed neatly in an oily waist-length plait. She couldn't be a day over twenty-five.

'Miss Ramakrishnan, may I remind you that this is a hostile takeover?'

I can listen to the suave MaMi chief, but something about this arrogant slip of a girl brings the bile to the top of my throat. 'Look, I think this is enough. You need to tell us in plain language what you want right now.'

'Just a second.' She snaps her fingers. 'Nalini, this has nothing to do with you. But as they say, in Mumbai, you do as MaMi tells you. Just one tweet, or text or update any status or photograph anywhere, and I promise you, girl, Baston will burn.' She emphasizes the American twang there.

Neelu flashes her braces, adjusts her knotted spaghetti strap and glares at her, unafraid. 'I'm the only one who has a phone. If you didn't want me to tweet stuff, you would've gotten my phone grabbed down there.'

'Fierce! You're a clever girl.'

'Can we speak to Saurabh, please?' I butt in before the squabble escalates further.

'You just heard him. He's left for a meeting with the chief minister.'

I guess the apartment has a secret tunnel or electronic underground cable car using which Saurabh has vanished; did not see him exiting from the front door. 'I think we've had enough of these games now.'

'Have you?' Madam Secretary gets up and takes two strides to look up into my face. For such a tiny person, she has a commanding personality. She also hasn't threaded her eyebrows or waxed her upper lips for weeks. A large black mole is twitching near one of her bushy brows. 'I don't think any of you understand how serious this is.' She tilts her head at Triple S. 'We have kidnapped your little kidnapping operation.'

'Why?' I'm beginning to feel dizzy.

'Because we're hijacking the RAA press conference today.' Little Bitch is speaking to the precise area between my breasts and neck. Triple S is now tapping on her shoulder. She ignores him.

'And why's that?'

'Because we have an announcement of our own to make.'

'That MaMi isn't responsible for the murder?'

'We don't owe anyone any explanations.'

The dizziness has evaporated. I feel a rush of adrenalin. 'The hell you do!' I burst out, my eyes boring into Sagar's.

'Don't talk to him. Sagar, tu za!'

'No. He stays.'

'Or what?'

An explosion occurs behind Little Bitch.

'T'chaila, bass!' Triple S looks wounded.

Little Bitch turns around, places a stern palm against his chest and shakes her head as if telling a frisky Dobermann to stay. An intensely personal look is exchanged between them.

Good lord, are they lovers?

'Look, whoever you are ...' I stutter.

'Katya. Kulkarni.'

'Great. But we are *not* speaking to a secretary.'

'I'm Saurabh's wife.'

'Oh.'

Strike at Thirty-Six is officially in the land of the terminally unhinged.

'Hutt, halkat!' The old woman is finally done with her peeling and is getting Pushkie to help heave her bulk off the floor. She slips twice, then throws him off to manage on her own, gathers her thali and plastic bags and starts waddling towards the spot from where everyone has been entering and leaving. Midway, she rolls to a halt and shouts at us. 'Amlet?'

'Maushi!' Katya, the terrorizing bitch, yells back at her. 'Aika everyone! Saurabh will be at the CM's bungalow for an hour and will join us at the hotel. We have an emergency on our hands. And we are very short of time. But first, we have the pooja.'

Ganpati Visarjan Day – the conclusion of one of Mumbai's biggest festivals – is on the eighth of September, specifically chosen by RAA's in-house astrologer as the most auspicious date for the *Yogi* announcement. I'd nagged Bala and AK for an entire day, almost begged to move the presscon to the fifth. Today. We couldn't have risked our operation on a day when the entire city was in celebration mode. It escaped my mind that they send Bappa home on each of the ten days of the festival.

'No whispering,' Katya booms. 'All gents, follow Tatya.'

Tatya turns out to be the oldest, tallest, swarthiest of the safari suits, with a walrus moustache and sparkling gold chain over his chest.

'All ladies, follow me to the kitchen. Shobhna, what are you looking at?'

'This is a democracy. If we are going anywhere, we are going out of the door.'

She turns to one of the younger guards and rolls her eyes. He snaps his heels, clicks some metal and points his rifle in my face.

'Oh please. Go ahead, if you dare.'

'Sho!'

'Uday, they're bluffing.'

'Why would they?'

She points at two more guards and snaps her fingers like a modern-day Marie Antoinette. Instead of approaching me, they go to Neelu and grab her by both arms. The kid screams like a banshee. 'Mama, they will rape. Mama, they will kill. Boston will burn. She's crazy!'

The safari suits are more likely to squash her like a fly than rape.

Uday puts on his famously stern, corporate expression. 'Let her go. We'll do what you say.'

Poda! Drama queens, all!

Tatya swings his enormous rifle upside down and raises it to the sky, ready to bring its heavy butt with full force on Neelu's dainty feet. Of course, he's not going to smash her up, but the effect upon Neelu is electrifying. 'No! Mudderfuckah! No!'

Uday grips my arm and commits my behalf, 'Look, that's enough. We'll do your thing.'

Tatya lowers his menacing rifle. The men let go of Neelu who continues to shake as she shuffles towards us. 'I'm calling Bhai, Mama!'

'You're not calling anybody. That phone will be used only when I allow. When I say you tweet, you tweet what I say. Okay?' growls Katya.

'Psycho bitch!'

'Yes.' It is Uday answering on behalf of Underage Pottymouth now.

'Good! Now the ladies will follow me. No screaming. No protest. As per tradition at the Mahajan family, all guests will help prepare for the pooja.'

Someone is going to pinch me and I am going to wake up.

But for now, there's no escaping MaMi.

15

(Thirty) Six Degrees of Separation

Udayan

Love and politics are extraordinary bedfellows.

The bizarreness of this whole situation is beginning to feel like three years ago in the Jordanian desert. Sho looked ethereal outlined against the sun, her red dupatta wrapped across her face, her walk cinematic and stilted, a flamboyant swing at the hip, even if she thought no one was watching. I never told her I fell in love with her then. The Arafat ghost hallucination seemed like an appropriate distraction. She was, every inch and curve, the tough and sexy female warrior. I never got over that flu.

It's 3.15 a.m. A cold shower with Hamam soap is a foolproof refresher. A gentle breeze appears to be blowing outside the bolted French window of this large but sparse room with a cold slate floor. I had showered barely five hours ago, but felt the need for another. Besides, Katya insisted that everybody bathe before the pooja, even though it's to be held only after daybreak. I need a puff, but the house is a strict no-smoking zone. Pushkar aka Pushkie informed me about the rules of the house before he left to go home, half an hour ago. He assured me that he would keep the Kinetic Activa safely at his place. All I had to do was send someone to John Sutari Chawl in Nagpada once all this 'tamasha' was over, and collect the scooter. My hunch was bang on. Pushkie and his gang had been trailing me right from the time I had my meeting in town with GMine. He swore Sagar 'Dada' was not with them while I was being trailed; in fact Sagar was with Saurabh 'Dada' all of the previous day. Then Pushkie clamped up, refusing to divulge more information about Sagar's involvement with MaMi or the Panthaki murder. So I had to change the topic.

'Who is this Gharpuré?'

He had given a nervous giggle. Nothing short of killing him would make him squeal. So, I let loose a few red-blooded curses, as Doshis of all persuasions are wont to do. As soon as he realized I was a native cusser, he lapsed into a rant, in a strong Belgaum dialect. These MaMi people are all mental and dangerous and unreliable, he warned. And they do not appreciate loyalty, and are very cruel. His heart lightened considerably, he left with another warning: 'Whatever you do, never, ever try to break open any of the windows here.'

The room reeked of agarbattis. Just like Doshi House at this time of the year. The Doshis' Ganpati celebrations are held alternately at Worli, and at Shruti and Bhavesh's penthouse on Napean Sea Road. At this time, Bhai gives up all other activities to personally supervise all decorations and arrangements for the eight-day stay of his favourite deity. This is the first time in the three decades I remember that the family isn't at home for the celebrations. Some internal logic that eludes me seems to be at work in the decision to please Shirdi Sai Baba during the Ganpati festival this year. I know they resent the fact that I've been away all this while. Bhai still thinks I'll come back to jewellery. My decision to propose to Monee is going to ease tensions to a great extent. That they'll love her is a given. And Bhai will finally forgive me for giving up on Sho.

But for now, there's no escaping the MaMi.

The inside of the house turned out to be a contrast to the austere and intimidating living room. We entered and walked in single file, although the corridor – lined with CCTV cameras – was wide enough to accommodate an elephant. The security men pushed their way between Neelu, Sho and me, and made sure we stayed apart. When I tried calling out to Neelu to check if she was good, the guard in front turned around and boomed, 'Tch tch, nahi sahib.' They looked professionally trained, beefy, and no-nonsense, and trying to break free from them seemed to make no sense. The walk through the corridor took a full minute, maybe more. On one side of the passage were several rooms. On the other hung MaMi memorabilia – framed photographs, saffron flags with the white-and-ochre MaMi logo. Of the photographs I managed to catch were some stunning landscape stills. Others had Saurabh posing alongside dignitaries like the chief ministers of Maharashtra and Gujarat, and one with his arm around the prime minister. There were some group photographs with his party workers and a life-size portrait of Saurabh in traditional regalia – a cream-coloured kurta and dhoti, accessorized with a bejewelled belt and an orange silk turban, holding a large sword in a bronze casket encrusted with uncut corals and pearls. The same sword hung, crossed over by its twin, at the end of the corridor. Saurabh was smiling in all the photographs. There was no picture to validate Katya's claims anywhere.

The end of the corridor broke into startling activity. It was an ante-room of sorts, much smaller than the living room, but alive with colour and at least a dozen men and women bustling about, yelling. The corridor was so long that we hadn't heard a whisper of this activity when in the living room. At the centre of this room was an enormous Ganpati idol, adorned with marigold, mogra and hibiscus garlands, and surrounded by typical home-made decorations. There was a canopy of colourful paper streamers and two brass pots containing large bunches of banana leaves on either side of the idol, which sat on a gaudy Thermocol throne with an elaborate backrest. Laid out in front of the idol was a jungle of toys, food items and sundry knick-knacks. There were plastic replicas of the local public transport, a red BEST bus and a black-and-yellow auto rickshaw. There were some dolls – one dressed in a nine-yard sari with a tiny mud pot on her head and others as farmers with little bullock carts. There was a large Japanese fan next to the idol and a bottle of Bvlgari perfume next to it. On the periphery were more than two dozen steel plates loaded with chaklis, laddoos, chivda, burfis and chirotas.

'Do you like? We made it,' came a voice from behind me. I turned around to see a little girl and a boy dressed in jeans and white kurta. That's when I realized that I was alone with the kids. The rest had disappeared. I didn't get a chance to ask the kids exactly what they had made since they were sent packing with a woman in a nine-yard sari who emerged from my right with Katya, who asked me why I hadn't gone to shower yet. The Mahajan household, she said, had a tradition of performing Ganpati pooja at dawn during the entire ten-day period of the festival. Attendance was compulsory for everyone in the vicinity, and all guests had to shower and put in an appearance in traditional clothes. Saurabh's mother was very strict about these things. I asked Katya if the lady peeling garlic back in the living room was Saurabh's mother. She said it was none of my business, pointed to a room, and ordered me to get in quick. She would send Tatya in with something suitable for me to wear.

I couldn't let her go without an explanation. So I blocked her way. She scowled fiercely. I said, in my nicest corporate voice, that she owed us an explanation. She retorted that we had no choice; nobody owed us any answers. I said they couldn't get away with it. She said they could get away with anything they wanted. I told her it was only a matter of hours before I found some way to get us out of this place and they'd have the police and press jumping on them. She laughed and said I'd been living in New York too long. Pity, she drawled, she didn't expect such naivety from one of corporate India's finest minions and Bhai Doshi's son.

Whatever she was, there was no way out with his hardcore woman. An enemy who does his homework is a dangerous one.

So I smiled, flopped on my knees, and launched into unashamed admiration of the Ganpati decorations. I admitted, truthfully, that I have a soft corner for the Marathi community, their artistic bent, and intelligent, cultured ways. She frowned and asked me – without any trace of mirth – to stick the flattery up my Gujarati bum. But she did bite her lower lip. If I went and took the bloody shower, she hissed, she would try to prep me for what would happen at the press conference in the evening. The woman in the nine-yard sari reappeared with two saris on hangers. After consulting both hangers, Katya told the woman that 'the little one who curses', being the same size as her, could wear the blue Paithani and the 'tall, screaming one who looks like Sridevi' would have to go with her mother-in-law's red cotton one. Her Marathi was impeccable, but had a hint of a foreign accent. I intervened; there was no need for this fancy dress; we had more important matters to discuss. She dismissed the maid and calmly told me there was nothing to 'discuss', stressing on the word with inverted commas in the air. The only way things got done here was her way. I could cooperate or keep standing near the Ganpati, looking like a prime ass. With that, she turned on her heel, leaving me with no alternative but to clean up in the room she pointed to before leaving.

I'm done now, and Pushkar has left after having dispensed cryptic advice. The room contains only a bed and a wardrobe with fresh linen. The grey-tiled bathroom had nothing except a new bar of green Hamam soap and a vial of Parachute hair oil. While I was bathing, someone left a cream-coloured oversized kurta and a lungi on the bed. Despite having quit ages ago, the familiar desperation to smoke makes an appearance. Tobacco is the only thing that can help me think, and stop the headache and fever. The solitary window in the room has a tiny rectangular metal box with a red light attached on the inside. The second I unbolt the window, a light flickers and an alarm goes off. I let it be and light up with my spare lighter anyway. Gazing out, I notice it's a steep jump. Down below, there's a mob, some vehicles, red lights. It's a bit like the one back in the living room, only less shrieky and more rhythmic. Within seconds, Tatya slams open the door with two of his men, all holding up their rifles. They circle the room like sniffing dogs, giving me enough time for a couple of deep, relaxing puffs, until Tatya snatches the stick from my fingers. Tatya's cell phone rings. He answers it and informs the person at the other end that all is fine, it was just a guest trying to smoke and opening one of the windows. 'Yes, I will explain to him,' he assures with a gruff voice and hangs up. There is a black thread above the gold chain around his thick neck, and a U-shaped white tikka on his forehead. He asks for the lighter, takes my cigarette, shakes his head and asks one of his men to get rid of it. His rifle – the one he'd poised over Neelu earlier – is slung over his arm.

'Is that a .250-3000 Savage?' I ask.

'Yes.'

'Were you in the army?'

'Yes.'

'I want my phone back.'

'No.'

'Can I use your phone to make a call? Only one. Please?'

He shakes his head and begins to walk out. When he's at the door, ready to shut it, I let loose a decoy. 'Mala sanga, Tatya. Tell me how someone like you can let these people do what they are doing?'

He pauses for a nanosecond, then bangs the door shut.

I rush over, open it and speak softly to his back. 'You don't look like someone who destroys his own home.'

No reaction. He's slipping away. I raise my voice, 'Why is a man who fears only God afraid to stand up to people who are nothing more than bullies?'

Tatya looks back and asks the other guard to carry on ahead. Striding back into the room, he shoves me in, shuts the door and asks me if I grew up in a naatak mandali. 'Dekho baba. We Konkani people are very simple and straightforward. But we know life and are not stupid enough to fall into the traps you suit-wearing people set for us. Who is not a goonda these days? Wearing a suit and talking in English doesn't make you smart. Or kind. You are also just another kind of goonda,' he sneers.

But I continue my efforts to get the man to flare up. 'These people are thugs. And now they have turned into murderers.'

'Who says that?'

'The TV, the newspapers.'

'And you are stupid enough to believe what those monkeys in suits say?'

There must be a MaMi training programme that turns easy-going Maharashtrians into nasty, suit-hating guard dogs.

I pump up the hyperbole. 'You people are no better than the terrorists across the border.'

'Must be. Why don't you say that to Vahini?'

'I will. Call her.'

'Nice try,' he gives me a scornful look-over. 'Wear the good clothes and come for the pooja.'

'Where are the girls?'

'All the ladies people are in the kitchen.'

'And that boy … Sagar?'

His eyes falter. They are steel grey eyes with a dull tomato-coloured rim, with the depths of wisdom that sixty-plus years bring. He holds his gun upright between us, looks into my eyes, and swears by Ganpati Bappa that he will kill me if I as much as touch Sagar.

'That boy suffered too much,' he says.

'Ridiculous,' I pretend to snap, and tell him it is his Sagar who has betrayed us and landed us in this mess.

'Sagar would not betray a stray cat,' Tatya snaps back, growling like a protective lion.

I ask him if he is related to the boy, to which he offers a sad smile and says that some relationships with strangers are thicker than blood.

'I don't know him,' I say. 'But if Sagar is such a morally

upstanding young man, why didn't he speak up in the living room? Why didn't he say he isn't a murderer?'

'I don't know.'

'Tatya, tell me honestly. Has he murdered that Parsi man?'

'How do I know? You ask him.'

'Where is he?'

'Nice try!' He marches out again, this time with a warning that if I don't get dressed in the next five minutes, bad things will happen that he will not be able to prevent.

'Wait, Tatya. I have never worn a lungi,' I call out.

'It's a dhoti. I'll send someone. Till then, hurry up and wear the jubba. One last thing; keep your mind open ... and trust in Bappa.'

They call a kurta a jubba. It is two sizes too big for me, and the khadi silk is rough. But it feels cool and roomy without jeans. Perhaps I can tie a lungi out of the dhoti. Just as I lift the kurta to wrap the cloth around my waist, the door opens and Sagar walks in. It's not the best way to confront Sho's beloved Triple S; I'm half naked, an XXL kurta hanging on me.

'Tatya said you need help with tying the dhoti. I told him you can go into hail, but he made me come. I cannot say no to Tatya.' He keeps standing close to the door, scowling. I walk over and hand him one end of the cloth. Thankfully, I'm wearing boxers. He continues scowling, but wraps it around my waist and ties a knot in the front. 'Hold the jubba in your teeth,' he orders and begins neatly pleating his end of the cloth. He reeks of hibiscus oil.

'What happened to your ...?'

'Polio.'

The pleats are done. He hands them to me, asking me to hold them tightly together, and examines me from the back to check the scene there.

'Why did you do this, Sagar? Shobhna trusted you.'

'That is her problaim. Giuve me that between your laigs.'

I fold both ends of the cloth inside my thighs and hand him the bunch. 'How can you betray a woman who has put her career and reputation at risk for you?'

'Hmmm. Roll it propurly around your laigs.'

I turn around, messing the dhoti over his arms. 'Exactly what is your problem?'

He is on one knee and mutters without looking up. 'You caanot wear a simple dhoti. That eez my problaim.'

'Jasta shahanpana karaicha nai, nahitar ek haath todun dusrya hatat dein ...'

He looks up. Telling him that I'll break one of his hands and place it in the other if he doesn't behave himself appears to have made a tiny dent in his armour. More importantly, he realizes he can't play the sullen son-of-the-soil card with me. He puts an unsure hand between my ankles, then decides it's better that I finish the dhoti-tying myself. He instructs me to take half the pleats between my legs and tuck them at the back of my waist ... no, not all of them! He is a strict but accurate instructor. Within minutes, the dhoti is securely tied and I've stepped back into my brogues.

Sagar lets out a growl of approval and begins to get off his knees, when he loses balance and falls to the floor. I try to give him a hand, but he refuses. But when I try to hold his hand, it is hot to the touch.

'Take your peeti to hail.' He collects himself and prepares to leave.

'You didn't murder the Parsi man?'

'Does eet matter what I say?'

'Yes. Are they forcing you in any way? To work for them?'

'No.' He looks me straight in the eye and answers without

thinking twice, but looks pained. Putting the weight of his body on his arms, he hauls himself up and adjusts his shirt.

'How can you work with these terrorists?'

'Eet is a fashun now to call aneeone who works for his own peepul a terrorist.'

'You destroy public property and beat up innocent people.'

'If the problaims of the wurld could be solved by non-vhiolence—' He begins limping towards the door.

'Bullshit. Violence is never the answer to anything.'

'Take yuar Oscar-weening dielog to hail!'

No ordinary foot soldier, this. He's shrewd and very sharp. On another day, in other circumstances, I could be on his side, but not now. I need to play him. Tatya was a wise old dog; Sagar a brilliant young man who is inexperienced and hot-headed. Unlike Sho, I am a bloke and I speak his language. We are on equal footing.

'Typical desi mentality! Blame your personal problems on the world. What else can one expect from a local party?'

'T'chaila, you peepul,' he rises to the bait. 'What do peepul like you who hauve one leg in New York and one in Mumbai and peesing on your own life, know about Vahini and Saurabh Dada?'

I tell him I know that they are petty and small-minded. I use a Marathi swear word that has him sucking on his cheekbones and tightening his fist. He opens the door, warns in his rich bass tone that he will not tolerate any insulting comments about his people and begins limping rapidly to the right side of the never-ending corridor. I have a finger on his pulse, and I'm all dressed anyway, so I follow him, hurling provocative words like a rabble-rousing politician. 'You are all cowards.'

He dismisses me, waving his hand in the air.

'Yeah right, go back under your vahini's apron. You're too afraid to make it on your own. You don't have the guts to believe in yourself even when a stranger risks everything because of her faith in you.'

He turns around. 'Bhau, you first deecide, are you talking about MaMi or me?'

'What is the difference?' I shout at the top my voice, hoping that would bring in Katya and her guards. 'Both of you, all of you are gutless.'

He pounces, aiming at my throat, face and chest. The bastard is sinewy and fast despite the limp, and a good inch taller than me. But I've been expecting this attack and take him down with an easy backhand lash. He tumbles down, arms protecting his ribs. 'Aai ga!' Prostrate on the ground, he kicks robustly, cussing with a vengeance and brushing off my attempts to get him off the floor.

'Liu me alone!'

Tatya materializes with a bunch of his boys. The younger guards help Sagar to his feet. Tatya pushes me to the wall and holds his gun horizontal to my chest. Before I can speak, Katya comes running down the corridor, pulling along the two children from earlier on. The kids have changed into traditional clothes and Katya into a yellow sari, worn in the nine-yard style. It hasn't made her any more approachable; she's still toting her iPad and the three handsets.

'Tatya! What is wrong with you people? Can you not solve a problem without violence?'

The girl, younger of the two kids, jumps up and latches on to Sagar's legs. 'Mommy, Mommy, don't yell at Saaguh.' She looks like her mother, but her accent, unlike Katya's, is all-American. She must be a couple of years younger than Sona from the AI flight. Katya reacts by whacking both the girl and the boy on their bums and handing over their custody to Tatya. 'Take them inside and make sure they stay out of everything.' Then she turns to me, eyes ablaze.

'He called us all cowards,' Sagar points to me.

'Yes I did,' I say. 'We are educated people. You cannot just kidnap and scare us. We will keep asking questions until someone gives us answers.'

'Is saheb trying to say the raist of us are unayducated?'

'*This*,' I jab my finger at Sagar. '*This* is your problem. Huge chips on your shoulders! Your entitlement issues are—'

'And you peepul toh bloody solve any problaim by sending SMS on Facebook, no? Make a grup, save the world with one cleeck, and you become bloody Bhagat Singh!'

Katya looks at him sharply to indicate that he better get moving.

I push Tatya's rifle off my chest. 'It's people like you, with your small-town mentalities, that keep Mumbai from achieving its full potential,' I yell in the direction of the anguished writer's back.

He turns around. 'You think it is only about Mumbai? T'chaila who cares! Call it Mumbai, Bombay, Queen Victoria Begum or ... t'chaila ... whatever you want.'

'If it doesn't mean anything to you, why don't you pack up and go back to your village, where you belong?'

'Correct! That is exactly what peepul like you want, right?' He needs to have all that bull-headedness knocked out of him. The smartest people need that done to them.

'I don't think Bhai Doshi will appreciate you slumming it at "our" level.' Katya appears to share my love for decoys and unleashes a lethal one of her own. She may be an Americanese-spouting NRI, but she's also the wily wife of a don.

'I don't know what connection you have with my dad, or

don't. If there is some blackmail involved in this, you need to come clean. We're getting nowhere with this you people–we people.' I am on high alert now that Bhai has been brought into the picture.

'That's exactly what you peepul say when you aren't gaiting what you want.'

She gestures Tatya to take Sagar away. He refuses. Tatya cajoles him quietly. He brushes off Tatya's arm, at which point the burly older man grabs him like a lion would its rowdy cub and drags him screaming and kicking in the direction of the living room. This leaves me and Katya and two guards in the middle of the corridor. She adjusts her two-inch pearl–ruby nose ring and gazes into my eyes. The diamond cluster in it glitters. 'Excellent coordination,' she says.

'What?' It is difficult to keep pace with her stream of consciousness.

She begins to walk away, handling the nine-yard drape gracefully. The guards march on either side of her. 'When she screams, you stay quiet. When she calms down, you fire up. You two are quite the team.'

'What have you done to Sho? Neelu?'

'Your niece and girlfriend are fine.'

'Ex.'

'I know. A pity.' She stops for a minute at the decoration to adjust the clothes on the Ganpati idol. I jump at the opportunity and grab her wrist. The guards click their rifles and get a bit wild, screaming for me to let go of 'Vahini' or they'll shoot. She holds them back with a wave of her head, not making any attempt to free her wrist from my grip, instead clamping her palm into a tight fist. 'You're crossing a line, Udayan.'

'I'm crossing a line?'

She pauses, frees a finger from her fist and wags it at me. Her eyes are fierce. Lots of facial hair. 'Udayan, the hero. Coming here from the Big Apple to first save your ex-girlfriend, and then save Mumbai from the clutches of the homeboys.'

I let go. She rubs her wrist. The guards drop their rifles to their sides.

'*We* people are not the enemy of *you* people, Udayan.' Her eyes scan the Ganpati decorations. 'In fact, I'm afraid I think we are all the same people. Cinema, politics, love, kidnapping ... we're all closer to one another than—' She shouts at one of the guards to get a fresh garland for the idol. Then she turns to me, smiles and waves her iPad in my face. 'The press falls for that sort of mush. Facebooking orgasm.'

'Daha is not on Facebook. Neither am I.'

So *progressive.*'

'You've lived in the States,' I pry.

'Yes. But what does that have to do with being progressive?' The woman is stuck in the previous conversation.

'And so Saurabh and you drop your mansion and stocks in Sacramento and return to Mumbai to form a chauvinistic, rowdy political party of petty goondas.'

'How perceptive! Would you like to join the ladies in the kitchen in making modaks?'

'What sort of name is Katya Kulkarni?'

'My father was a Russophile.' She's speeding along another corridor, taking zigzag steps, so I'm forced to walk behind her, the guards almost sticking to me.

'That's where you get your fascist leanings?'

She smiles. Like a tiny, scary cat. Without warning, she stops and turns around. I stumble on her.

'You're an attractive man, Udayan.'

'Yes.'

'Shobhna is an attractive woman.'

'Yes.'

'Do you believe in the theory of Six Degrees of Separation?'

'Yes.'

'I don't. But I think we're all fated to be here together this day. Something binds us.'

'I guess.'

'No. I know.'

'Who is Gharpuré?'

'I don't know.'

'Did Sagar murder Panthaki?'

'I don't know.'

I almost smile.

'Why are you playing us?'

'Let's just say, it's complicated.'

16

Kitchen Politics

SHOBHNA

'Sole muttar amlet?'

I'm sitting cross-legged next to a dimpled giant grandma, struggling to shape a sweet dumpling and retain my sanity. Yet again on this incredulous day, I ask myself: how did it come to this?

Neelu was beside herself with excitement. When they led us in from the living room through the corridor, she held on to my hand and squealed in glee. Only a noughties brat could interpret a hostile takeover as a sign to party. We tried calling out to Uday, but there were more than a couple of those guards and that freaky Katya tailing our heels. The wall to our right was fully decorated, but I didn't get a look. My mind continued somersaulting even as Neelu's voice echoed faintly in the background. Why was this happening to Strike at Thirty-Six? I had spent an entire month carefully stitching up every probable loose end. I'd destroyed my residual reputation in the fashion world to get those overpriced barbies. The word is probably spreading out there right now that Shobhna Ramakrishnan is seriously dipping and dabbing, and I hadn't even mentioned H for Heroin yet. I had kept a tight leash on MM. I'd pretended all was well with AK, even though the sight of the man made my blood boil. And I'd tolerated that murdering genius writer. Honestly, the worst scenario that I'd run over in my mind was that AK would super-heroically resist the barbies and emerge to give us all a spanking, and Triple S would be back in Baramati and MM and I would be out of jobs. But *this*?

'Whom has he murdered? The limping fella?' It was Uday's brat.

The kid knows how to get on people's nerves for sure. 'He's a writer,' I replied.

I could sense her pitch rising. 'And a murderer?'

'Why not? Why can't a writer be a murderer?'

'I'm a blogger,' came the inexplicable retort. It turned out Neelu sometimes ghostwrites for something called Boston 'Blah'min, a blog started by a political science dropout and whose girlfriend— At that point, I had to stop her.

My antennae were on overdrive, picking up on the interiors of the mafia den instead of focussing on how to get us out of there. In that maelstrom of emotion and sensory overload, and Neelu's low-pitched chattering, we lost Udayan and found ourselves being herded via an '80s-style curtained arch into the world's biggest kitchen. Of the goons, only Katya and Tatya entered with us. It was at least a 1000 square feet space of grey stone and cement, with the regular L-shaped cuddapah platform and a low sink. On the far end, there was what looked like the kitchen-gadgets corner, lorded over by an industrial-size oven. The corner was deserted, but the area on the other side of the sink was a hub of frantic activity. Ten or more bejewelled women in brightly coloured saris were bent over big degchis and kadhais. The combined smell of coconut, oil and condensed milk was sickening, but it was nullified by the overpowering scent of sonchafa flowers, which most of the women wore in their plaits and decorated hair buns with. A petite young girl, around Neelu's age, was manning the chapatti section. Pot-bellied Paati from the living room was squatting on the floor next to a kerosene stove, stirring a pot of something that fumed furiously and reeked of burning gram flour. Katya called her 'Atya', which I knew meant aunt. We were ordered to bathe, change into something 'dee-saint', and to help Katya's atya prepare the prasadam for the Ganpati pooja. I glanced at Neelu, who was blown away.

It made sense, in that sinister vaudeville environment, to follow Katya's finger to a bedroom facing the kitchen. Just as we left, someone began to char brinjals in the kitchen.

Tatya was ordered to stand outside the room and make sure we emerged in exactly thirty minutes. The room was bare except for a cupboard, a life-size mirror and a clock on the wall. It was at 2.45 a.m. Neelu flopped on the bed, while I hunted for possible exits. The entire house – or whatever we'd seen of it – was crawling with CCTVs, and boxy equipment was stuck to all windows. I blanked out and couldn't think what to do next until the doorbell rang. A woman in a nine-yard sari stood outside, with two saris on hangers. The blouse on the blue one was smaller, so that went to Neelu, while the brown one – which did nothing to nobody's skin tone – went to me.

Neelu sprang up; it was going to be her first time in a sari. 'Booyah!' A personal milestone. Within minutes, she flung off her balloon pants and top on the bed and jumped in the shower, belting out '*Miss Invisible*' at a volume that made me want to go in and sock her senseless. Mundam! There was no network on her phone.

She emerged refreshed enough to update me on car crashes and dorm crushes. And to think I'd thought she was just Uday's mousy niece. I mentally signed out, stripping off my jeans, and attempted three minutes of anulom–vilom in the midst of her incessant chatter. I tried making sense of the past, present and future of Strike at Thirty-Six. Breathe in. Breathe out. Breathe in. Breathe out. This was precisely why I wrote to Uday and begged him to help out. We are writers, not crisis managers. I genuinely thought I had Strike at Thirty-Six down pat, right to the fiery speech that Triple S was to deliver to the cream of Mumbai's press. He'd protested violently; the concept of a speech in Hindi jangled every nerve of his being. Sunny, MM and I spent three days coddling, cussing and wearing him down, until he agreed to speak in Hindi 'using regular Marathi words that any idiot living in Maharashtra would understand'. Despite our differences and the fact that my palms always itched to slap him, I thought Triple S and I had connected, as artistes. Never in my wildest dreams did I imagine him involved with the MaMi.

Or had I?

Makku plastri, Sho, what an idiot! 'Why can't a writer be a murderer?'

A killer concept, I'll admit. Murdering writers make great press. Especially for a movie as revolutionary as *The Dhaal*. Is Triple S smart enough to have orchestrated this real-to-reel conundrum? I would think not.

A good hour or more later, we're scrubbed with the Hamam soap we both swore at, overdressed and wide awake. The shower felt good and the sari is comfortably pleated and tucked in. The blouse fits perfectly. *Do they have every inmate's measurements here?* Neelu insists I drape her sari Gujarati style; it's like the bleeding garba night at the Doshis' all over again.

There's no sign of Tatya when we leave the room. Another guard escorts us to the kitchen. It is even more frenetic now; the women are rushing in and out with plates of food, marigold garlands and banana leaves, and everyone is yelling instructions in full volume. The pressure cookers are whistling and someone's frying batches of pakoras. No sign of Katya, Uday, Tatya or that bastard. Three lady hawaldars in khaki saris are hanging around a vat of boiling dal while Pot-bellied Paati is busy placing finished snowy white modaks in a thali. Modaks – Ganpati's favourite snack – are delish. But making them takes skill and practice. I have neither. So I hover next to Paati, playing with the loose end of my sari.

Neelu, meanwhile, is whizzing around the kitchen. The elderly women indulge her; some shoo her away and one even hits her with a spoon, none of which dampens her enthusiasm. Having surveyed the menu and the cooking team, she has gravitated towards the petite girl who's almost done with her kilo or two of chapattis. The two strike up a conversation.

Amongst the rush of women, I spy Orange Gajra from Saayba, who is dragging two large cans of milk out of the kitchen with the help of a man wearing all white, including a Nehru cap. She espies me, drops her cans and slides across to ask where my 'mister' is. I tell her – very loudly so everyone can hear – that Uday is not my 'mister' and instead demand to know the whereabouts of Triple S or her Mohawk-sporting son or nephew or whatever, both of whom are directly responsible for getting us into this mess. Before she can respond, Pot-bellied Paati pulls my pallu and rumbles, 'Amlet?' What the proposition to serve 'amlet' is doing in this conservative Hindu fortress on a pooja day is anybody's guess.

Neelu gestures from across the room at the culinary exploits of a woman – wedged between her and Chapatti Girl – dressed in a blinding rainbow-hued sari. Orange Gajra suggests that I relax and get on with making the prasadam because Vahini will be here any minute, and the rest of the offerings are ready. 'Screw Vahini,' I mutter, attracting the attention of her male companion who strides over to ask what the matter is. I yank my pallu out of Paati's grip and push aside Orange Gajra, yelling for Neelu. We're leaving this kitchen.

'A woman who can't manage herself in a kitchen can't manage her life.' That's Katya at the door, Uday by her side. Even in a kurta two sizes too large, Uday rocks the dhoti. Neelu whistles from across the room.

Mafia Bitch has changed into a yellow, nine-yard sari. An oversized pearl nose ring covers half her face, and does a wonderful job enhancing her evil aura. 'Why aren't you making modaks? We need twenty-one for the pooja. It's getting late.' When she opens her mouth, the nose ring lurches off her lips as if it would tear her nose off.

'Late pourquoi? What are you going to pull at our presscon?' I inquire.

Udayan assesses the kitchen and looks relieved to find Neelu in a jolly mood. He looks bompued. Have they been talking? What did the bitch tell him? Where is Triple S? Off shooting bullets into another decent, law-abiding citizen's chest?

'Sho, do as she says. Now!' He's brusque, but the aquamarine eyes quickly run over my sari-clad body with a glint of fulsome approval and he gives me the slightest nod. I sit cross-legged near Pot-bellied Paati, who pushes my hand towards the dough and filling, indicating that I begin making modaks of my own. Suddenly, half the kitchen is crowding around us. Orange Gajra was right; everyone's done cooking and is free to gawk at me.

Away from me, across the kitchen, Neelu sticks her head

out from behind the shoulder of a bony woman with a dark, menacing face: 'Di, check this out. Awesome balls!'

'It's called litti chokha. A popular Bihari snack.' Correction by Katya.

Why a woman is whipping up a Bihari snack in the kitchen of a fundamentalist Maratha fortress is anybody's guess. I'd rather concentrate, bompu-like, on getting the modaks right. I've been here, I've seen this. Anita's mother tried teaching me how to make modaks when she came over from Ratnagiri two years ago. It takes a lifetime to master the delicate folds of this sweet teardrop dumpling. I dip my fingers in the bowl of water, place the flattened dough on my upturned palm, place the stuffing and begin to fold. It's tricky; the dough is small and delicate and the stuffing restricts attempts to fold it. I finish making one modak in two minutes and place it on a brass thali offered by Paati. There is a group silence. Uday is expressionless. Katya's nose ring shivers. Most unexpectedly, Pot-bellied Paati's chubby cheeks give way to form two massive dimples and she lets out an infantile giggle. The policewomen release raspy sniggers as well.

Uday folds the elephant sleeves of his kurta and sits down cross-legged beside me. Pot-bellied Paati's giggles haven't subsided yet. Uday flashes a dimple and picks up one of the snowy pancakes. For a split second, the significance of the ex and self in traditional gear, sitting down together to make prasadam for Ganpati pooja, heckles. This is how Bhai Doshi, Amma, Appa and Roja would have wanted us – man and wife laden with all the jewellery in the Doshi lockers.

C'est la friggin' vie.

Efficiently, quickly, he spoons in the filling, removes the excess and, to the now-admiring gaze of a rapt audience, deftly pinches the dough between his long, artistic forefinger and thumb to create almost a dozen delicate folds which he then proceeds – and this is the excruciatingly difficult part – to gather expertly, in vertical alliance, into a slim tip. This work of art placed in the thali makes my modest effort look like a grotesque little gnome.

It's not like Uday to perform for an audience. Scanning his face, I know his intention isn't to upstage me, neither is he indulging in strange games to hoodwink the terrorists. There is something else in his face I can't quite read. He cocks his head to one side and begins to talk to Pot-bellied Paati in Marathi. The old woman slaps his thigh encouragingly, spitting out unfamiliar curses: 'Wah Gharpuré chi d****, wah Gharpuré chi d****.' She pronounces it Ghaar-poo-reh. In between, she throws her 'amlet' and her sagging jowls jiggle in joy.

Even as they bond, Uday produces three more divinely plump modaks. I try to offer assistance, but he refuses, indicating that everything is under control. Convinced that the first modak wasn't a fluke, the audience is rapturous. It's an act worthy of an ovation: the fair and handsome NRI tossing up a notoriously complicated delicacy that even the most adroit housewives struggle to perfect. You can't buy authentic steamed modaks off the shelf; the shops sell tiny mawa replicas. The modak is the Chhatrapati Shivaji Maharaj of Maharashtrian cuisine. Not my own words. This wisdom was fed to me by Anita's mother, accompanied by superb raw jackfruit bhaji.

Before one can flit over to the next thought, Uday has finished his artful construction of all twenty-one modaks. His adoring female audience is now cheering lasciviously. Pot-bellied Paati's hand hasn't moved from his thigh. Her tobacco-stained teeth are bared wide. The word Baramati echoes through their rapid-fire chatter. Katya taps my head. I brush her hand off and stand up. If she doesn't keep her bony fingers off me, I might just give in to the urge to indulge in a catfight in saris. Besides, it's a bit uncomfortable sitting next to Uday like this. The knot in the petticoat is a bit loose.

'You are from Baramati?' asks Triple S, who is spewing fire at the threshold of the kitchen. As per house rules, he's changed into a crisp white kurta and churidar, with a saffron sash around his waist and matching turban – tied Maratha-style, with a stiff fan blooming out of the top and a tail hanging down the back – on his head. I suppose he's bathed.

'I was born there,' comes Udayan's reply.

'Why?'

Before Udayan can answer that metaphysical question, Triple S growls at me, 'Why didn't you tell me thees?'

Before I can open my mouth, Katya has left my side and apparated beside him. There is something sinister about the way she touches him. Despite barely reaching his waist, she towers above him.

Uday is still cross-legged and in full bompu mode. I didn't know he was born in Baramati. Does it matter? Maybe he's just lying.

'Oh, Bhau!'

Bhau? While I was changing into a sari, my boys formed a brotherhood?

'What does it matter whether I lived in Baramati?'

'Aaf course it does. I was not told about eet.'

'Why should you be told? My life is not any of your business.'

'T'chaila, everything izh a beezhness for you peepul.'

A deep look passes between the boys.

Bromance brewing much?

The mention of Baramati has thrown a bucketful of water on Sagar's simmering surliness. He's splattering. He's blistering. He's shouting at the audience to get on with their work. The Nehru Cap Man yells asking why the food is being held up. They're getting late. Triple S hollers back, telling 'Anna' to shut up. This has a domino effect. The assault on their man irritates the women and they begin to disperse, curse and create further anarchy. The kitchen is now clearly split into four groups.

Straight ahead of us, there's a swarm of worker bees, mostly very old women, carrying large, covered containers of hot, fresh food out of the kitchen. Blocking the kitchen entrance are Katya, Uday and Triple S, embroiled in the pointless Baramati controversy. Katya is standing on the elevated threshold, where a toran made of golden foil and mango leaves dangles above her head. To our left is Nehru Cap Man, surrounded by quibbling women. The Bihari woman in the rainbow-coloured sari carries a plastic tub filled with her fresh litti chokhas and dives into this section with her tribe's characteristic enthusiasm. 'Ek kaan pe bajayi?' she lassoes the irate Nehru Cap Man. And at the back end, standing by the sink, are Neelu, Pot-bellied Paati and I. Neelu has gathered the pallu of her blue Paithani around her neck like a scarf.

Is it wrong that this does not feel unreal anymore?

I draw my pallu over the other shoulder, elbow into the Triple S–Katya–Uday section, and grab Triple S by the neck of his collarless, starched kurta. 'You! Don't raise your voice at Uday!'

He tears his eyes away from Katya and pins them upon me. 'Pleeezhe take yuvar hand away from my kudta.'

'This is my plan. My Strike at Thirty-Six—'

'... which izh illa without me.'

'You ungrateful dog!'

'Ekzhactlee!' He seizes my arm.

Katya pokes Triple S's arm with the edge of her iPad.

'T'chaila. Finally, you admeet that I'm a dog. You petronizhe me. Just like your Khansaab petronizhes you.'

Just do it, Sho. This is a big kitchen. There must be a knife somewhere sharp enough to plunge into his ungrateful heart!

'Sagar, shh!' Katya instructs.

'Vahini, bass jhala.'

'Sho, get off him,' Uday hollers.

'Periya pista nu nenapu?' I retort.

'Shobhna, behave yourself!' Uday has succeeded in wresting my hands out of Triple S's iron grip and is holding him back successfully, though with what looks like extreme effort. Some of the women from Nehru Cap Man's faction have broken out and are crowding around us, demanding to know what's happening. The 5'10" Bihari woman – the tallest and presumably strongest of the lot – throws her hand into the fray, hurling the word 'kuthiya' into the air several times.

Smack! Triple S just socked Uday in the eye. Uday pummels his fist into Triple S's stomach.

A couple of kids are tugging at Katya's sari, calling her 'Mommy'. In the distance, turning around the corridor, in blurring slow motion, closely pursued by his boys, I see the rapidly advancing outline of Tatya.

Kkuii-aiee-aii-eee ...

A storm kicks in from the corridor. Tatya turns around at the first screech of the alarm, but runs back within a couple of seconds. There is a scuffle on the other side. The guards yell 'stop' and 'ID'. A couple of gunshots. This doesn't appear to freak out any of the kitchen inmates. Between the gunshots, there's the sound of fast footsteps and a grating sort of noise, along with the soft thud of hooves.

Hooves?

'Roja!'

She's galloped straight and jumped on Uday – vaulted upon his shoulders and, as always, pinned him to the ground, dribbling uncontrollably – in a kitchen where prasadam is being prepared!

Why does he always allow her to get away with it?

Sunny follows, heckled by a bunch of guards and a couple of plain-clothes men. Behind them, Tatya rolls in a wheelchair that has my boss, AK, dressed in a shiny brown Pathani suit – the kind that men at kebab stalls on Mohammad Ali Road wear – and a skull cap. And blue Bata chappals. He's grown a stubble, I hadn't noticed that earlier.

For the love of Allah, is he dead?

Katya is the first to react. Grabbing the pleats of her sari, she surges towards Sunny with the intent of a big cat about to devour a rat. But before she can take a couple of steps towards her target, the strangest creature emerges from the opposite end of the corridor. Surprisingly, nobody seems unnerved by the appearance of a strapping Great Dane pummelling a grown man to the floor. But the bedlam magically comes to a standstill at the altar of the new entrant.

Dressed in a purple zari nine-yard sari with the heavy pallu drawn over her tiny head, it's a little old woman, with cracked alabaster skin. She can't be younger than ninety, looking like she could step into her funeral pyre any minute now. A traditional nose ring larger than Katya's looms over her petal-like lips. She's leaning on a gold-coloured walker.

'Pahuné?' her thin but authoritative voice echoes in the rapt silence.

Roja barks. Uday must have tickled her ear.

'Where are aawur guests?' she kindly translates.

Exhibit Four of the MaMi madhouse.

Wizened Nonagenarian dispenses uneven dollops of Marathi. Her frail, white hands are covered with at least three dozen thick gold bangles. Two large necklaces hang on her neck, right down to her abdomen. All the women, including Bihari Snack Lady and Nehru Cap Man, begin to file out of the kitchen in the manner of students who know better than to argue with the dying headmaster. I dash towards AK while Uday untangles himself from Roja's embrace. Tatya is standing guard over AK who – head slumped to one side, eyes shut, that same stupid smile on his lips – has got both his hands on the wheelchair armrests.

'What is this?' I ask Sagar and Sunny.

'Double M Kaka got new Pathan dress. But sir wanted to wear suit only.'

'Sunny, where is MM?' I ask a little sharply.

He stops admiring Sagar's saffron robe and turns to me, his eyes wide pools of innocence. He's wearing a satiny white shirt with black skinny jeans and white laces. 'Double M Kaka parking and coming.'

'Sunny, you bastard. All those lies. Those tears! Using his mother—'

'Aai shapath. I did not lie. Sagar's mother is sick. I swear!'

AK's head is bobbing. Uday and Katya have caught up with Wizened Nonagenarian and the phalanx of security is hovering around them. Only Triple S is crouching behind Sunny, waving his hands in front of AK's face.

'How long have all of you been members of MaMi?' I ask.

'No maimbership. This is aawar family!'

'Yoowar family is murdering innocent citizens and smashing chemistry labs and who knows, bombing our presscon,' I sneer. But when one thinks about it, that possibility is terrifying.

Sunny's eyes light up with a childlike enthusiasm that doesn't indicate mass murder. 'Yes, lots many camayras are there. All foreign channels also. Politicul peepul.'

'What political people?'

'Prime Minister.'

Why is the PM coming to a film announcement presscon? Does Bala know? 'Does Bala know?'

'Hees presscon. He must be knowing.'

At the least, they could have asked me to put on make-up!

'Akkasaheb wants to know if your dog has had a bath.'

'Huh?'

Katya stands beside Wizened Nonagenarian and holds her arm while the old woman thrusts her walker at Roja, saying, 'If he hasn't had a bath, he can stand outside the corridor and hear the pooja. The rest of you, hurry.'

'Can't do.' I put my foot down.

'Akkasaheb is Saurabh's mother, Shobhna. She owns this house.' There's a hint of metal in Katya's voice.

'Ooh, I'm scared! What's she going to *do*? Lie and cheat to *Ganpati* and steal his thunder *too*?' There are tears in my eyes, at the sorry remnant of Strike at Thirty-Six. My gang – ex-boyfriend, his niece, and a genius-writer-turned-goon – has collected to the left. Roja is sticking to Uday's legs, but is looking at Triple S. As always, he saluted her when they met.

Wizened Nonagenarian aka Akkasaheb takes a long look at me and whispers energetically into Katya's ear, then breaks into a toothless smile.

'Akkasaheb says that if you do not move the dog's feet right now, she will ask Bandu to take it downstairs, strip his skin, cut him into little pieces and throw all the pieces down the Bandra–Worli bridge.'

Akkasaheb's furrowed petal lips shrivel and curl. Katya continues to address the congregation on her mean mother-in-law's behalf: 'Murder is easy. Kidnapping is easier. Lying, cheating is okay. God will not judge you on that. The real question he will finally ask is, how far did go for what you believed in.'

Akkasaheb pokes Katya's chin with her golden walker.

'And of course ... did you ever really know what you believed in?'

'Hoye!' Triple S raises a hand in the air, and pumps his fist up and down. 'Jayostuté! Jayostuté!'

Everyone, including the few MuPo officers, raises their fists and repeats the slogan.

Roja is now looking from Uday to Triple S. Then she looks at me, tears rolling involuntarily down my face, and cocks her head to one side, gently twitching her ears to the rhythm of the slogans.

'Jayostuté! Jayostuté!'

Somewhere, I can hear AK's voice too. Squeaking from within the bedlam: 'Hurr, Gharpuré?'

17

Cymbalism

'Sukhkarta dukhharta
Varta vighnachi
Noorvi poorvi prem krupya jayachi
Sarwangi sundar utishendu rachi
Kanthi jhalke maad mukhta padhanchi ...'

It is 4 a.m. in the Mahajan household in Rajputana building in Vile Parle. The fragrance of mogras and jasmine, sonchafas and agarbattis pervades the 6000 square feet penthouse. Close to seventy people are gathered in the covered gazebo next to the kitchen, chanting and clapping in front of a 4-foot sitting idol of Ganpati, dressed in a yellow dhoti, fuschia shoulder wrap, orange turban and forty kilos of gold jewellery studded with pearls and yellow sapphires.

Right in front of the mandap is a row of eleven children aged between three and twelve, clanging their little cymbals and ghantas out of tune. Behind them are Akkasaheb; Katya holding an enormous pooja thali – which is clearly too big for her petite frame – with ease; the family priest standing beside her, chanting in an ear-splitting nasal timbre; Pot-bellied Paati; and AK in his wheelchair. MM – his eyes closed in piety but opening once in a while to check if AK is dribbling saliva or beginning to ask about Gharpuré – stands behind AK, holding the backrest of his wheelchair. Akkasaheb seems to be aware of AK's kidnapped status, which is why she is keeping her good eye – she has no vision in the other one – upon the kidnappers Udayan, Shobhna and Sunny, who are standing on either side of AK and MM. Bringing up the rear is Sagar, who has untied the saffron sash around his waist and hung it over his shoulders. Despite his jagged speaking voice, he sings in a deep baritone with an even pitch and heartfelt passion that makes the rendition soar above everyone else's. There's a deep red gash on the side of his neck, where someone's nails have just scratched and bled him. Uday – left eye smashed black and blue, and his little briefcase stuffed uncomfortably in the back of the waist of his dhoti – sings in a low-pitched voice, but seems to know each word and its perfect intonation. Sho's face is tear-stained. Sunny's eyes are closed, and he is clapping his hands, swaying and singing the aarti at the top of his voice. Tatya and four of his boys stand surrounding the kidnappers. Just by the Ganpati dais, Neelu is recording the pooja on her mobile phone. She still hasn't recovered network, but Katya has had her swear before the idol that there was no way she will blog for the Boston 'Blah'-min or tweet a single word or photo before she gets permission from the Mahajan couple. Neelu is in top form, the official and only photographer of the event. Neelu jumps up and shivers with delight every time somebody talks to her. She's tickled pink with this mafia angle.

'Lambodar pitaambar phanivar vandana
Saral sond vakratunda trinayana ...'

Behind them, the kitchen gang is clapping and warbling in varying levels of proficiency. The safari suits – all twenty-five of them – cordoning off the exits, spill into the corridor. Roja is alone in the living room, staring balefully at the framed photos of the old man on the wall. There is a steel bowl of condensed, sweetened almond milk in front of her, untouched – nobody apart from Sho knows that Roja stopped drinking milk and consuming dairy products ever since Uday and Sho split up.

The aarti rises to a climax and ends with a hearty call to the elephant-headed god to return next year. 'Ganpati Bappa morya. Pudhcha varshi lavkar ya.'

As soon as the large hall is filled with a brief but profound silence, AK's voice rings out, loud and clear. 'Jai ho! Hurr hurr.'

Everyone turns around to look at him. MM kneels down beside AK, places a gentle hand on his shoulder and murmurs, 'Saheb, okay?'

AK bats his eyes at the quintet staring into his face – MM, Katya, Akkasaheb, Pot-bellied Paati and Sunny.

Pot-bellied Paati re-launches her pitch. 'Amlet?'

AK bobs his head.

She fattens the bait, '*Masala* amlet?'

He ponders over the offer for a minute, then speaks slowly, but clearly: 'Hidiot traitor!'

Someone cuts through the group. It's the Mahajans' bare-chested family priest, clad in white and gold, struggling with the gargantuan pooja thali that Katya handled with ease. The thali holds, amongst other goodies, a roaring silver lamp and a bowl of yellow pedas with liquid saffron centres. Everyone seeks the blessings of the deity by cupping their palms over the flame and then touching their own eyes. Akkasaheb, being the eldest, directs the smoke of the flame towards AK's face and pops a peda into his mouth. He gobbles it appreciatively. Then she thrusts some more of the creamy yellow gobs into his right palm and pats it shut.

'Hidiot traitor,' AK repeats, scanning the room, smacking his lips. It seems the particular turncoat he wants to address is not exactly in front of him.

Martand Murkute aka MM was the reason why Sho went ahead with Strike at Thirty-Six. While she was entranced by Sagar's writing prowess, bizarre imagination and abrasive personality, she knew he was as much of a loose cannon as she herself was. They needed someone solid. Fifty-six-year-old MM was one of that rare species. A Mumbai native, he had never known the world outside AK's office and home, but she'd seen him gaze at Sagar kind-heartedly in AK's office, and also knew that anyone working with AK over a period of time was bound to develop a touchy nerve regarding the Pathan's not-terribly-subtle class condescension.

As soon as Sagar agreed to be part of Strike at Thirty-Six, Sho pushed Sagar to convince MM to bat for them. She and Sunny had to force Sagar to meet MM, but once the maverick writer sat facing the old man outside his house at Khotachiwadi in Girgaum, the boy from Baramati shone. Being sons of the soil, their connection was instantaneous. Sagar gave MM a rapid-fire narration of *The Dhaal*. The old man fingered his pepper-and-salt whiskers for the entire fifty-five minutes, but it was clear he was sold. They asked if MM could slip two barbie-spiked jujubes to AK on xyz date and drive him to a spot from where they could relocate him to Sho's house. Later, he'd also have the honour of convincing Bala and the RAA board that AK was safe, did not want to disclose his location, and that the old man would surface at the presscon. Nobody would dare suspect MM of wrongdoing. Including MM himself.

Why – MM wanted to know, after pondering the situation – were they so desperate to humiliate Khansaab? 'Who will speak for the small people then, MM?' pleaded Sho. He nodded. But there was an unspoken agreement that Strike at Thirty-Six was built using bricks of personal vendettas.

Now, as MM looks at Sho, waves of guilt and embarrassment radiate from both parties.

Katya bends to touch the priest's feet, and retreats from the core group as the horde of devotees scrambles for their share of the holy flame and sweets. Before Sho or Uday can contemplate any action of their own, Tatya ushers them to AK's side. By now, Sunny has placed himself at AK's feet and is looking searchingly into his eyes. Sagar stands at a distance, re-tying his turban and sash. Some of the other young men in similar clothes come to chat him up. He acknowledges everyone, but his attention is focussed on AK.

Sunny narrates what happened at Sho's house six hours ago, right after she left to meet Uday at Saayba. Sunny had administered the last dose of barbies at 10 p.m. the earlier night. Just like during the past two days, the old man was awake by 10.30 p.m. and had accepted his dinner – seviyan cooked with jaggery and dried nuts – in a complete daze. But his eyes had turned bloodshot after five spoons of the kheer and he'd pointed towards Roja and begun bawling. This was soon after Sho's last call, post which her cell phone was not reachable. When the Pathan got up from his bed and swayed 'like a big bhoot', shouting 'kaafira, kaafira!' at him, Sunny panicked. Thankfully, just then – Sunny's eyes lower and he blushes as he says it – Vahini called and told him that MM was on his way to take all of them to the pooja, and everyone, including the dog, was ordered to be present at Saurabh Dada's house. MM had brought the fancy outfit and had to suffer many slaps and screams from AK before he could stuff the old man into it.

'Munni,' mumbles AK.

Sho realizes the old man is looking directly into her eyes, his gaze lucid and resolute.

'But you gave him the injection, didn't you, Sunny?'

'No, he was scaring the sheet of me. He wanted to know everything. Look at his size and mine. How I'll say "no"?' So, says Sunny, he skipped the dose.

AK shifts his considerable weight from his left forearm to his right so he can fix his disapproving peepers on Uday. He holds his palm out to Sunny, who picks out a peda for him and respectfully places it in his mouth. Uday's black eye catches AK's attention: 'Who hit you, bete-jaan?'

'It's a long story.'

AK shakes his head and looks around for Sagar, who is arguing with Katya. His gaze veers back to Uday as he sucks in a mouthful of air and ejects it in a potent sigh.

Sho pushes Sunny away and kneels in front of the wheelchair and bores her eyes into AK's large violet orbs.

'AK, this is the MaMi. They're taking over the *Yogi* presscon.'

'The one *you* were supposed to take over?'

'Yeah.'

Katya butts in, clapping her hands, calling in the prisoners. 'Five minutes. Everyone goes down. The Ganpati programme begins in fifteen.'

The gathering races towards the main door. The guards bark out instructions in Marathi and Hindi – everybody needs to be out in five minutes, else the security system will lock them in till late in the evening; all presents, garlands and coconuts are to be deposited on the table to the left of the main door; nobody will go beyond the Ganpati pandal, except family members, under any condition; whoever hasn't received the prasad should raise their hands.

Except for Neelu's, all cell phones in the room have already been deposited into a shelf at the entrance of the apartment.

Sagar approaches AK's wheelchair and announces that the gang of kidnappers and kidnappees have to exit via the private elevator. He gently adds a caveat; before anyone from the group should consider objecting, they should check their black eyes and sprained wrists. AK begins to wheel himself when Sunny takes over and begins to move it to the back of the Ganpati dais. The rest follow. Akkasaheb decides she will stay back with Pot-bellied Paati, because you cannot leave the divine guest alone at home.

'Where's Roja?' Uday asks.

Akkasaheb replies that Roja has had a bit too much basundi and is staying back. 'As long as you children behave,' she drawls in English, 'your big dog is safe here. Or remember, dog meat and blood at Chowpatty.'

Despite a location change, the threat remains forceful.

There is a door behind the pandal, which Katya opens. Everybody walks out, upon which the door slides back with an electronic beep. There is a slim elevator at the end of the tiny passage behind the door. They squeeze in, too close for comfort, a strange bunch – MM, Sagar, Katya, Sho, Uday, Sunny in possession of AK in the wheelchair, and two Safari Suits.

The uncomfortable silence is finally broken by Neelu. 'What's the prog?'

Sagar volunteers. In another ten minutes, the annual MaMi

powada will begin, powada being a Marathi folk ballad tradition, in which the poets aka shahirs narrate historical events in an entertaining storytelling format.

'Are you a poet?' Neelu asks, edging closer to him.

'I was.'

'The chief guest is here.' Katya adjusts her pallu to cover her head, sticks her toes into her bronze Kolhapuri chappals and gracefully steps out of the elevator into a phalanx of security men.

The grounds around Rajputana building are now enveloped by a towering, billowing white-and-red mandap. In the rust-tinged glow of pre-dawn and the harshness of a dozen neons, the place looks all set to host a political rally. The action is centred around a semi-circular area which is lined with thick, dirty white mattresses, cushions and armrests. Facing the seating arrangement is a crude mud-and-stone replica of a Maratha fortress, complete with a saffron flag and a bust of Shivaji. Lording over the arrangements as the background to the 'stage' is an eighteen-foot Ganpati idol, this one an eco-friendly version fashioned with coconuts and grass. The band of saffron boys from upstairs are starting to bring in musical instruments and fussing over their turbans. The crowd from upstairs has surged down to dissolve in a gathering of people thrice its size. It's a motley mix of blue- and white-collared guests. Katya's security cordon cuts her off from the others and leads her to a fat lady in a red silk sari, accompanied by an equally obese pre-teen boy and two male bouncers.

'I've seen the big auntie somewhere,' says Sho.

'She's the mayor,' Uday turns to her, incredulous.

'Of what?'

'Mumbai. You live in the city, don't you?'

Sho replies with a scowl.

By the chai stall to the far left of the mandap, three lovely ladies chat excitedly – Farah Master, current editor of *X'Quisite*; Archana Patel, PR maven; and Aashi Kappu, high-flying starlet. Before Sho can grasp the deeper significance of the presence of Mumbai's top fluff girls at a fundamentalist political organization's Ganpati bash, Tatya deposits four of his men by their side and orders: 'Sit with Khansaab there.'

Sagar walks up to AK's wheelchair and holds out an arm to help the old man stand up. AK refuses with a smile, heaves his weight off the armrest, waddles two steps and stumbles, falling into Sagar's lean and muscular arms. Sho and Uday rush over.

'Where are you taking him?' Uday asks Sagar.

'He is the chief guest.'

'And you knew *all* of this?' asks Sho, some hurt creeping into her voice.

'No, nothing. Vahini and Dada told me in the night.'

'Bullshit!'

'Look hiyer, I am not lying.'

'While you're not lying, here's another question …' Uday treads cautiously.

'Yais.'

'Did you murder that Panthaki fellow?'

'No, but I was there. Also, I was there when we smashed the chaimistry labs.'

AK looks at Sho and Uday – standing beside each other in sari and kurta–dhoti – and whispers: 'Beautiful, bete-jaan.'

The duo pretends it hasn't heard him.

Sho picks up the trail of the interrogation. 'Do they know you are a writer and not a … party worker?'

'I can do both.'

'And look where that's got you!'

'They are my faimilie.'

'And we? The idiots who had faith in your talent?' Uday thunders, then seems to realize what he has just said.

Sho seems shaken by the sudden outburst. The weight of what has just been uttered seems to sink in slowly. Uday takes a step ahead of Sho. She steps back.

'I am sorry. But I hauve to go and perform,' says Sagar dismissively.

'And what happens at the presscon?'

'I reyaylly don't know. Dada did not tail me.'

'Do you even remember the speech we wrote for the presscon?'

The speech – contained within two A4 sheets – was written by Sagar and vetted by Sho, MM and Sunny. It had taken over a week to prepare, and passionately pleaded the cause of *The Dhaal*, and how it would change the face of Indian cinema. The file remained in Sho's Vaio, with the typos she'd corrected. It was etched, verbatim, in Sagar's head. Just like the rustic powada he was about to launch into.

18

The Morning After

UDAYAN

An unusual comparison, but more than two years ago, I was in the same situation as Sagar. Only in a different context. But unlike him, I made a choice.

A day after Sho had behaved like a psycho at the Andheri café and I'd walked out on her, Rohini had called me. Sho's appa and amma were perplexed and she wouldn't say a word, except that we'd broken up. 'I'll be honest, da. Sho needs you more than you need her,' Rohini had said. She'd urged me to patch up with Sho, or at least meet Appa. I had just about begun to consider the possibility when Motabhai called to announce that Daha was setting up shop in NYC. I went up to Bhai and announced that I was leaving for New York the following week. It was the angriest I had ever seen him. He'd called me 'harami', an endearment he normally reserved for errant servants. It was like water off a duck's back. At that point, I was sick of being the good apple. I wanted some respite. If Sho wanted to make amends, she could have called. She hadn't.

Present moment. Sho and I are seated at the far right of the semi-circular seating arrangements, with Tatya's men standing guard. Khansaab is up front, seated between the mayor and Katya. There is a camera crew at the back, but it has been asked to keep its equipment shut. Having returned from the CM's house twenty minutes ago, Saurabh is on the stage with Neelu, giving her instructions. Katya's people are rounding up wandering guests. The programme will begin any minute. The boys on stage are testing their daflis and throats. Sagar has assumed control; speaking individually to the boys and his background chorus, tweaking the musical instruments and keeping Sunny at bay.

I haven't seen 'Afzal Khanacha Vadh', but I've been to a couple of powadas, and know this one is about the historic meeting between the Maratha warrior king Shivaji and the terrorizing Mughal general. Anyone who's studied up to fourth grade in Maharashtra knows this story – when the cunning and gigantic Khan requested a meeting with his arch enemy, Shivaji prepared for the worst by arming himself with concealed daggers and tiger claws. They say, Afzal Khan stabbed him in the back under the pretext of hugging the Napoleon-sized warrior, at which point Shivaji stuck the claws into the giant's stomach.

Highly unusual for an Indian political–cultural affair, there are no speeches, garlanding or thanking of the chief guest. Sagar and his band launch right into the act. There is a simple rap-ish rhythmic quality to the powada; even if you don't understand the language, you can clap your hands or sway to the beat. After extolling Shivaji Raje's exploits, every stanza ends with a reverberating 'ho jee jee jee jee jee'. The chorus is strong, but Sagar's voice – as the shahir or poet–narrator – rises above the others'. He is gifted in the art of storytelling and has the audience hooked. I turn to see Sho's expression, but can't find her next to me. I look around. Nada. I look towards Neelu, but the girl is lost in recording Sagar's performance.

I get up and turn to the guard behind. He informs me that Sho left with Paresh and Prakash ten minutes ago. Where did they go, I ask, assuming Paresh and Prakash to be two of the guards and not another pair of Sho's protégés. He says he doesn't know, but he'll go search. He's bored with the show, and readily clicks his heels, rubbing his rifle with glee.

There must be close to 500 people, including children and curious neighbours, packed cheek-by-jowl in the limited space. I say we'll search together. The policeman warns that he's served in the Maratha Light Infantry, one of Indian army's most prolific battalions, for fifteen years, hence I shouldn't try any funny business with him.

A mini-truck with a bumper proclaiming 'Hak Farid Ya Farid' has arrived late and is dropping off a large group of women in saris, abayas and two dozen children in Pathani suits, skull caps and lehengas. Perhaps, they're being paid to stage a secular circus for MaMi. But the press is nowhere to be seen. A frustrated camera crew is smoking by its vans.

Someone taps my shoulder. It's Martand Murkute, AK's trusted aide. He's brought me a stainless steel tiffin box. It's the prasad, he says. Akkasaheb has got it packed for them to carry home after the presscon. He points towards the chai stall and murmurs, 'Shobhna Tai.' But MM's hand is still planted firmly on my shoulder and so I cannot begin moving towards where he is pointing.

'You are from Baramati?'

'I was born there. We went back when I was seven and spent five years there, at my mother's maternal home, when

Bhai was travelling. That does not, in any way, make me sympathetic to the cause of your party.'

'And what is aawur cause? You tail me. You know better.'

Before I can speak, MM shifts his hand to my elbow and tells me that AK had accepted MaMi's invitation for the powada several weeks before Sho approached him to be part of Strike at Thirty-Six. Khansaab, Murkute says, is a connoisseur of Marathi literature and culture.

'But why didn't you tell Shobhna? Why did you have to humiliate her?'

'Chalo, walk with me,' he says, slides his gentle grip down to my hand and leads me in a zigzagging motion into the crowd, courteously requesting people to make way. One of the guards trails us, barking at everyone, while the policeman I originally set out with seems to have got lost in the melee. As we snake through the throng, Murkute spills the beans. He knew that Khansaab was a long-time patron of MaMi, but didn't know that the party was in any way concerned with Khansaab's kidnapping and the presscon. It appears that MM was suddenly 'picked' up by the MaMi people the previous night from his home in Girgaum – where he hurriedly packed in one of AK's fancy clothes from his personal stash of his employer's emergency clothes – and taken to Sho's house where they then picked up Sunny, Roja and Khansaab.

'They were … they had guns,' MM whispers.

'They are bullies. This is what they do.'

'No, beta. The MaMi is very popular for the work they do in the villages.'

'Then maybe they should stay there!'

He smiles kindly and pats the tiffin box in his hand. 'That is exactly what Khansaab said about Sagar. He told me. "Let him stay in the village." We can say that to a boy like Sagar also. Stay in the village. Let him work with the village children and do small theatre. That is why I decided to help Shobhna Tai.'

He speaks good English. Three decades with Khansaab can do that.

'Do you know what they are going to do at the presscon,' I prod.

'No.'

We're around 500 yards away from the stage, at the mouth of the gully that leads to Rajputana. The powada has reached an electrifying pre-climax; Shivaji has dug his tiger claws into Afzal Khan and his band of guerrilla soldiers have been given the signal to attack the Mughal army. Deep and resonant, Sagar's voice has reached a crescendo, and the crowd has got into the mood and is adding to the chorus strain of 'ho jee jee jee jee jee'.

'Do you remember when you and Shobhna Tai went to the Japanese hotel? I followed you. Khansaab said you looked biutiful. Together.'

'What does that have to do with this, kaka?'

Before I can drill Murkute further, we've reached the hideout. It's a compact and ramshackle security cabin, double the size of a phone booth, sitting at the dead end of the gully. Why on earth would someone have a security cabin here? Murkute points his finger and suggests I go speak to Shobhna alone. 'I will call everyone,' he says, pulling out Sho and my phones from his pocket and handing them to me. 'We can leave for the press conference as soon as everything gets over here.'

There is nothing in the cabin except a chair, a table, a telephone, a couple of notebooks, a mobile phone, and much dust and cobwebs. One of the guards is leaning against the table and stands to attention as soon as I step in. He points to a broken door opening out to a small backyard with a couple of dry trees and some flowering shrubs. There is the faintest scent of jasmine in the air. The other guard is squatting near the steps, polishing his rifle with his handkerchief. At the end of the pathetic little garden, Sho stands facing the sun, a cigarette between her lips, her lustrous hair tousled by the light morning breeze.

'I didn't know you smoke!'

She tears her eyes away from the sun to look at me. 'I didn't know you lived in Baramati. Got the ciggie from the guard.' She holds out the pack of Classic.

'Don't smoke; it's deadly,' I advise but pick a couple of sticks for myself, cursing my own resurgent impulse. The guard gets up and lights a match for me. Sho and I stare out at the sun peeking out of the filthy mass of concrete beyond. Typical of the city, a garbage bin can be seen spilling out in the horizon.

'How's the dhoti doing?'

Now that she mentions it, it is extremely comfortable. 'Thanks for letting me read *The Dhaal*.'

She dangles the cancer stick loosely between her lips and breathes deep. 'It is phenomenal. The reason why I got into the business.'

The guards Paresh and Prakash eavesdrop openly on our conversation; the space is so small, nobody minds.

'Daha will be happy to produce it. On the scale you want. And Sagar.'

'That was never the point.'

'Saris always suited you.'

We puff in silence for another five minutes. I move closer to tuck a curly lock behind her ear.

Before we can get any closer, a voice calls from the back. 'Need a room?'

The guards snap to attention upon being caught unawares by Katya. She is standing right behind us, arms crossed over her chest, a pocket-sized shadow in the dimly lit room. Prakash and Paresh fumble into apologies. Sho just wanted a cigarette, they stutter. Katya claps her hands briskly, dismissing them. But before Paresh walks out, she asks him to leave the pack of cigarettes and the matchbox with me. 'You didn't like the powada?'

'Been there, heard that,' I answer.

'I'm asking your ex-girlfriend.'

Sho shakes her head and grins, but rises gracefully above the tease. The woman blows hot and cold. If I had waited it out and called her back, things would have been different.

'Sagar is a natural performer,' I muse, puffing.

Sho shakes her head again. Katya holds her hand out for a cigarette, which I light using Paresh's match and hand over to her. She drags the half-broken table to the door, removes her Kolhapuris, and jumps up to perch comfortably on it. I hadn't noticed earlier; she has a diamond toe-ring.

'You're checking out my bling.'

I nod.

'Wondering how such an ugly lower-middle-class Indian can speak such smooth American?'

'Something like that.'

She fixes her gaze upon her shiny toe-ring.

'We stayed there for ten years. Saurabh and I, the toast of

Silicon Valley; the brownest of browns who triumphed over their brownness. I was barely twenty-three when Saurabh and I got married and shifted there. Just like him, I learnt quickly, very quickly, how to speak American, and to genuinely love and appreciate America. We came back because I think we were fated to be back. Do you know Saurabh doesn't spend much time in Mumbai? He's usually working in the smaller towns. That's what he always wanted to do. Be a part of something bigger than himself ...'

'Why did you come back?'

'Let's just say it involved Akkasaheb visiting us, a dinner in her honour, a beef steak and a Chinese-and-Irish couple.' There is still no hint of emotion on Katya's face, though she has shifted her gaze from the toe-ring to her glittering mangalsutra.

'The thing is, I didn't know I was a fundamentalist until my fundamentals were challenged. I was chuffed, yes. It was a dream any small-town Indian girl would die for. At least that is what is assumed of her. I had reinvented myself. I threw the best omakase and sake dinners in the Valley. I was on the VVIP list of Neiman Marcus. This ... I had this specially made by Harry Winston.'

'I recognize that pink bezel. They had something similar at the place where I got the engagement ring,' I add.

'For his Bengali girlfriend.' Katya fills in the blanks for Sho, whose eyes are wide in astonishment.

So, I finally said it! Awkward, but it's out of the bag.

'Have you been carrying diamonds in that pansy Hobo all this time?'

'No, it's got some papers—'

'He's carrying around a copy of *The Dhaal*. Like a besotted lover,' Katya interjects.

Is there *anything* this bizarre little woman *doesn't* have on us? She's right, though. The bag has been with me ever since I landed in Mumbai.

Katya has jumped off the table and stubbed her stick. Now she claps her hands. We're back to playing Marie Antoinette. 'Okay exes, let's snap to it. The presscon is at four this evening.'

Sho seems meditative, incapable of being rattled any more. Or just on autopilot.

'You do want Sagar to practise his speech, don't you? He's a homeboy. His Hindi is atrocious. But if you're looking for any sort of national coverage, he has to talk in Hindi.' The little woman sure knows how to grab the eyeballs.

A Land Cruiser has just appeared outside the cabin. Sunny is on the driver's seat, Sagar next to him, and Neelu poking her face out of the rear window. Next to Neelu are Khansaab and Murkute. Katya clicks her fingers at Sagar, signalling him to shift to the backseat of the SUV, signalling Sho and me to get in the front with her. 'Saurabh will join us at the presscon. He has gone for the visarjan. Any questions?'

Pin drop silence.

I'm feeling surer by the minute that Katya is the mastermind behind MaMi, playing an entire city.

The first lady of home-grown terror claps her hands and barks at Sunny.

'What are you waiting for? Chalo!'

19

Who the Fuck Is Gharpuré?

SHOBHNA

'It's a cow.'

'We can see that.'

'Why is it so fat? Why is it not moving? Fatty, move.'

'Honk it, honk it.'

'Wait, what is tied under its stomach?'

'Shit.'

'Nothing is tied. She's pregnant, ya.'

Let's just get some last-minute perspective here.

The backseat of the Cruiser has been ripped out to accommodate a couple of phones, a TV screen and a fridge. AK is sitting bang opposite me, cradling a foot-long clay Ganpati idol in his hands. Some sort of souvenirs for MaMi's moneybags sponsors, one guesses. His eyes have reached full dilation and are looking at me.

Yes, AK, I was wrong. You obviously know how the business works. Tell me, did you get yourself kidnapped just so I could look stupid?

Neelu is squeezed next to him, her sleepy head occasionally hitting his shoulder. But she's still spirited enough to yell out at pregnant cows in the middle of the road.

No guesses for what'll be trending on Twitter tonight, from Bori Bunder to Boston. The hottest scoop on Maximum City's mental people!

Given AK's girth, Triple S, Uday and I have no choice but to squeeze together in the other seat. Triple S's turban and sash are with Sunny. Uday's dhoti is hitched up to his knees. His left leg touching my right; he's lost to the world, blowing smoke in concentric circles outside his window.

Can't live without his cancer, can't live without his fiancée. Never thought one could accuse Uday of being needy.

Katya, upright in the front seat, back-to-back with Sagar, is on the phone with Saurabh, and speaking in a rapid-fire mix of English and Marathi. There are loud mentions of the CM, a certain Tripathi, 'Yes, we'll be there in an hour' and 'Haan, they're all here'. She barks at Sunny to drive carefully, avoiding all future cows. The Eastern Expressway is clear; it's a beautiful morning. A cavalcade of cars and jeeps is trailing us.

'Is everything ready for the presscon?' AK's voice is back in its commandeering terrain.

Barbies, blah!

'Call Priyanka, Merhernosh, Ranjan. Everything should start on time.'

'AK, where's MM?' I ask, doing away with any trace of remorse at my deeds I might have let slip out unwittingly.

'I fired him.'

'But—'

'You're fired too.'

Oh, so I can't even diss you now with an 'I resign too, old man'.

Triple S turns to look at AK. Minutes fly by. Our mobile phones are back with us, but none of us is using them.

'Look at you children. So innocent,' AK flaps.

Innocent. Idiot savant. Same difference.

'You artistes are such babies ...'

Yeah, taunt us.

'You never grow up, hai na, bete-jaan?'

This is directed at Uday, who reacts incredibly rudely by blowing out bigger smoke rings.

'Martand would never have left me if I didn't fire him. His son and daughter-in-law have started a catering business in Alibaug. They need his help. He needs to spend time with his grandkids. It is time for him to get some rest and peace. Some people are always and will always be a part of you. You have to push them away, for their own good.'

AK arranges the blood-red shawl around the shoulders of the little silver Ganpati in his lap. Udayan pulls down his dhoti to cover his legs up to the ankles and drops the stub out of the window.

'Khansaab, we're sorry.'

'I know you are not.'

AK drums his fingers on Ganpati's hips, like an Afghani drug lord.

'Do you know the MaMi office at Worli is owned by Bhai Doshi? They've only rented it out.'

'Shh ... you're giving away our secrets, Khansaab,' Katya heckles from the front.

'Khansaab, they are murderers.'

'Is that so bad, bete-jaan? One murder?'

'There have been others, Khansaab,' Katya smiles broadly.

AK grins and shakes his head. They obviously share a mysterious camaraderie.

The vehicle brakes harshly and the door on Uday's side slides open – it has been opened by someone outside. The surroundings are dimly lit and dank. Saurabh pops his head in, nods at everyone and squeezes in next to Katya. One of the bodyguards standing outside hands him a silver thali, which he extends to AK, who places his silver Ganpati idol in it and touches its tiny feet with his fingers.

'Dhanyawaad, Khansaab. Are you all right?'

'Alive, beta.' AK grins.

'How is everybody doing?' Saurabh purrs.

Katya hands Saurabh his titanium Vertu, another phone, and a small blue velvet drawstring pouch. Settling himself beside Triple S, he opens the pouch and brings out tiny, exquisitely crafted little jewels in gold. A little necklace. A baby crown. With great reverence, he begins to adorn the Ganpati idol in AK's lap and initiates a monologue with the idol.

'We've been asking for the resignation of the health minister of the state for five months now. He is a fraud, a cheat and a major ass. But the high point of his career was last year when the entire funds for the Central milk scheme for government schools in twenty-five districts across western Maharashtra went into his personal account. We've shouted and threatened, but they won't touch him—'

'Because he is a Dalit,' Triple S cuts in.

Oh!

'What does this have to do with Panthaki's murder?' asks Uday.

'Nothing. We are politicians. We loot and murder. That's what we do.' With the exception of Sunny, Saurabh has the sunniest smile in the group. 'Come, Neelu, we're here,' he beams at our perky little rabbit, who hops out obediently.

We file out into a swanky car park, the basement of the Four Seasons hotel, one guesses. A few of the vehicles from the cars trailing us are parking themselves at close range, including Sunny's Pajero. Tatya emerges from one of the cars and propels himself to the tip of Saurabh's security platoon. I try to get by him, to check on Roja, but he assures me she's fine. The safari suits from Rajputana have formed a thick semi-circle around us. Other uniformed guards, belonging to the hotel, one presumes, pour in from across the tube-light-illuminated vast expanse beyond. From within that huddle, a short, spiry man in an olive-green safari suit jumps out and heads straight towards our coterie. Spotting the bejewelled Ganpati idol in AK's hands, he rushes forth and makes a big fuss of kissing its tiny feet.

'Arre, Vahini, kahe der lagayi?' he pouts, turning to Katya.

'Tiwariji, from the CM's office,' Saurabh introduces.

'This is the one?' Tiwariji booms, staring at Sagar. Katya nods.

'Nice, nice. Amitaabachchan, angry young man. Camera will love him,' the little bureaucratic powerhouse nods, pleased.

'Aur ye, Bhai—' before Saurabh can finish properly introducing Uday, Tiwari's eyes light up.

'We have mate.'

'No.'

'Yes. You have forgotten everything. We mate when you were still in Mumbai, in your family Ganpati.'

Tiwariji hustles us towards the elevators, insisting that we avoid the press which is camped all around the foyer and the ballroom. Does anyone want him to call any family or friends, he wants to know, texting vigorously on his Samsung tablet whilst hurling instructions in chaste Hindi to two sidekicks who've emerged from the shadows. Saurabh tells him that all of us have our cell phones and appear to have chosen not to use them. His affability seems to have dulled at the edges with Tiwari's arrival. He takes the little man aside to confer at the far end of the security cordon. Saurabh's face and posture seem to harden and look tenser by the second; Tiwari shakes his head.

Saurabh nods his and points to our group. Tiwari waggles his tablet. Saurabh shakes his head. Tiwari throws up his hands. They return. Meanwhile, the hotel security makes way for a cheerful gent in a rose-and-beige suit, who introduces himself as the GM and ushers us behind a glass façade towards two service elevators.

'Sir, the presscon party. The presscon party! The press conference party.'

'They've arrived,' the GM whispers discreetly.

We're thick in it now. These moments will go down in the Ramakrishnan–Doshi–Sonawane–Khan history as the 'daze' of our lives.

It's 1.30 p.m. Having finally run out of things to say to each other, we – Uday and I – are resting against the French windows of the Pavilion, which open out on the lawns of the Four Seasons. Uday is looking sexy in his dhoti–kurta and one-day stubble. I've always liked him in anything but a suit, but always suspected whether he liked himself in anything but a suit.

Minutes pass by. No sign of Neelu or Saurabh. Just right for a power burst of untoward introspection.

My relationship with Josef, the Czech photographer I briefly hooked up with while at *X'Quisite*, had concluded within one week. The bitter end to the short affair had him accusing me of pistanthrophobia – the fear of trusting people. That was pretty rich, coming from a logophile who'd hopped cities and been unable to settle in any country or relationship since he was eighteen. He had deluded himself into believing he was a free spirit when, in fact, he had severe intimacy issues with women and commitment problems in life in general.

I'd sworn I'd do better than Josef. And I almost did. We almost did.

I'm staring at Uday. He's staring at me. Then, unexpectedly, he makes a move. 'Happy birthday, Sho.' He cups my face in his right palm, then jerks it away.

Of course he remembers! He knew why I'd called this operation Strike at Thirty-Six – right from the day I called him in NYC.

Today, 5 September 2012, is my thirty-sixth birthday.

Of course he didn't forget!

We're no longer just ex-lovers. By co-conspiring in Strike at Thirty-Six, we've been forged by fate into becoming a modern, urban, dysfunctional family. The operative word here is family. It doesn't matter if Uday is getting married to his Bong beauty and if Triple S is bonking Katya. Willy-nilly, we're all in it now – Uday, Triple S, AK, MM, Sunny, Roja, and since last night, assorted characters in the MaMi madhouse: Katya, Saurabh, Pot-bellied Paati (currently envisioned feeding masala amlets to Roja), Pushkie and sundry others.

I'm ringing in my thirty-sixth birthday. Like this! In this merry menagerie.

And yet, beyond the mayhem and the mental cartwheels, beyond the scent of Uday next to me and the warmth of his palm soothing my cheek, the future is no longer a blur. There's light at the end of this deranged black and white and grey tunnel.

The Dhaal.

In my turquoise-walled office at RAA, amongst other objets d'art collected by AK, there's a small framed poster in burnt orange with an anonymous quote: 'You are not always the hero of your own story.'

For now, in the midst of what can correctly be termed pandemonium, I feel at peace.

I've made a decision. From my feelings for Uday, from our friendship, from my attraction or repulsion for Triple S, from my resentment towards AK and my gnawing disappointment at my own inability to pull my life together, I have chosen one, just one cause to concentrate on. *The Dhaal*.

I am the hero in *The Dhaal*'s life.

The *Yogi* presscon is fashionably late. The theme is tropical rainforest-meets-2050, so there are streaks of green and brown with a midnight blue background. The seating arrangements are au naturel, in something Bala calls 'distressed wood'. A champagne waterfall gushes around a trunk in the middle of the room. At least twenty people buzz about, preparing for the press that should arrive any minute now. Bala is in spanking CEO mode, dispensing multiple instructions to the RAA team that arrived a couple of hours earlier. He was so overjoyed at seeing AK, he really didn't care if the boss had been vacationing in the Bahamas or tortured by the Taliban. Rohit was promptly despatched back to Juhu to grab a couple of Savile Row suits from AK's wardrobe. Priyanka, along with Mehernosh, one of her assistants, is fussing over the Brit deejay and the contemporary dancers from LA, feeding them and escorting them to and from their suites. Out-of-town press is also lunched and wined and made to feel very important. Sunny is whirling around, as happy and smiling as Neelu, helping with everything from the sound system to the LCDs to the hors d'oeuvres.

It's time now. The models are stationed at the entrance. The bubbly fountain is in soft whirl mode, the pretty little bites are in the pantry oven, and the servers are putting final touches to their bow ties. Featuring shadowy silhouettes of the film's lead stars Aashi Kappu and Aatish Khan in blue paint and pointy-eared avatars, five vinyl *Yogi* cut-outs loom above us. 'This summer,' they scream, 'get ready to return to the future.' The two actors, Bala informed us, are doing an exclusive photo shoot for *Vogue* in the Tapan Terrace on the second floor. They will be here soon, to make their grand entrance to flashbulbs and the most important press reporters and editors in the city calling out their names.

Or so they think.

Yogi is about to be walloped by *The Dhaal*. And *The Dhaal* in turn, walloped by MaMi.

Triple S is in the anteroom. He went in quietly, with no resistance or snarky comments at all to Kappu's make-up man dabbing him with a bit of concealer. After overseeing the ironing of Triple S's kurta, Neelu has been texting Uday furiously. It appears Triple S – or Hot Guy, as Neelu's taken to calling him – is also in a meditative state of mind.

hot guy's cool

reading speech. his hindi wierd

dat catya chick sd i cn tweet now

hot guy askin bot u mama

hes sorta qute iz di dating im?

da catya comin atcha

Even as Uday shows me Neelu's last text message, Katya joins us by the French windows. The three of us are greeted with goggle-eyed stares – we're still draped in our occasion-inappropriate clothes. After every five minutes, someone hovers past us respectfully, with pink flutes or cheese platters and crocs of tapenade. Occasionally, people wave at Uday and me, unapologetically gaping at seeing us together. Others come by to offer obeisance to Katya who swats them away like pesky flies. Saurabh left two hours ago for a last bout of super-urgent negotiations with the CM. Tiwariji stayed with us, trailed around the hotel by two of Tatya's men. Taking advantage of Tiwariji's declaration of kinship with the Doshis, Uday tried to wheedle out insider information about MaMi's power game with the government regarding the vile health minister's resignation. Tiwariji left as soon as the uncomfortable questions began flowing. But this real-life intrigue of the state health minister's involvement in a milk scam and MaMi baying for his blood has begun to eerily and uncomfortably resemble *The Dhaal*'s plot. How tangled is Triple S in this web?

But I'm the rock in *The Dhaal*'s life now. And my faith in Triple S's genius must supersede his past or future with MaMi. I don't know if I planned Strike at Thirty-Six, or whether it planned itself using me. It's back to all questions, no answers. But this time, I'm not spazzing. I'm not spilling coffee. I'm not taking the escape route.

The Pavilion is filling up quick. Cameras are being positioned. Reporters are getting their pens ready. RAA's PR team is on fire. Priyanka totters up to us in her five-inch heels, smiling at Uday and Katya. 'What the hell are you wearing, Sho? Where is Bala? He said he's going to fetch AK. Who found AK? Where was he? What happened to him?'

The volley of questions is answered by AK's arrival. Having changed into a light grey linen suit with a salmon pink tie, he toddles – the barbies haven't exited his system completely – from the double doors to the dais, acknowledging a few faces, looking blankly at most, and smiling glassy-eyed for the cameras which descend upon him en masse. Whispers grow into waves rippling across the room.

'Khansaab, where were you?'

'Khansaab, were you kidnapped?'

'Khansaab, look here. Was there a ransom? How much did RAA pay?'

'AK, are you having an affair with Rashmiji?'

'Mr Khan, is apaharan ke peeche kiska haath tha?'

'Look here. Look here. Khansaab, who are you wearing?'

For a minute there, AK loses his balance as he is just about to reach the podium. Before any of us can react, Katya – surging forth like an agile cat from beside me, in the manner of her husband – jostles back a couple of cameras, pokes a reporter in the ribs and grabs AK by his podgy elbow.

A bearded cameraman from the back yells, 'Katya Mahajan!' Thus identified, the entire horde of press guys tumbles towards Katya, who hovers protectively over AK.

'Mrs Mahajan, why are you here?'

'Mrs Mahajan, do you know the Quit Mumbai protestors are on a hunger strike from tomorrow morning?'

'Katyaji, what does MaMi have to say to the tax-paying public of Bombay?'

'Mrs Mahajan, the Mumbai Police are saying they've identified Panthaki's murderer. Is it a MaMi man, Mrs Mahajan?'

'Katya, Katya, who are you wearing?'

Bala and Priyanka squeeze in between Uday and me, acknowledging my ex-lover cheerily.

'Hola handsome, long time no see,' Priyanka trills at Uday, overcompensating for the extreme shock at seeing us together, togged out in traditional gear.

'Looking good, bro.' Bala beams at Uday before hissing into my ear: 'Who the hell is that woman and what is she doing with AK?'

'She's Saurabh Mahajan's wife. Did you know AK was involved with MaMi?'

'Yes. You *didn't*?'

'No.'

'He's on their board of directors.'

'The MaMi has a fucking board? Why didn't you tell me?'

'You didn't ask. Wish me luck.' He buttons his blazer and strides ahead, iPad in hand. That must be the *Yogi* launch speech. Meanwhile, like Humpty Dumpty and the Red Queen, AK and Katya have climbed up the podium and positioned themselves right in front of a large cut-out of Kappu's futuristic, pointy bazookas. Bala creeps up, joins his hands to greet Katya, and squeezes between her and AK. The emcee – a popular television actress who has been trying to attract Uday's attention over the past hour – eyes the unlikely trio on stage and begins the proceedings, apologizing insincerely for the delay. The presence of AK and Katya on the stage has got the photographers in a tizzy.

Getting away from the melee, we have found a vantage position at a corner of the front of the room. We can see the end of Triple S's orange sash and Neelu's shoes – they are standing backstage, along with Sunny.

The cacophony of camera flashes and requests for poses begins to drown out Sexy Emcee's pleasantries. Minutes tick by ominously. RAA's chic soiree is threatening to turn into a wholesale fish market. AK picks up a champagne flute, clinks it gently to his mobile phone and coughs. For a second there, he looks like he's going to faint. Priyanka, Uday and I surge forward in single file. Before any of us can get on the podium, Katya grabs Sexy Emcee's little microphone and begins shushing the crowd. 'Shh. Stop. Shh. Settle down, everyone!'

Amazingly enough, the whispers subside and the rowdy

press begins to settle, as if hypnotized by Katya's scorpion gaze. She has crossed her arms and is tapping the microphone, like a school marm waiting for the juvenile class to quieten down. Sexy Emcee steps back. Bala sticks around near AK and continues to grin for the cameras, eyeing Katya with dread and awe. Sinuous LA dancers in shiny satin bodysuits pose beside the podium for a clutch of lowbrow publications and TV channels. The Brit deejay is rounding off some deeply progressive funk into a soft purr. AK reaches into the breast pocket of his jacket, brings out a mint green jujube, pops it in his mouth and clears his throat.

'Ladies and gentlemen of the industry and the press. I am sure you have been wondering where I've been over the past few days. There have been some rumours of a kidnapping and extortion which, some have been speculating, was an inside job. Let me clarify everything right now ... But how presumptuous of me! There's so much happening in the city, maybe none of you noticed I was gone!'

The crowd applauds. Chuckles erupt. A couple of whistles fly in from the back of the room.

'But enough about me, because that's another story and another blockbuster.'

Another round of applause and cheers.

'The reason we are all gathered here today is to announce Ramrakha Amina and Associates' most ambitious project ever.'

Brit Deejay takes that as his cue to send psychedelic sound waves shimmying across the room. The dancers spin their arms and sway their waists. Bala takes a step forward, brandishing his iPad, but Katya swiftly – and softly – places her palm on his elbow and smiles.

'I,' AK coughs, 'don't want to sound like an old man on his deathbed, so I will make this brief. RAA has always believed that there are no permanent friends, enemies or memories. There is only one force that cuts across people and parties and business and ideologies …'

Katya flashes another lopsided mafiaso smile.

'That force, my friends, is art. All great art cuts across boundaries, nations and petty politics.'

Katya strikes a mock horrified look, promptly earning more flashbulbs and whistles. They're playing to the gallery, like only pros can. But there's showmanship and there's sincerity. Triple S, despite his flaws, hopefully has a combination of both. If these two limelight-hoggers would only let him take centre stage.

If Strike at Thirty-Six had gone according to plan, AK would be in a wheelchair right now, Sagar on the podium, I – architect of brilliance – smiling proudly by his side and Katya in her Maratha fortress. But some things are not meant to be. *You go with the flow.*

'In an undeprece … umpreee … unda …' AK falters before composing himself. 'In an unprecedented move for our industry, our fantastic new project is an unusual collaboration between the most outstanding talents in cinema.'

Bala steps forward again. Katya stops him. AK's tubby hand, I notice, is pointing in the general direction of Uday and me, motioning us to come closer. The cameras swing towards us.

'Doshi! Udayan Doshi!' A faceless voice from the crowd grants Uday a Bond-ish suavity.

'Come up, beta,' AK booms, smiling at me.

Uday urges me on, placing his palm on the small of my back. I pull the end of the pallu around my hips and try to glide gracefully to the podium. Priyanka and Mehernosh are following us, so there's no turning back.

'Sho! Sho! Hey, Shobhna!' Another faceless voice bellows from deep within the crowd.

Smiles all around. The scent of an impending politico-cinematic coup has put everyone in a jolly good mood. You cannot buy this sort of heart-thumping thrill even with the best booze, hors d'oeuvres and PR-coordinated stunts.

'Please give a big round of applause to one of our dearest friends, CEO of New York-based Daha Films and one of the brightest young producers we have, Mr Udayan Doshi.'

Uday acknowledges with a single, terse nod. His gentle but firm warm hand is still on my back.

'Let me now call on stage the lovely lady accompanying Uday this afternoon. One of our fiercest talents at RAA, Miss Shobhna Ramakrishnan.'

WTF does this mean? Should I go up alone? Or drag Uday up too, the way I dragged him into this circus? What should I do about the sari petticoat that is getting increasingly slippery at the waist? Before I can get another minute to think, AK continues. 'And I take the greatest pleasure in inviting to join us, the star of this afternoon.'

With that, he hands the mic to Katya. Uday and I are at the edge of the podium. If we're going to make an entrance, we aren't sharing the stage with this crafty crowd-pleaser. An excited Neelu and an expressionless Triple S are now fully visible from where we stand. Triple S's kurta is ironed. His hands are clasped behind his back – significantly, not bullishly crossed over his chest – and he's glaring at Katya.

'Mrs Mahajan, aho, Mrs Mahajan,' the bearded journo from the back of the room, who'd earlier identified Katya, calls out. 'What do you have to say to Mr Panthaki's grieving family?'

'Spill the beans, Katya!' one of the powder-puff girls from the front row screeches.

Katya daintily touches AK's feet, seeking his blessings. He clasps both her bangle-filled hands and pats her head. A swift, effective show of paternal warmth. Touché!

'I'll make it brief. Maharashtra Mitra will be releasing an official statement soon. Meanwhile – and Khansaab will agree with me – it's best if you concentrate on something more productive than rumours.'

She declares this with a dismissive wave of her palm and an authority that naturally discourages follow-up questions. Besides, the press is busy making sense of the priceless news bytes she's beginning to hurl in rapid succession.

'They say politics, business and art do not make good bedfellows. It's a conspiracy theory; do not let those fundamentalists and purists convince you. I don't know how many of you are aware, Mr Mahajan ... Saurabh was an award-winning graphic designer and art director before he entered public life.'

Eh! Wasn't Saurabh an *IT professional?* I turn to Uday. 'The IT guy has been turned into an "award-winning graphic designer" for the press! Hah!' I hiss.

'No, Katya was the IT girl. Saurabh shifted to the US to be with her. Katya told me.' Uday has that half-distracted, dismissive look I have seen so many times before.

Adequately chastised, I shut up.

'... We support a number of private funds that send young Indian artists to intern at the best ad agencies and graphic design companies in Shanghai, California, Milan. The Art School of Chicago has instituted a scholarship on Saurabh's father's name, which includes full tuition and accommodation for two of India's brightest young artistic talents from our smaller towns ... That's from all over India, not just Maharashtra ... But of course, you don't want to know about that, do you? Mr

Mohit Swaraj from *Indian Headlines?*' She points to the bearded gentleman at the back, who responds with a mock 'salaam' and a wide smile. 'So without further ado, I am proud to bring you our very own artistic genius, someone – and you can note this as an official statement – whom MaMi endorses as *the* cinematic talent to watch out for from India. And like everything else we do, we endorse him forcefully and vehemently. Ladies and gentlemen – Sagar Saraswati Sonawane.'

By now, Bala is rather vexed, and the dancers aren't shaking their booty any more. Katya drapes her pallu across her shoulder and looks at us.

'Shobhna, Sagar, the floor is yours. Jai Hind. Jai Maharashtra.'

20

Couplehood of the Divinely Discontented

UDAYAN

I never met Sho's mother. We only spoke on the phone.

The last time, Amma had called me two mornings after the day Sho and I broke up. She hadn't pried for details; only asked me if we were ever going to make up. I'd said I didn't know. She'd consoled me saying there was an astrological affliction in Sho's birth chart. Cancer in Leo or Mars in Leo, or something to that effect. It's known as Divine Discontentment – she'd asked me to Google it – an inner urge to unsettle, fuelled by being overwhelmed when it came to dealing with emotions. Amma had no doubt that we were in love, and passionately committed. But passions, she'd warned, couldn't sustain a marriage.

It had taken Bhai to put the situation in perspective. With the wedding-planning dinner with Appa and Rohini cancelled, he'd hounded, wheedled and threatened me until I spoke to him the night before I left for New York. It seemed right then, to repeat the Divine Discontentment theory to try and explain Sho's inexplicable behaviour. 'Aem ke?' he'd sneered, a little sad. That cryptic parental riposte had said it all. Sho wasn't the only emotionally malfunctioning aspect of our relationship.

There was no reason for me to have shown up at Beans & Booze with Archana Patel that day, no reason for me not to have gone back to her, no justification for me having lied about liking Sho's script. She – with her self-awareness and instinct for brilliance – knew it was a run-of-the-mill money-spinner. It could have raked in millions, but it hadn't hit even its own creator in her gut, let alone me. Unlike *The Dhaal*.

She – the birthday girl – is up there now with Sagar. They're seizing the moment. After cold-calling Daha as *The Dhaal*'s co-producer, Khansaab tried to drag me up on stage too. Katya intervened – snapping her fingers and letting AK know how things ought to be run – from where she sat on the stage, making sure I sat in the front row instead, between Tiwariji, who got up in a hurry and rushed out five minutes ago, and a clutch of industry big-wigs with whom I'm desperately trying to avoid conversing. With my attire and the bruised eye, they deem it better to just stare, not talk. Neelu, almost falling out on the stage, is clicking furiously with her phone. On stage, behind Sho and Sagar, Bala is arguing with AK. If anyone's been completely caught off guard, it's him. Katya is least bothered about the fact that she is seated in full view, and is alternately looking at Sho and texting on her phone.

Behind and around me, tablets, dictaphones and cameras are on an overdrive. The press has sensed something unprecedented here – real news. Photogs are crawling all over, but there's no heckling or dissing. Or shouts of 'Uday, are you and Shobhna having another affair?' Nobody appears to know about Monee or the engagement. Thank god until that happens.

Sho speaks first, briefly and graciously describing her profile at RAA and her first meeting with Sunny and Sagar.

She is funny and charming; the press loves her and laughs at all her witticisms. Sho doesn't play to the gallery like Katya or Khansaab, but she can more than outshine the cleverest of orators when she really believes in something or someone. Her narration of how she met Sagar and was blown away by *The Dhaal* is not mushy or full of hyperbole, yet it holds attention – the mark of a fine storyteller. In her crumpled red cotton sari, without any make-up, and after an exhausting night, she's shining. Adrenalin's always been her choice of poison and red her colour.

She's handed the microphone to Sagar. Her right hand instinctively moves to his back while the other one opens out to the crowd. She's smiling, but there's the protective proud parent in her too, showing off the prodigy. Sagar looks into her eyes, unsmiling. They make a striking partnership. There's potential there for it to develop into something more.

'Sanjay. Sanjay! Idhar dekho. Look here!' A female voice from my right yells at Sagar.

He squints in the direction of the voice and makes a single movement with his palm, still unsmiling. Then he kneels and touches the tips of his fingers to the stage, and then to his forehead. It's a quick movement, not orchestrated for the cameras.

'Who's the new wolf?' a socialite journo seated next to me leans over the back of her chair and leers across to someone seated on the same row. There is a commotion at the entrance. Everyone turns around. A fresh batch of gun-toting security guards has swept in. It's Saurabh. The cameras lunge at him, but the guards hold them at a distance. Saurabh walks rapidly to the front row and occupies Tiwariji's seat. There is another man with him, fair skinned and well dressed. One of the guards requests a producer sitting next to me to vacate his seat, and offers him one towards the side. I offer to vacate my chair, but Saurabh raises his hand. The well-dressed man sits next to me and wants to shake my hand. Saurabh leans over and introduces us. 'Udayan, meet Gustap. The Panthakis' lawyer, and a very dear friend of ours.'

'Hello, a pleasure,' Gustap smiles, his deep blue eyes twinkling. His accent is a strange mix – European with a south-Indian twang. Meanwhile, Sagar has given the microphone to Katya who requests the press to stand back: Saurabh will make an official announcement later. Her request sounds like a command. The reporters protest feebly.

'Mr Mahajan. Saurabh. Say something!'

Saurabh smiles and nods his head, indicating that they should allow Sagar to speak.

'Saurabh, how do you know Shobhna? What does MaMi have to do with RAA?'

'Saurabh, who are you wearing?'

'Mr Mahajan, you owe this to Bombay.'

Sagar taps the microphone. 'Namaskar. My name is Sagar Saraswati Sonawane. I am from MaMi. And I hauve a confession.'

The booming baritone has brought the ballroom back from the brink of bedlam.

The confession begins in heavily accented Hindi. But his voice is clear, calm, and instantly in command. The petulance has disappeared. The anger is reigned in. The intensity is palpable. Like Sho, he has risen to the occasion. They make a striking couple.

His focus is *The Dhaal*. He isn't revealing anything about the plot, but his real story is riveting, delivered in a thunderous monotone. A small-town boy. Poverty. Polio. A theatre group of disadvantaged children. Struggles. Disappointments. Deaths.

Debts. A script called *The Dhaal*, not based on 'mere bachche' but inspired by the frustration of what they deserve and what he cannot give them. An ailing mother. And then coming to the city to be sidelined and ignored and told to pimp his writing for barely enough money to buy an overpriced cup of coffee. If it wasn't for his best friend, Sunny, he would have stopped writing and gone back to Baramati and his kids. The choice in this city, he says, was between wearing a cap, calling college kids younger than him 'ma'am' and 'sir' and serving them fried food at an international food chain while begging people in the film industry to read his script, or working with MaMi.

Sagar's is a different kind of playing to the galleries. He's not witty like Sho. His is an unsophisticated, guttural desi arrogance, the kind that is in short supply these days. Even as he's talking, he's walking casually across the stage, like one accustomed to it. Occasionally, when a camera flash hits him, he's startled, but immediately gains control. It is obvious this speech isn't the one he is alleged to have rehearsed.

Whether the press likes Sagar or not, they cannot ignore him.

The boy is a game changer. Daha needs him. We're going to bat for him, despite the huge chip on his shoulder, or because of it. Monee had mentioned once that I have a soft corner for people with entitlement issues. 'For our sake, I just hope you don't sleep with any of them,' she'd joked.

'Main Saurabh Dada aur Katya Vahini ko sirf ek saal se jaanta hoon,' he continues. They, he adds without melodrama, were the only people who understood *The Dhaal*, until ... he pauses for a few seconds, Shobhna and ... he pauses longer ... Khansaab and ... he looks at me ... Udayanji came into the picture.

The 'ji', I think, is a little muted.

A few flashes capture what I hope is my politely expressionless face.

Sho pulls the end of her sari around her waist, looks at me and cocks her head to one side. Just like Roja.

'Jaise Katya Vahini ne kaha, business, politics and art are not good baidfellows. Maibee. Maibee note.' He's noted some of the blank faces at his Hindi-only speech and is inserting English words to get the interest up. He's still not smiling, though. For the sake of his kids, he says, and maybe for his future, totally out of selfishness, he made a big mistake. 'Maine ek bahut badi galati ki hai.'

Khansaab has wrenched himself away from Bala and come up to Sagar, smiling genially at him. Katya has come up on his other side, close to Sho. A guard stationed next to Saurabh bends down and hands him his phone. Saurabh reads the screen and nods at Katya, then leans across me and whispers cheerfully to Gustap, 'We're good to go, saheb.'

'Come, Uday,' he turns his wide smile on me.

'I'm fine. Thanks.'

'Uday, you're in this now. There is absolutely no escape. You are now a MaMi man. Yes, Gustap?'

Gustap shakes his head and mumbles something which I can't hear because I'm trying to listen to what Sagar is saying next. AK has placed one hand on the star writer's shoulder and the other on Sho's.

'Maine galati ki. I took a reesk. I mixed my art with my poltics and their bizhness with my art—'

'And the result, ladies and gentlemen, is the film of the year, that begins filming three months from now – *The Dhaal*.' Khansaab's roaring voice doesn't need a microphone anymore. He's beckoned Bala, who was moaning aimlessly by the ignored *Yogi* posters. They're all standing in a line now – Bala, AK, Katya, Sagar and Sho. Khansaab gestures at me to join them.

As I begin walking towards the stage, I am restrained by an extended hand.

'Nice purse ...' It is Gustap.

'What?'

'Udayan, Gustap is speaking to you,' offers Saurabh who is seated nearby, now flanked by armed guards.

The blue-eyed man's eyes twinkle again and he wants to shake my hand again. He likes my 'purse', Monee's gift. 'Udayan, I am Gustap Gharpuré, Homi Panthaki's lawyer. Mr Panthaki was murdered by goons sent by his own brother. MaMi and Sagar have nothing to do with it.'

'But the Mumbai Police is looking for you,' I say.

'What? Must be some other Gharpuré.'

Yes, must be some other Gharpuré. But how many Gharpurés can one encounter within a span of a couple of days in this incredibly mad city of mine? I didn't peg him to be a blue-eyed Gustap either. But for now, there's no choice other than the willing suspension of disbelief.

'But Sagar ... he smashed those chemistry labs, didn't he?'

Saurabh gets up from his chair. '*Our* Sagar? He wouldn't hurt a stray cat! Come now, I have an official statement to make on the Quit Fucking Mumbai movement. And we're expecting the PM any time.'

'So he's not your goonda?'

'The Prime Minister?'

'Sagar.'

'I didn't say that,' he smiles.

Meanwhile, the people on the stage are getting restive and are standing around, whispering to each other in an attempt to dispel the awkwardness. I was supposed to have gone up a good minute ago.

The wordplay with Saurabh can happen later. I nod to him and cover the distance between the stage and me in brisk strides. Cameras flash furiously. In that minute, a million questions explode through my head, crashing into an earlier impatient lot of unanswered ones.

Why has Khansaab suddenly turned around on *The Dhaal* and Sagar? Was he just testing Sho all along? Is this a trap? If so, for whom? If not, who's to benefit from this unlikely partnership between cinema and politics? Why, at no point of time, have I protested against what's going on?

'Would you like to say a few words, Udayan?' Katya is back at the microphone. Neelu has sidled from backstage to the edge of the stage and is now standing in front of Katya, alternatively clicking and punching on her phone. Saurabh, who has followed me to the stage, genially waves aside the throng of reporters and camerapersons jostling for him, and taking the microphone from Katya, holds it in my direction.

'I'm good. Thanks.' I shake Saurabh's hand, give him a half-hug, and pat Sagar vigorously on the back. It seems the right thing to do. Then I turn to Khansaab and attempt to fall at his feet, before which he pulls me up and thumps me on the back. Just like that, we're sealing a business deal.

Should I hug or shake hands with Sho?

The press is lusting for more. It is not every day that you are invited for the announcement of one film and introduced to another. Moreover, Saurabh's presence on the stage, holding MaMi's official statement, has got them more agitated. For all we know, the CM could land up any minute to announce resignations and the PM could air-dash from Delhi to congratulate Khansaab.

'Uday! *Uday*! We heard you're getting married next month?' A shrill-voiced reporter raises her hand.

Standing between Sagar and Sho, I slide to cover Sho from the audience so she's free to fiddle with whatever it is in her sari that has been bothering her over the past five minutes.

'Bloody petticoat ... thanks,' she whispers after half a minute, her breath on my stubble.

'I found Gharpuré ... the wrong one.' I turn my head and smile.

'Wha ...?'

'Sagar hasn't murdered anyon—'

'T'chaila, what did you theenk? You peepul ...'

'Not now. Not now!' Sho hisses at Sagar.

Saurabh is seconds away from blowing the lid off the state government.

'Uday! Are you and Shobh—' The pesky reporter, now jumping up and down in the crowd, refuses to give up.

'You're hot,' Sho grabs my palm in hers.

'No personal questions, please!' Saurabh's voice shoots across the room.

'Hey, Uday! New York or Bombay?'

'You're feverish,' Sho presses my palm harder.

'I'm not.'

'Choose, Uday. Choose.' The voice echoes.

'Why the fuck are you so hot?' Sho's eyes blaze.

Have I caught Sagar's fever? My back is still hurting.

'To kyaare?' Bhai's voice rings in my ear.

What now, Uday?

The reporter is still shrieking for a headline-worthy sound bite.

I look around. I see Mumbai, putrid hellhole of my dreams.

And then, there's *The Dhaal*.

Saurabh, smoothly ignoring the yelping reporter, clears his throat. 'This is a new chapter in the history of …'

Acknowledgements

Thank you to my parents for delighting in every published word I've written, even while lamenting my appalling life choices. Thanks to my sister – I couldn't ask for a cooler sibling – and other family members. A big shout out to friends (especially my curly-haired namesake from school) and colleagues who've opened their hearts and homes for me in Mumbai and around the world. Without your company, food and good spirits, I couldn't have survived and don't hope to survive writing. Please continue to feed, humour and tolerate me.

A big, grateful hug to readers who enjoy discovering layers to humour and will not dismiss funny as flippant.

Also, bundles of gratitude towards the magazine editors I've written and continue to write for.

Most important, much thanks to the lovely team at HarperCollins for all the support, enthusiasm and very enticing carrots.